# SUBSTITUTE

## ALSO BY SUSI HOLLIDAY

## Writing as SJI Holliday:

*Black Wood*

*Willow Walk*

*The Damselfly*

*The Lingering*

*Violet*

*Mr Sandman*

## Writing as Susi Holliday:

*The Deaths of December*

*The Last Resort*

# SUBSTITUTE

## SUSI HOLLIDAY

THOMAS & MERCER

Published by Thomas & Mercer, Seattle

www.apub.com

Amazon, the Amazon logo, and Thomas & Mercer are trademarks of Amazon.com, Inc., or its affiliates.

ISBN-13: 9781542020046
ISBN-10: 1542020042

Cover design by The Brewster Project

Printed in the United States of America

*To all of my family and
friends . . .
because it would be impossible to
choose only three.*

'Most of the evil in this world is done by people with good intentions.'

—*T. S. Eliot*

# Prologue

The room is stark, yet stifling. Clean white walls, standard-issue bed, two plastic chairs. Both occupied.

He sits by her bed, waiting for the inevitable, keeping a watchful eye on the doctor who sits silently in the corner. The monitor beeps a steady rhythm, her chest rises and falls . . .

His head buzzes.

*She's like a doll,* he thinks, lying there with the blankets pulled up to her chin. Her face is shrunken, waxen. Her eyes have been closed for some time now. They won't open again, unless—

The door swings open and the nurse's urgent, whispered voice interrupts his thoughts. 'It's for you.' She's holding a cordless phone, one hand over the mouthpiece. 'It's your daughter. She wants to come here . . .'

He turns to the doctor in the corner, watches him stand, smooth down the creases in his white coat. His face, his whole demeanour, is impassive. He frowns, but still says nothing.

He turns back to the nurse. 'How did she get this number?'

'I don't know,' the nurse says. There's a hint of guilt in her voice, as if she might somehow be responsible, but she can't be. He knows this.

'Hang up,' he says, calmer than he feels. Trying to breathe. Trying to push it all away. What a *mess.*

The monitor's high-pitched screech stops anyone else from replying.

Flatline.

*No! Not yet.* His heart is hammering, the harsh sound of the machine cuts through him. 'Please,' he says, turning to the doctor. Pleading. Desperate. 'Are you sure you can't do something? We've got five minutes from this point, right? Can't you at least—'

The doctor walks slowly around the bed and switches off the machine. No urgency at all. He shakes his head. 'Not this time. We've been through all this. You've been unlucky, that's all.'

He bunches his hands into fists. There's no point arguing.

'Your daughter?' the nurse says to him.

He swallows. Feels like his throat is closing up. Feels like he might choke. Feels like he might want to. He looks down at the bed, then back at the nurse. He shakes his head, slowly.

'Just tell her that I'm sorry.'

# PART 1

PART 1

# One

## Chrissie (Now)

She spots him from the bedroom window. Jittery. Anxious. Cheap suit and battered briefcase. He shifts from one foot to the other. Rings the doorbell, rattles the knocker for good measure. Glances at his watch. She stands back, concealing herself behind the curtain so that if he looks up he won't see her.

She doesn't have time for this today – this dishcloth sales-man or Jehovah or whatever he is. She's been kind to them in the past – buying overpriced J-cloths from ex-cons, promising to read the *Watchtower* thrust into her hands. But today she can't face going through the motions of a polite, awkward conversa-tion with a stranger.

Unfortunately, he glances up at the window just then, face etched into a frown, and she's pretty sure he's seen her. He rings the doorbell again and stares right at her, then looks away and rattles the knocker once more.

She responds by backing further into the bedroom, so she can only see the top of his head, where a blossoming bald patch glints in the sunlight. Finally, he rattles the letterbox and a sharp stab of irritation pierces the base of her skull. Persistent little bugger.

He's not going away.

Her sigh turns into a stream of muttered obscenities as she slowly makes her way down the stairs.

*Careful, careful.*

It's what she's trained Holly to say to herself before she goes up or down. These stairs are so bloody steep.

She's past the halfway landing when the letterbox snaps open and a pair of dark, curranty eyes appear in the slot.

'Mrs Tate? Christina Tate? Please don't ignore me, Mrs Tate . . .'

The letterbox snaps shut.

She leans on the bannister, sucks in a breath. *How does he know my name?* She never uses her full name anymore. She's Chrissie, now. Has been for a long time. A million thoughts whizz through her head. Taxman? Has there been some catastrophic error? No. She's good at sorting out the finances. Is it Nathan? Has something happened? No. They'd send uniformed police for that, wouldn't they? They'd come as a pair and they wouldn't be so shifty. Her heart stops.

*Holly . . .*

No.

Holly is at nursery. Wendy picked her up at 8.30 a.m. and took her there, just as she does every other weekday, while Nathan is out at work and Chrissie works from home trying to deal with an ever-expanding and ever-more-demanding client list. No. This man is *not* from the nursery. Her heart restarts, as if defibrillated.

She's still going through the possibilities when the letterbox opens again. 'Tell me, Mrs Tate – have you ever experienced grief?'

*Snap.*

A Jehovah, then, not dishcloths. It's her soul he's after, not her cash.

Quite the opening, though.

*Have you ever experienced grief?*

Of *course* she has. Hasn't everyone? A vision of her mother at the end slides in front of her eyes. Small and wizened and nothing like the strong, capable woman she once was. And then . . . nowhere. Gone. Chrissie didn't even get a chance to say goodbye.

Twenty years ago, but it still feels like yesterday.

Chrissie had muddled her way through until the pregnancy had triggered PTSD. She'd been a wreck, after that. Nathan had tried his best, but he hadn't lost anyone at all, so how could he really understand? She'd suffered dark thoughts, back then. Sometimes now. Most of the last few years have passed by in a blur.

She still wishes that someone else had died instead. Why do the insufferable bastards get to live out their lives yet the good ones get taken too soon?

It's normal, she knows – this angry stage. But she hadn't realised how much it would affect her. How it would almost swallow her whole. How long it would last. *It's been years, Chrissie.* Nathan's frustrated voice. *I thought we were past the crying stage?*

She continues down the stairs, hanging back against the wall.

*Funny you should ask. Yes, I* have *experienced grief, as it happens. You got something for that?*

The letterbox snaps open again, the man's voice drifting through. 'What if I could ensure that you never had to experience that again, Mrs Tate? Would that be something that might interest you?'

She stomps down the final few stairs and yanks open the door. 'Who *are* you?'

The man stands up straight, smoothing down his jacket where it has crumpled. He extends a bony hand, revealing ragged nails in painful-looking shades of purple and black. Hers is not the first letterbox he's invaded, she suspects.

'My name is Joseph Marshall. You don't know me, but you've been recommended by someone who thought you would benefit from my services. Please, may I come in?'

Her first thought is to slam the door in his face, but then those images of her ever-diminishing mother float across her vision again. That loss, that grief, hot and fresh as the day it was inflicted upon her. If losing her mother has branded her like this, how could she possibly survive losing Nathan . . . or, good God, Holly . . .

'Mrs Tate?'

Joseph Marshall takes a step forward, and she hesitates, just for a moment. *Could* there be something in what he is selling? She shakes her head. *Don't be ridiculous.* She retreats back into the house, letting the door close in front of her, shutting the strange little man and his outrageous notions safely outside.

'No, thank you,' she says. 'Please go away.'

*But* . . .

She stands behind the closed door for a moment, holding her breath. Imagining that she can hear his breathing through the oak panelling. She stares at the door for a moment longer, then turns away. She's only taken a few steps when she hears the rattle of the letterbox again, and his reedy voice, drifting through.

'Not to worry, Mrs Tate . . . I'll come back.'

She turns and catches a brief glimpse of thin, bruised fingers poking their way into her house. A business card flutters through the letterbox, spiralling gently to the floor.

*Snap.*

# Two

## Chrissie (Now)

Rain is starting to spit against the windows, so she hurries out into the back garden, grabbing the washing off the line. The high-pitched squeals of children in the playground behind the house fly across the low back fence, and she pauses for a moment, watching as frantic parents and childminders try to round up their small charges before everyone gets soaked. The adventure play area is a new addition to the park, and Holly loves it even though she's a bit too small for most of the activities.

Back inside, Chrissie dumps the wash-basket on the kitchen floor, flicks the kettle on and runs a finger across the trackpad of her laptop, waking up the screen. She was only outside for a few minutes, but she feels damp and cold, and she's not in the mood for work.

She is in the middle of designing a logo for a new restaurant on Ealing Broadway. There has been an endless procession of businesses in the space, none of them making a go of it for longer than six months. She's not sure if it's a holding company who keeps shutting it down as one restaurant and opening it as another, or if there are some nefarious goings-on, but if they were to ask *her* opinion, she'd say there was very little chance of success with a unit in that location. It might be on the main drag, but it has a tiny frontage that's more than eclipsed by the ubiquitous chains on either side. Those places are always packed.

Drink in place, she checks her scribbled notes that are spread across the worktop and clicks open a new window, ready to start all over again. The work she'd done earlier is all wrong. She'd been unsure before, but after popping upstairs to get one of her design books, and being interrupted by that very strange man, she's now certain. The brief was brief, as they often are, but she's going to have to rethink this one entirely. She taps out a quick text message to the client, asking him to call her. It'd be good if he got back to her tonight, so she could make another start on the design in the morning.

She takes a sip of her coffee and opens the fridge, realising that she's forgotten to do the online shop. Glancing at the time on the microwave clock, she knows it's too late to pop out before Holly comes home, and sure enough, just as she closes the fridge door, wrinkling her nose at the faint but unmistakable smell of something on the turn, she hears the sound of the key in the lock, followed by the pattering of small, excited footsteps.

'Mummy, Mummy, I'm home!'

Holly barrels into the kitchen, flinging her arms around her mother's legs, before pulling away and wrestling with her Peppa Pig backpack, tangling her pigtails under the straps in the process.

'Ow, I'm stuck, Mummy!' she cries, just as Wendy appears in the doorway behind her, looping the straps off and freeing her hair before Chrissie has a chance to put her mug down and help.

'I did a painting,' Holly continues, unperturbed, her voice high-pitched and breathless, her cheeks pink, like fresh apples.

'Slow down, honey,' says Chrissie, smiling across at Wendy.

'She ran most of the way back. Ran and chattered. It's been an exciting morning at the hell-mouth.' Wendy rolls her eyes and picks

Holly's discarded backpack off the floor. 'Have you seen the state of those concrete planters at the end of the road? I know they're meant to be there to stop the cars from using the street as a rat run, but someone's managed to tip one of them over. Soil and smashed begonias all over the road. They must've had a bloody forklift . . .'

Chrissie crouches down and pulls her daughter in for a hug. 'Are you going to tell Mummy what happened?'

Wendy opens the fridge and takes out a carton of apple juice, piercing the little hole on top with a straw.

'Tommy Cole wet himself at break time and Sally Johnstone slipped in his puddle of wee and started crying and then Annabel Freer started laughing and then Tommy pushed her and she fell over and then Miss Barr got cross and said a bad word that—'

'Holly, honey, you need to slow down a bit, OK? And take a drink before you tell me the rest, you're all hot and sweaty.' She takes the box of juice from Wendy and hands it to Holly, who sucks down a huge gulp, then seems to calm down at last. She turns to Wendy. 'Did you two get caught in the rain?'

Wendy shrugs. 'It's only drizzling.'

Holly grabs Chrissie around one leg. 'Can I watch *Peppa Pig*?'

'Of course. Let's get your shoes off first and then I'll switch it on, OK?'

Holly nods, kicking off her shoes as she wanders through to the sitting room. Chrissie switches the programme on for her, and within moments, Holly is curled up on the sofa, transfixed.

'Peace for half an hour then,' Wendy says.

Chrissie turns to her friend. 'I don't think they're concrete.'

Wendy looks at her, confused.

'The planters . . . I think they have to be movable for the emergency services. I don't know what the point of them actually is. Nobody likes them.'

Wendy shakes her head and follows her back through to the kitchen. She flops on to one of the kitchen chairs and peers at Chrissie's computer. 'You're doing a logo for Meet-4-Meat?'

'For all the good it'll do. Didn't work as a pizza place, a café, a noodle shop or a bakery. I can't see that a badly named Argentinian BBQ is going to do much better, but they're paying a decent amount so I'm determined to come up with something that might work.'

'I'm sure it's a money-laundering front. Are they paying cash?'

Chrissie nods, glances over at her mug on the counter. 'Coffee or wine?'

'What do *you* think? It's nearly one p.m. I've no child-minding clients this afternoon. I've had the morning from hell—'

'What did Miss Barr say then?' She hands her friend a bottle of red wine and a corkscrew, then sets two glasses on the table.

'Poor Gilly. The *fuck* was out of her mouth before she had a chance to stop it. I mean, it's mad in that place most days, but it was the combination of it all – not to mention that Annabel had been winding Tommy up all morning as it was, little madam that she is. Gilly had separated them three times already, and then Tommy swiped Annabel's drink and gulped it down straight after his own, so it's not surprising that he couldn't keep it in . . .' She takes a mouthful of wine. 'I had to speak to his mother when she arrived, and you know what that's like.'

Oh yes. Chrissie's met Karen Cole on more than one occasion. In fact, she can't escape her now that she's working at the Co-op up the road, which is the one Chrissie always uses when she's forgotten the online order – which is more often than not, these days. How a woman like that could pass an interview for a store manager is a mystery to everyone who crosses her path.

'I'm sure she made every excuse for her little cherub.'

Wendy drains her glass and picks up the bottle. 'Obviously.'

'Well, I've had a bit of a morning myself, actually,' she says, picking up her own glass and taking a sip. 'Some weirdo came to the door. At first I thought he was trying to sell dishcloths or whatever. Out of a briefcase!' She pauses to take another sip. 'Anyway, he knew my name.' *Christina*. She winces. 'Shouted it through the letterbox . . .'

Wendy raises her eyebrows. 'Intriguing,' she says. 'You don't think it's got anything to do with this work you're doing, do you? I'm telling you, I'm sure that client is dodgy – do you even have the name of who owns the place?'

'Nope. I told you. It's always a different manager when I go in there. I'm sure you're right that there's something weird going on, but it's not for me to investigate. I'm a graphic designer, not Miss bloody Marple.'

'Maybe you should ditch this work, Chrissie. Do you really need it?'

She swallows back a sharp retort. *No, I don't need it, do I. Nathan's salary pays the bills. Only my little hobby this, isn't it?* She knows she'll only sound defensive. It's her work that pays for the fancy holidays, Nathan's salary not quite stretching that far, with most of his extra money going to overpay the mortgage and reduce their monthly bills. It might not be a huge house, and it's only a semi-detached, but it's in an area where square footage costs a premium. Even if it does come with neighbours on the other side of the party wall who don't want to speak to you. Wendy doesn't know all this, of course. Why would she?

'Forget that,' she says. 'This man was nothing to do with Meet-4-Meat. He asked me a weird question about grief . . . said he could stop me from having to suffer it ever again.'

Wendy snorts. 'Well, that's ridiculous.' She takes another large mouthful of wine.

'I know. Of course it is. But I don't know . . . It unsettled me. Made me think of Mum.'

Wendy leans over and puts a hand over hers, giving it a little squeeze. 'Maybe it's time for you to talk about your mum . . . and your dad? You've never—'

Chrissie yanks her hand away and Wendy jumps back, startled. Silence falls between them, only punctuated by the grunts and high-pitched voices coming from Peppa and the rest of the pig family on the TV.

'Sorry,' Wendy says, pushing her chair back and standing up. 'That was a stupid thing to say.' She gives Chrissie a brief smile, then turns towards the sitting room, calling out 'Bye sweetie, see you tomorrow' to Holly – who doesn't reply.

Chrissie walks Wendy to the door. 'No, I'm sorry,' she says. 'I overreacted. It's just . . .'

'I know,' Wendy says. 'Look, just forget about it. Forget about all of it. When I come round tomorrow, let's arrange a night out for us, OK? It's been too long since we just went out and forgot about work and nursery chatter and all of that. We need a girls' night. High heels. Drinks. Sexy barmen. What do you reckon?'

'Yes,' Chrissie says, feeling her mood lift at the thought. 'Nathan can curtail some of his late nights for a change. I'm sure his clients don't need him quite as often as he makes out . . .'

Wendy gives her a brief, odd look and then smiles. 'Oh, talking of Nathan – Holly's done him a painting. It's rolled up in her backpack.' She leans in and kisses Chrissie on the cheek, and then she's gone.

Chrissie picks up Holly's backpack and pulls out the rolled piece of paper. She feels a small ping of annoyance, as if someone has flicked her ear. Another painting for Nathan? How come it's the parent she sees the least that their daughter seems to favour the most?

# Three

## CHRISSIE (NOW)

She's thrown the wine bottle into the recycling, rinsed the glasses, and is tidying away her laptop and her notes when Holly appears in the doorway, thumb jammed into her mouth.

'Mummy, can I play upstairs now?'

'Of course you can, sweetie.' She leans down and gently pulls Holly's hand away from her mouth, kissing her thumb. 'Daddy will be home soon.' She kisses Holly's thumb again. 'We'll go out to the park . . .' She kisses her thumb once more. 'Then we'll have something yummy for tea. OK?'

'Pizza?'

Chrissie smiles. Her daughter knows her only too well. 'I think pizza sounds just perfect.'

'Don't forget to give Daddy my picture,' Holly says, running through the dining room. She stops at the bottom of the stairs and turns back to Chrissie with a big grin and a thumbs up. 'Careful, careful,' she whispers.

'Careful, careful.' Chrissie grins back, then waits at the bottom of the stairs while Holly climbs up. The only thing that she hates about this house are the stairs. Too narrow, too steep. But there's not much they can do except train Holly to walk up and down rather than run, and to follow the same advice themselves. Once Holly is safely past the halfway landing and her footsteps have broken into a run along the top hallway, Chrissie breathes a sigh of relief. One day, she'll stop being terrified of these stairs.

Maybe.

She turns around and pushes the inside doormat against the doorframe with her foot, straightening it up, and as she does, she notices the business card from earlier, wedged underneath. She'd forgotten about it after seeing it drifting in through the letterbox. It must've been disturbed when Wendy opened the door and Holly flew in like the little tornado that she is.

She picks it up and slides it into the back pocket of her jeans.

She's back in the kitchen, arranging a selection of takeaway leaflets across the table in a fanned horseshoe design, when she hears the key in the lock.

Nathan stomps into the kitchen. 'Seriously?' He tosses his work bag on to the table, sending the leaflets flying. 'Takeaway again?'

She can smell beer on his breath, but says nothing. She's hardly one to talk today.

'I've had a total nightmare of a day,' he says. 'Some idiot nearly knocked me off the platform on to the tracks. Bumped me from behind.' He opens the fridge and takes out a bottle of beer, flipping off the cap. 'Bloody dangerous. One of these days it'll be more than a near miss.' He takes a pull of his beer. 'Aren't you going to say anything? What've you been doing, anyway?' He nods towards her laptop.

She takes a deep breath, counting to ten before answering. It's not the first time he's come home complaining about the commute, or about his job. Trying to insinuate she's not pulling her weight, when she's the one who has to juggle working from home with looking after the house, and Holly, save for the few hours she's out at nursery. She watches as he drains the rest of his beer, then sets the bottle down on the worktop with a sigh.

'I'm sorry,' he says. 'I'm just tired. I think I need a bath and an early night . . .'

Chrissie forces a smile into her voice. 'Let's pop to the park first, OK? The rain's off and I really think it's good for us all to stick to the family routine.' She pauses. 'You hardly see her during the week.' She waits for the inevitable explosion, but it doesn't come.

Nathan rubs a hand across his stubbled chin. He *does* look tired. 'OK.'

'Oh, I almost forgot,' Chrissie says. 'This is for you.' She hands him Holly's rolled-up drawing.

He unrolls it, and she can't help but look. Four people in this one. A man in the centre – Nathan, presumably – a woman on either side. The women look the same, except one has an upturned curve for a mouth and the other's is downturned. They're all holding hands. In front of them, a small girl on roller skates that she assumes is Holly. Holly doesn't have roller skates, but it's all she talks about at the moment.

'A woman either side, eh? You are a lucky Daddy.'

'I wish.' Nathan laughs. 'I think these are both you,' he says. 'You're such an omnipresent force, she's had to draw two of you. The two faces of Chrissie Tate. That sounds like a movie—'

'Oh shut up! Go and get Holly, will you?'

He lets go of one side, and the painting re-rolls itself. He hands it to her like a baton before he heads out of the room. She unfurls it once more, takes a pack of Blu-Tack from the drawer, ready to put it up beside the others that decorate the walls of the kitchen. But there's something about this one that she doesn't like very much. She re-rolls it tightly then puts it in the corner next to the stacks of paper and the paints and pens and all the crafting paraphernalia. Perhaps Holly will forget about it and do another. She makes a mental note to ask her daughter about it one day. About the two women. And about why the paintings are always given to Nathan, and not her.

She sits down at the table, squaring away her laptop and work notes. After a moment, she hears pattering feet and squeals, followed by the careful *thump thump* of Holly making her way down the stairs.

Holly runs into the kitchen, frowning. 'I was making a blanket fort for the bears!'

Chrissie smiles. 'I know you were, sweetie. You can leave them in there all nice and cosy, while we pop out to the park for a little while. How does that sound?'

'OK!' Holly runs to the back door, reaching up to lean on the handle, trying to pull it down.

'Shoes!' Nathan calls, following her into the kitchen. He gives Chrissie a brief smile and a small shrug – his usual *sorry* gesture – before bending down to push Holly's shoes on to her feet. He opens the back door.

'Phone!' Chrissie calls after him, and Nathan takes his phone out of his pocket and slides it along the worktop, where it comes to rest by the kettle. She lays hers beside it. *No phones*, is her rule for family time before Holly goes to bed. They'd barely speak to each other otherwise. She hesitates for a moment, thinking about the client. She *wants* them to call back tonight. It'd be Sod's Law they'd call when she doesn't have her phone, but she doesn't want to break her own rules – that'd be the start of it and Nathan would gladly pull her up, and just like that, her carefully curated family time would be ruined. She sighs, then picks the phone up again and turns the ringer volume to maximum. If they ring, she'll hear it from the park and come back in – it's literally thirty seconds' walk from the back door to the park entrance, crossing the narrow alleyway that runs along the back of the houses. Their house

18

is practically *in* the park, which is a nuisance when she's trying to work and there are kids out there shrieking. If the client doesn't call, she'll try them again when Holly is in bed.

'I'll cook something nice for us tomorrow,' she shouts to Nathan as she steps outside. He's halfway down the back path. 'One of your favourites. Extra-cheesy mac 'n' cheese? Spicy chicken wraps and sweet-potato wedges? You can pick.'

'Maybe I'll cook for a change,' he shouts back. 'Hardly rocket science, is it?'

*I'll believe it when I see it*, Chrissie thinks. But says nothing. She doesn't want to spoil the mood.

# Four

## JOSEPH (NOW)

Joseph waits patiently in the queue for the lanyards. There are a couple of people in front of him, both taking longer than they should to locate their own names from the neat rows of name badges lined across the long table. Even from where he's standing, without having to strain, he can see that the names are in alphabetical order. How hard can it be? He shifts from foot to foot, smooths his hands down his trousers. Then takes a step forward when it's finally his turn, keeping his eyes down as he scans the rows of cards close up.

'Good evening, sir. May I take your name?' The woman behind the table smiles up at him. She has no reason to doubt him. Why would she? He's got just as much right to be here as anyone else. Well, he would do. Had he purchased a ticket. Thankfully, unlike the other two before him, who've both marched off through the swinging glass doors, he's prepared for this.

He chooses a name and raises his eyes to meet hers. 'It's Terrence Bowman,' he says, remembering to smile and trying not to fidget. 'Orchard Scientific.'

The woman nods and runs a finger down the 'B's, passing 'Bannatyne' and 'Beecham' before coming to rest on the name he's given her.

'Here you go.' She takes a long silver chain from a box to her right, then hands him the name badge, a brochure and the chain in a well-practised move. 'Enjoy the conference,' she says, already turning away to deal with the next person in the queue.

Joseph slips the chain through the hole and secures it, then slides it over his head. He flips the badge so it faces his chest and mentally congratulates himself for a job well done.

There are so many attendees to deal with, by the time the real Terrence Bowman arrives the woman will have forgotten his face. Joseph had seen the box next to the chains, filled with stacks of blank cards and plastic sleeves. A couple of Sharpies lying in wait, for any missing names to be handwritten if required.

Observant. Excellent attention to detail. Always two of his strongest suits.

He pushes open the glass door and vanishes into the throng. Just another conference attendee.

He scans the room. A wide, airy space lined with small tables, some with partitions – most with some kind of advertising banner or sign board either behind or to one side. The ceilings are high and the chattering noise is a dull roar. Directly in front of him is an information booth, a screen behind it showing a map of the various rooms, interrupted by scrolling banner adverts along the top and the bottom. There are smaller screens at either side of the desk. He remembers to smile at the young man behind the booth, then makes his way to the unoccupied screen on the left. He taps it to wake it up, then slides his finger along the bottom until he finds what he's looking for.

Attendees.

He has to scroll through three pages to find her. Dr Ris Anderson – GenYSis Therapeutics. *Ris*. He wonders why she's chosen this version of her name. It's unusual, certainly. Perhaps she wants to be memorable.

He's certain she will be that.

Once he's checked her location on the floor plan, he taps the screen again to get it back home.

He takes his time as he passes the various booths. Stops occasionally to read some of the posters. Remembers to smile at the people stationed beside them. Some desperate to push whatever it is they are there to sell. Others with pained expressions suggesting they've drawn the short straw, would clearly prefer to be anywhere but here.

He used to enjoy things like this. But that was a lifetime ago, and besides, he's not here to enjoy himself. He has someone to find.

He has a job to do.

She's sitting down behind her table, flicking through the brochure, when he arrives in front of her. Sensing him, she looks up – and for a moment she looks startled, before composing herself quickly.

'Good afternoon,' he says, launching straight into it. He takes a good look at her face. It's definitely her. He made sure to memorise her face from the information on her company website. He can't afford to make a mistake here.

It'd been easier with Mrs Tate. He knew where she lived, because she works from home and that was the address he'd found for her on her company's website. But Dr Anderson had proven trickier to pin down without raising any red flags. This was the issue with him not being allowed access to all resources. His relationship with his employers and his level of security access was a complex situation. Luckily it had been easy enough to find out Dr Anderson's whereabouts today. Once he'd got the details of who she worked for, the company website had helped him along by proudly displaying their esteemed representatives and their involvement in this conference.

*GenYSis Therapeutics: Medical advances in rare genetic diseases.*
So appropriate.

She looks at him expectantly, waiting for him to say more, and when he doesn't, she says, 'Hello. Welcome to GenYSis Therapeutics. I'm Dr Ris Anderson. Were you happy to browse through the materials on show, or did you have any specific questions for me?'

He feels a little flurry of excitement. He quickly taps his watch, glances down to check the reading. 70bpm. Bit high, but well within the safe limits.

'As a matter of fact, I do, Doctor.' He lifts his head to look her in the eye; remembers to smile. 'Tell me, Dr Anderson, have you ever experienced grief?'

# Five

Holly and Nathan are already in the playground when she walks through the gate. The park is quieter than normal, the recent rain sending most people on their way. Chrissie recognises the young, red-haired mum with the boisterous twins and gives her a little wave. She hopes the woman doesn't beckon her over. She's not really up for a chat. Far across the park, a couple of older kids are playing on the tyre-swing, while a lone jogger does circuits of the park's perimeter. She starts towards the bench near the gate that she often sits on, then stops herself. It's occupied. An old man is sitting at one end of it, his umbrella still up despite the rain having stopped. If she sits at the other end, she'll have to talk to him. But really, she should be trying to talk to her husband. She hurries across to rejoin her family.

'Watch me, Daddy!' Holly shoots off across the damp bark-mulch that covers the ground and jumps on to the see-saw. She tries to push herself up, but her feet don't quite touch the ground. 'Daddy! You push the other end,' she shouts, her little voice excited and impatient. She grips on tightly and grins.

Nathan climbs on to the other end and moves up and down gently, giving her enough of a lift and a bump to make her giggle, but not enough that she slides off the seat. The see-saw is for bigger children, really, but trying to tell Holly that is a complete waste of time. She has a routine that she likes. See-saw, swings, treehouse. It takes her an age to climb the ladder, but she seems to like the challenge.

'Swings now,' Holly shouts, and Nathan climbs off the see-saw before slowly lowering her down. She slides off the seat and stumbles to the ground briefly, giggling. Then she runs off towards the swings. Chrissie falls into step beside Nathan.

'Feeling better now?' She's referring to his earlier mood, hoping that the fresh air and laughter of his daughter is enough to lift him.

He grunts, non-committally.

Chrissie wants to shake him, or start an argument – anything to force him into the moment with them. With *her*. Does he not realise how lonely it is for her at home all day? She misses the company of adults. The banter of the workplace. She hadn't felt ready to go back into the office for a long time, but she's starting to think she needs it.

Holly has made it to the swings and is attempting to climb into one of the ones with the enclosed seats and the bar to hold on to, but it's too high off the ground. She turns around to face them, raises her arms. 'Come *on*!'

Chrissie laughs. Holly is a cute, funny kid. Always keeping them entertained. She's just turned to say something to Nathan about what a good job they did creating her, but he's moving away from her.

'I'm just going for a wander around the park,' he says. 'I need to clear my head.'

And with that he's off out of the children's play area, towards the far end of the park.

Great.

'Come on, Mummy!' Holly is attempting to climb into the swing again and Chrissie jogs over, grabs her by the waist and plops her inside it, then steps back, pulling her high, pushing her hard. Holly squeals. 'Higher, higher!' Chrissie pushes the swing again, mumbles replies to Holly's inane chatter, all the while watching Nathan as he walks around the perimeter of the park.

For a moment she thinks he's talking to someone on his phone. But he can't be. She saw him leave it in the kitchen. He must be talking to himself instead. Hopefully he's telling himself to stop being such a moany git and have some fun with his family.

'Nuff now,' Holly says, bringing Chrissie back from her musings about her grumpy, distracted husband. She lifts Holly out of the swing and she's barely touched the floor before she's racing across the park again towards the treehouse.

One of the twins is climbing the ladder, and Holly waits patiently at the bottom for him to get to the top. The child's mum is sitting on the bench now, near the person with the umbrella. She's trying to keep an eye on both of her kids, the other one currently spinning himself dizzy on a mini-roundabout thing that Holly hates. The first twin launches himself down the scramble net on the other side of the treehouse, and disappears underneath, before running away, waving his arms, roaring about being a monster. The woman is a marvel. Chrissie can't imagine how she would keep track of two Hollys.

Holly is in the treehouse now, standing in the open doorway that leads out to the fireman's pole. Most of the bigger kids step out and grab the pole, sliding down, but it's too far for Holly to reach, so her usual game is to launch herself off the treehouse platform into Chrissie's arms instead. Sometimes Chrissie pretends to fall, and they roll about in the bark-mulch for a minute, throwing the shaved wooden flakes at each other. But it's too wet for that today.

'Ready, Mummy?' Holly calls down from the treehouse. The first twin from before is on the ladder again, climbing up.

'One sec, sweetie.' Chrissie scans the park for Nathan, but she can't see him. The park is a decent size, but not so big that she wouldn't be able to see him even at the far side. Her stomach does a small somersault, wondering where the hell he is, but then she senses him, and whirls around to find him standing behind her. He's grinning, but it looks forced.

'I'm back!' he says with fake enthusiasm. 'What's happening here then?'

'Oh, you're just in time for Holly's very special game . . .' But he's already left her side, and is now leaning against the back of the bench, hands in pockets.

Chrissie is about to say something else, when a loud ringing makes her jump. *Christ, I really did turn the volume up.* Chrissie checks on Holly, sees her take a step backwards into the depths of the treehouse. The little boy squeezes past her and flings himself down the fireman's pole, landing in a heap at the bottom and grabbing a handful of bark-mulch and flinging it into the air as he jumps back up.

'Back in one second,' Chrissie tells Holly, and jogs off towards the house. 'Watch her, Nathan,' she calls over her shoulder from the path.

In the kitchen, she snatches up the phone and swipes to answer it. 'Hello?' There's no number on the screen. Must be the client. It always comes up as a private number. 'This is Chrissie,' she says. 'Are you there?'

No one answers. The phone hisses with static.

'Oh for God's sake,' she mutters under her breath, her mouth away from the microphone. 'Hello?' she says again.

The hiss is replaced by a dialling tone. The call has been ended.

She sighs, dropping the phone back on to the worktop. She should go back outside to finish off playtime, but Nathan will be back with Holly before long. He clearly isn't up for it today and she's tired now too, and beginning to get hungry. Her stomach growls in agreement. She walks over to pick up the takeaway leaflets. One of them has slid across the wooden floor right into the living room, and that's where she is, crouched down picking it up, when Nathan storms into the house. She hears him before she sees him, his voice loud, his words punctuated by ragged gasps of breath.

'Chrissie, where the hell are you?'

She steps back through from the living room into the kitchen, as Nathan appears, Holly in his arms. His eyes are wide and wild.

'Holly? Oh God, Holly . . . Nathan, what the—'

'She jumped out of the bloody treehouse, Chrissie. Landed flat on her back. She was watching that other kid, the little ginger one running wild . . .'

Chrissie's breath sticks in her throat. 'You're supposed to catch her, Nathan. This is what she does. This is her game. You would know that if you ever paid any bloody attention! Oh God . . .' She takes a step towards him.

Holly lies limp in his arms.

Chrissie tries to swallow. Her throat has constricted so much that she feels like she's going to choke. 'Holly!'

'I think she's just winded herself . . .' Nathan says, his voice calm. He carries her through to the living room and lays her on the sofa. Holly's eyes are closed, her face pale.

'Nathan!' *How can he be so calm?* Chrissie is screaming now, pushing herself into the space between her husband and her daughter. 'What's wrong with her . . . Oh God . . .'

'Calm down, Chrissie!' he snaps. 'Please. Give us some air.'

'Holly!' Chrissie cries, kneeling down against the sofa. Nathan gently pushes her away. 'Chrissie, for fuck's sake. Call an ambulance!' Then he is talking to Holly, in a gentle, sing-song voice. 'Holly? Can you hear me, honey?' He turns his head to the side and leans down over her face, listening for her breath.

'Jesus, Nathan, I can't . . .' Chrissie shuffles backwards, away from the sofa, manages to stand up. Her mobile is in the kitchen. Her chest is tight, she can barely breathe. She can't lose Holly. She's already lost so much. Her chest tightens further, and she feels like she might pass out. She staggers through to the kitchen and grabs her phone, leans against the counter as she tries to tap in the number to call for help. Her fingers refuse to cooperate.

From the living room, Nathan's voice is drifting through. 'Come on, Holly, wake up for Daddy. You're all right. You're all right.'

She manages to dial 999. Manages to tell them she needs an ambulance. Then the pain in her chest tightens another notch, and she feels herself slipping, sliding further down until everything goes black.

◆　◆　◆

The banging on the door brings her to enough to get to her feet, but she opens it in a haze, her hand absentmindedly touching the back of her head where she hit it on the counter as she fell. The green-uniformed paramedics come inside, and one of them comes to her, tries to talk to *her*, though she's mumbling, 'No, it's Holly, it's Holly.'

At last the woman understands. 'But we need to see to you too, my love. Can you tell me your name?'

'Chrissie . . . It's Chrissie. I'm fine. I just—'

'Let's get you on to a chair, eh. Make you a bit more comfortable. Did you hit your head, Chrissie?'

'I think so, but I'm fine . . .' She lets the woman help her on to a chair. Wonders if she can smell the alcohol off her. It was only two glasses. Or was it three? She's not a drinker. Not like that.

Then Nathan is there in front of her, cradling Holly in his arms, her face pressed into his shoulder. She's crying softly. Gripping tightly to her dad's neck.

The male paramedic walks in behind him. 'Quite the hero, your husband. Perfect resus skills. We might have to offer him a job.'

'Are you going to take her in?' Nathan says. 'Check her over?'

He nods. 'I think that's best, sir. Just to be on the safe side. Her airway is clear and she's breathing fine, but it wouldn't hurt to take her in. I'm sure she'll be out again in no time. I doubt they'll need her overnight.'

'Might like to get your wife checked over too?' the female paramedic says. 'She's had a nasty shock.'

Holly's sobs are muffled, but so full of anguish that Chrissie bursts into tears herself.

'Shhh,' Nathan says, 'everyone's all right now. Shhh . . .' He crouches down to Chrissie, extends an arm, gesturing towards her. Pulling her in. She hugs into him tightly, feeling the warmth of her husband. The shaking fear of her child.

It's OK. Everyone is OK.

This time.

◆ ◆ ◆

Back home, several hours later – pizza demolished, coffee brewing, Nathan upstairs reading Holly a story – she texts Wendy:

So Holly had a little accident today . . . flung herself out of the treehouse before Nathan could catch her.

Oh shit! Is she OK?

She's fine . . . luckily. A little egg on the back of her head and a few tears. Knocked the breath out of her. It's lucky there was a soft landing. Bloody Nathan! I don't know what he was playing at. He was totally distracted in the park.

Bet you were terrified. Want me to come round?

Nah. It's fine. Look, I wanted to apologise for earlier.

You didn't do anything.

I was snappy. I didn't mean to be. I love you, you know.

I love you too, you daft cow.

Can we definitely sort out that night out soon?

#HELLYEAH.

Haha!

Oh wait . . . meant to tell you earlier – I bumped into your neighbour when I left . . .

Oh?

Yeah. He gave me a filthy look. You been throwing wine
bottles in their recycling bin or something?

Ha! You know, I don't know what's up there. I haven't seen
Maureen for ages, but whenever I see Arthur he looks like
he's just found something disgusting on his shoe.

That sounds about right. You always did have a way with
words. Glad to know it's not just me he's taken a dislike to.

Bit odd though, I agree. Thanks for telling me.

No worries. Night night, babe xx

Night x

Chrissie tiptoes upstairs and into Holly's room, where both Holly
and Nathan are sound asleep. His long legs curled up to his chest,
Holly squeezed in beside him. She feels a surge of pure love, like
a lump that spreads across her whole chest, gripping her tight.
Anchoring her here. She turns off Holly's night light and pulls the
door closed, leaving just a small gap. The way she likes it.

She goes into her own bedroom, pulls off her jeans.

The business card falls to the floor, and she bends to pick it up.

*Joseph Marshall*
*Consultant*

He'd sounded so ridiculous, talking through her letterbox like that.
*What if I could ensure that you never had to experience that again?* He
was clearly a lunatic, some kind of freak. But now she can't stop
thinking . . . what if he, or someone, or anything *could* ensure that?

What if there really was something that could be done about the pain, the never-ending misery of it all? There's not, of course. That's not how the world works. She lays the business card on the bedside cabinet and climbs into bed.

For a while, she just lies there, staring up at the ceiling – thinking about Holly, her limp body in Nathan's arms. Thinking about Nathan, his quick actions when it really mattered – despite it being his stupid fault that he didn't catch her. And about Wendy, her best friend. What would she do without any one of them? Her head spins with the possibilities. She misses her mum. Her heart aches when she thinks about how much she would have loved Holly. Tears slide down her cheeks and she leaves them there to dry, leaving tight, itchy trails. She closes her eyes, and, eventually, she falls asleep.

# Six

## MICHAEL (JULY 1980)

Michael takes a step back from the microscope and sucks in a quick, sharp breath. He removes the slide and places it back into the protective case. His hands are shaking, and he clenches them into fists, releases. Does it again. A bubble of excitement pops in his stomach. Can this really be happening? He flips the cover over the eyepiece and starts pacing up and down between the two lab benches. He glances around, checking that no one is paying him any attention, before doing a little air punch.

Then he composes himself.

He slips the little case containing the slide into the pocket of his lab coat and hurries out of the room.

Edward's office door is closed, but Michael doesn't bother to knock.

'It's happening,' Michael says. He's trying his best to sound calm. Act like the serious post-doctoral scientist that he's meant to be. But he can't keep the excitement out of his voice.

Edward looks up from behind the stack of papers on his desk. His hair is sticking up in clumps, from where he has been fiddling with it, and his glasses are perched on top of his head.

'Babooshka' by Kate Bush fades in and out, and as the chorus starts, Michael has a sudden urge to fling his arms in the air and screech along.

'This better be good, Mike.' Edward stretches over the papers to turn the radio off. 'I've got fourteen more of these buggers to mark.'

'Forget first-year experiments, Edward. We've got bigger fish to fry.' Michael lays the slide case on the desk, on top of the nearest pile of papers. 'You need to look at this, now.'

Edward's eyebrows shoot up.

Michael is already pulling Edward's microscope out from the wall where it has been pushed out of the way to make space for several boxes of lab supplies: Petri dishes, slides, glass beakers. More stacks of papers. When did Edward last do any *real* work, Michael wonders absently. He's never been one for full-on experiments, but he seems to be doing more schmoozing and less of anything else, lately.

Edward slides his glasses down on to his face and comes around to the other side of the desk. 'What's going on? What've you got?'

'I've got regeneration. That's what.' He slots the slide into place, puts his eye on the eyepiece, adjusting the focus.

'That sounds like some serious *Doctor Who* shit, Mikey.' He elbows him out of the way. 'Come on then, let me see . . .'

Michael steps back and lets Edward into his place.

'*Cell* regeneration,' Michael says. 'Unless I'm seeing things.'

Edward readjusts the focus for his own eyes. The room is silent, except for their breathing.

Michael swallows. Maybe he's got it wrong. Maybe he *is* seeing things. He's been at this for so long, and today he's so damn tired. Maybe there's something wrong with his eyes. Floaters. His retina is detaching and he's about to go blind . . .

'Holy shit!' Edward steps back from the microscope, eyes wide. His mouth hangs open for a moment before it stretches into a wide grin. 'Tell me . . . is this . . .'

Michael takes a deep breath. 'It's early days yet.'

'Just tell me . . . is this your virus? Have you finally got it to work?'

'Like I said, it's early days. But yes. I infused it into a batch of blood cells from a newly deceased rodent specimen.' He pauses, takes a breath. 'The rodent was killed quickly, by running an electric current into its tank. Heart failure. I drew the blood, and I infused it with the virus. Higher viral load than normal. Highest I've tried. To be honest, I was on the verge of giving up, creating yet *another* new batch . . .'

Edward puts his eye back on to the microscope. Michael knows what he's seeing: the fluorescent-dyed cells puffing up like hundreds of tiny blooming flowers.

'It's still going,' Edward says. 'It's like watching a kaleidoscope. It's beautiful, Mike. You absolute *genius.*'

'Let's not get carried away. It's worked in vitro . . . Doesn't mean it'll work in vivo.'

Edward steps away again, still grinning. 'Well, then. How many mice have you got left?'

'Only one . . . I need to order some—'

'One it is, then. I assume you still have some of that infusion ready to go?'

'Well, yes, but—'

'So we can inject it straight in, right? Into the actual mouse – not just play around with its blood? Give it a heart attack – just like you did with the other . . . What's the difference? If it works in the test tube, it'll work in the body, right?'

'In theory, yes, but we're not there yet – this is the first time it's worked in a test-tube culture. I need to repeat that several times, monitor it – before I even consider injecting it into an actual animal.'

'Come on, Mike. Live a little. Who's going to know? If it works, then we've got a proper breakthrough on our hands . . . If not, we order some more mice. Carry on with your in vitro testing.'

'It's not ethical, Edward. You know I can't go straight from in vitro to in vivo after one success. We need these results to be robust. To hold up to peer scrutiny. We can't just start cutting corners and injecting into live animals on a whim. I need to monitor these blood cells . . .' He trails off, knowing it's a lost cause. Scientific protocol has never been Edward's forte.

'Humour me, Mike. Come on . . . Listen, I've got these potential investors. You want to do something big, right? You want to save the bloody world, right?'

'Well, of course I do, but—'

'Well, nothing. Let's go and kill our little furry friend, and bring him back to life!'

◆  ◆  ◆

Michael stabs the key into the lock a few times before it finally goes in. He pauses, takes a breath. Every part of his body seems to be wobbling. He's never been much of a drinker, but after the breakthrough, it'd been hard not to be carried along with Edward's excitement – even if it was a little premature. The first pint had slid down like water, as if he'd been stranded on an island, dehydrated for days. After the second, he'd expressed his worry at injecting the mouse. Scared that he was playing God . . . but Edward had waved his concerns away with a whisky chaser.

'It's one mouse, Mike. You need to think big. Think about the future . . . This could make us . . .'

'*Us*,' he'd muttered into his pint. But Edward hadn't heard him, or chosen not to.

Edward has let his own work slide over the past few months. Feeling jaded, Michael supposes. No one had told them that a life in research would be easy – in fact, several had tried to put them off it, suggested they get jobs in industry, where they'd be paid more and frustrated less. But that wasn't him – although he is still surprised that Edward hadn't chosen the smoother, more lucrative path.

If this works, though, Edward has plans for them both.

Michael just wants the damn mouse to survive.

'Mike, is that you?' The voice comes from behind the as yet unopened door. He's successfully inserted the key but still not managed to turn it. For a moment, the voice is disembodied, disorientating. He starts to laugh.

'This is me, but who are *yoooou*,' he says, falling against the door, just as it is pulled sharply inwards, drawing him in with it.

He staggers inside, pitches forward, lands with a thud on his hands and knees. Luckily he's too drunk to notice the pain.

After a few moments of confusion, he looks behind him and up. Blinks. She's staring down at him from far, far away. 'Sandy? Is that you?' He turns, tugs on the bottom of her nightdress.

'For goodness' sake! Get up,' she says. 'Look at the state of you.'

He takes a steadying breath, then pushes himself to his feet. The room tilts slightly, and he has to lean on the wall to stop it spinning.

'Where have you been?' Her voice has softened. 'I was worried . . .'

He grabs hold of his wife and kisses her hard on the mouth. She stiffens, briefly, before relaxing into his arms and kissing him back. Her arms go around his neck. He squeezes her tightly, runs a hand down her back. Lifts up her nightdress.

She pulls away, just a little. Her words come out in short bursts: 'I think we need to continue this somewhere a little more comfortable, don't you?'

◆　◆　◆

Afterwards, Michael lies in bed, wrapped up in blankets. He can't stop smiling. Thinking about what happened in the lab. Early days. *Very* early days. But something, at last, to make the years of hard work worthwhile. Long days and disappointments are the norm. Not everyone can hack it. Edward, for example – he's sure that he was on the verge of quitting. He'd seen a glossy magazine on top of the many piles of paperwork in his office. *Science Today* open at the jobs page. Edward is being lured by industry. By money. He can't blame him for that, but he'd always hoped that the two of them could do something together . . . and finally, it seems like it might not be such a pipe dream after all.

He's still musing when Sandra comes back into the room carrying a wide tray. Michael can smell the sharp tang of cheese, the comforting charred aroma of toast. He props himself up on the stack of pillows, and she lays the tray on the bed.

'Cheese on toast and tea in bed,' he says. 'You're far too good to me, my darling.'

Sandra climbs in beside him and lifts a piece of toast, a string of cheese stretching up from another on the plate, until it snaps and sticks to her chin. Michael takes the other half and demolishes half of it in one go.

'You know,' he says, pausing to lick a piece of cheese from the roof of his mouth, 'if this works out—'

'*When* it works out,' she chides, smiling.

'Sorry, *when* it works out . . . when Edward has secured this funding that he's so certain he can get us . . . once we have something to sell . . .'

'We can move somewhere bigger?' She snuggles in next to him. 'Somewhere with a second bedroom, perhaps?'

He leans in and kisses her, savouring the warm, tangy grease on her lips.

'That's exactly what I was thinking.'

She leans across and pulls out her bedside drawer. She turns back to him, presents the packet of birth-control pills like a trophy. 'Maybe I shouldn't bother about seeing Dr Holden for a new prescription then?'

He grins and drags her under the covers.

'Wait, watch the tray . . .' she says.

'Forget the tray.'

He's in the process of peeling off her nightdress when the phone rings, startling them both.

'Oh for goodness' sake, ignore it,' she says.

He slides himself out from under the covers. 'One second,' he says, fumbling for the phone on his bedside cabinet. It's late now, and late calls are never good news. He can't just ignore it.

Sandra gives a little grunt of displeasure and slides out from the other side of the bed, picking up the tray and setting it down on the floor.

Michael picks up the phone. 'Do you know what time it is?' he says.

'It's me,' Edward says.

Michael stands up, stretching the cord. When he'd left him a few hours ago, Edward had been excited, jovial and most definitely drunk. He's sober now. This isn't good. Michael grips the phone tighter. 'Are you calling me from the police station?'

Edward gives him a small, dry laugh. 'Not this time.'

'Then what—'

'I came back to the lab. Wanted to check on our little friend. See if he needed anything. I was expecting to find him spinning away on that wheel of his . . .'

Michael's heart sinks. He doesn't need to hear the rest. 'I shouldn't have left him alone,' he says. 'Not so soon after the infusion.'

'Too late now, Mike.' Edward pauses, and Michael can hear him dragging on a cigarette. 'He's dead.'

# Seven

## CHRISSIE (NOW)

'It's nice, having breakfast together,' Chrissie says to Nathan, as she watches Holly draw smiley faces on her plate with ketchup. Normally she'd tell her off for making a mess, but seeing her there, the hint of dark circles under her eyes on her still-pale face, it seems cruel. Chrissie had woken up twice in the night, panicked and sweating – both times, going in to check that Holly was OK. Nathan had slept there all night, curled around her like a protective blanket.

'Don't we have breakfast together at the weekend?' Nathan says, from behind the paper. He'd got up earlier than usual to go up to the shop for bacon and eggs, a little treat instead of the usual weekday cereal rush, and he was hanging around longer than usual too. Did it take their daughter falling out of the treehouse to get him to spend some time with them?

'We don't, actually,' Chrissie says. 'You're usually off out to the gym first thing.'

'And Mummy and me like to have toast in bed,' Holly pipes up. She's moving scrambled egg around the plate now, turning it into hair for her ketchup-man.

'Oh, is that right?' Nathan drops the paper and steals a finger of toast from Holly's plate. 'Don't see much toast-eating today, missy.'

'Hey,' Holly says. 'That's for his eyebrow.'

Nathan stands up and squeezes himself around the back of the table, starts tickling Holly under her armpits. 'I love eyebrows the bestest,' he says, kissing her forehead, pretending to nibble on it. Holly giggles.

The doorbell rings, and Chrissie jumps. Glances at the clock. 'Oh . . . time to wash your face and get to nursery, kiddo.'

'Time for me to go too,' Nathan says. He kisses Chrissie on the head and disappears into the hall, while Chrissie takes Holly through to the downstairs bathroom to get her cleaned up.

Holly is chattering happily while she washes her face, then brushes her teeth, spraying toothpaste on the mirror.

Chrissie hears hushed voices, then the front door being closed. Wendy appears in the bathroom, her face flushed.

'Good morning, my favourite girls,' she says. 'How's our little treehouse-jumper this morning?'

Holly grins a toothpastey smile into the mirror. 'Look . . . I've got an egg,' she says, pointing to the back of her head with her toothbrush. 'You want to touch it?'

Chrissie rolls her eyes. 'You'd never know anything happened. She's like a rubber ball, this one. Thank God.'

Wendy picks up a pink hairbrush and starts to untangle Holly's hair. 'Nathan was late, wasn't he? He's not usually here when I arrive.'

'He nipped out and got us a fancy breakfast. Didn't he, sweetpea?'

Holly nods, jerking the hairbrush out of Wendy's hand. 'Can I have bunches?'

'Can I have bunches, *please*, Wendy,' Chrissie says.

Holly sighs. '*Pleeeease*, Wendy?'

43

'Of course you can.'

She catches Chrissie's eye in the mirror, and Chrissie sees tension in her face, her dark circles matching Holly's. Wendy starts wrapping a hairband with a ladybird around Holly's first bunch.

'You OK, Wends?' Chrissie says.

'Fine. Didn't sleep too well, worrying about this little one.' She wraps the tie around the second bunch, then tugs them both, grinning at Holly in the mirror. She looks like she wants to say more, but then changes her mind and looks away.

Once the house is cleared up, Chrissie fires up her laptop and opens the graphics file with the restaurant logo. She frowns. It's just not coming to her, this one. Probably because she hates the name of the place, and it seems that whatever design she tries just looks cheap and tacky with the 'Meet-4-Meat' name attached. She'd meant to contact them again last night after that aborted call, but then Holly had happened.

She sighs and pushes the laptop away.

It's times like this that she misses being in an office. When she'd worked at the design agency in Holborn, she'd had plenty of people to brainstorm ideas with. Plenty of resources too – a wall of design books, far more stock-image libraries than she has now, plus just that buzzy feeling of being around other creatives. Even a rubbish design could end up half-decent after a few pairs of eyes had scanned over it, people suggesting tweaks that could turn things right around.

She misses Andy, too.

The place was supposedly a hot-desking environment – meant to encourage multiple collaborations, prevent people getting stale – but somehow she and Andy had ended up on the same double-desk right from when he started, and no one had done anything to stop them. It'd helped both of them advance their design skills – he was a whizz at finding anything at all that she needed online, and she was the expert at finding the right combination of images for the mood-boards that helped shape every campaign they managed.

He'd tried to keep in touch after she left . . . when she'd found herself unexpectedly pregnant, suffering a resurgence of grief at her mum not being there to share this huge milestone with her. Numb and confused, she'd retreated from him, from her work – from everything in her old life.

The pregnancy had triggered an episode of PTSD. The trauma of the circumstances of her mother's death never far from her mind, the guilt eating away at her. The blame she attached to her father was only a distraction against her own part in it all. She should've been there. All she could do now was be there for her own daughter. Since the day she was born, all Chrissie had done was focus on keeping Holly safe and alive . . . and trying her hardest to keep herself sane.

Maybe she should contact him? His last message to her had been an email – telling her that although he was hurt by her lack of contact, he understood that she was dealing with a lot . . . and he'd always be there for her.

She's not quite ready, though . . . and besides, she knows what Andy would say. They'd dealt with more than one tricky client in their time.

'Just remember,' he'd say. 'The client doesn't actually know what they want at all. That's what you're here for. It's up to *you* to tell them what they *really* want.'

The restaurant is closed.

Not only closed, but it looks like it has no intention of opening up any time soon. The windows are smeared white with Windolene. A cardboard sign is stuck to the inside pane on the door: CLOSED FOR REFURBISHMENT. There's a phone number underneath. She frowns, pulling out her phone and tapping the number in. She hits the green button to dial, and while she's waiting, tries to find a bit of glass that hasn't been smeared out, cups her hands and peers inside. No luck. And no answer. She leaves a terse message.

That's the end of that then.

Maybe they finally listened to someone and they're trying to come up with a better concept for the place? Whatever the reason, she's not going to waste any more time on the logo.

They could've at least had the decency to contact her. Maybe Wendy's right. Maybe the whole thing is some sort of front. She kicks a stone into the gutter and it flips expertly through the bars of a drain, landing in the water below with a satisfying plop.

◆ ◆ ◆

She stops at the Co-op on the way home. Determined that they won't eat any more junk this week, she's thrown as many fruits and vegetables into her basket as she can fit and is inspecting the ripeness of an avocado when she senses someone standing close behind her.

'Afternoon, Chrissie.' Karen Cole is dressed in the typical store-manager's uniform. The shirt is gaping a bit across her chest, her name badge pinned above her breast. 'Not seen you for a while – been shopping elsewhere, have you?'

Chrissie tries to smile. 'Ah, you know me, Karen. Like to mix things up a bit.'

Karen tries to smile, but it's more of a sneer. 'You know our produce is much fresher than anything you order online. That stuff's been in a warehouse for months before they even put it on the shelves.' She nods at Chrissie's basket. 'Look at the colour of those bananas. Nice and bright and *natural*, aren't they?' Her eyes flick upwards towards Chrissie's dyed blonde hair.

She knows her roots are due a touch-up, but it's not that bad, is it? Why is it that anything Karen says or does manages to rub her up the wrong way?

'I hear Tommy was in trouble yesterday—'

It's out of her mouth before she can stop herself. She usually tries not to respond to Karen's needling, but she's lacking patience today.

Karen's fake smile has vanished. She leans in close. 'Don't you be saying things about my boy. He's a *good* boy, my Tommy.' She pauses for a moment, and then the smile is back on her face. 'Have a lovely day, *Mrs Tate*.'

Chrissie squeezes the avocado so hard that her fingernails pierce the flesh. She glances around quickly, then, sure that no one has seen, drops it back into the display crate and pushes it under the others. Then she squeezes another, making sure it has just the right amount of give, before placing it in her basket.

When Wendy arrives back with Holly, Chrissie's tempted to offer wine again, but she doesn't want to fall into that habit, so she brews a pot of fresh mint tea while Holly scampers through for her TV fix.

'I was thinking we could do this Saturday,' Chrissie says, inhaling the fresh scent of the mint and feeling her head clear at last.

Wendy is flicking through a glossy magazine at the table. 'Military-style coats are back for the winter, apparently.'

'It's July. That magazine is ancient.'

Wendy flips it over to the front. 'So it is. These are last year's coats. Maybe they'll be in the sale.'

'How can you think about winter coats when it's glorious sunshine outside?'

'Yeah. Let's do Saturday. We can get the train into Waterloo. You OK to drive to the station or is Minnie Mouse heading back to the garage?'

Chrissie smiles at the pet name for her treasured little car. It's an original Mini Cooper from the 1980s, racing green with a white stripe. It had been her mum's pride and joy, and Chrissie had tried to look after it as best she could, but it was an old car and it was prone to things falling apart on a regular basis, the latest issue being the loose seat-belt clip on the passenger side and the driver's side lock not popping down properly, meaning that most of the time it's unlocked. Nathan thinks it's a clunky rust-bucket and refuses to drive it, which suits Chrissie just fine.

'Nah, not yet. I couldn't get an appointment until the end of the month.' She looks at her friend. 'Are you OK, Wendy? You seem a bit distracted.'

Wendy folds the magazine shut and places it back on the stack of them next to the table. 'Sorry,' she says. 'I'm just a bit tired, still.' She takes a sip of her tea. 'Nathan's all right with babysitting on Saturday then?'

Chrissie laughs. 'You mean, *being a parent*? And yes, of course. Not that I've asked him yet, but I imagine his plans will involve pizza and a Pixar movie. I might get him to take her out in the day too, so I can have some time to myself.'

Wendy takes another sip of her tea. Smiles.

'Looking forward to it. This night out is just what we both need.'

# Eight

## Chrissie (Now)

'So, I've been thinking . . .' Chrissie says, propping herself up on one elbow. She pokes Nathan in the back and he grunts. 'Don't pretend to be asleep.'

'What time is it? And why are you awake before me?'

'Couldn't sleep . . . Too much stuff whirring around in my head.'

He rolls on to his back, turns his head towards her. 'So what have you been thinking, exactly? Don't tell me . . . If this night out goes well, you want to go away for a weekend? Next thing you'll be telling me you're going for a month's hiking in Nepal.'

Chrissie laughs. 'As if.'

'I told you. Gareth at work's missus did that. Came back a completely different person. They're divorced now. She lives with a woman.'

'Maybe she was rebelling against being called someone's *missus*.'

'Oh, don't start going all feminist on me, woman – it's too bloody early.' Before she can protest, he grabs her and drags her on top of him. Kisses her hard. Then pulls back. Kisses her again, softer. This time she responds. 'I've missed this,' he murmurs into her neck.

She feels him getting hard, and she shifts position. Not ready. Not yet.

'Wait . . .' She sits up, shuffles herself off him. Moves back to a place beside him, and tries to snuggle in.

He sighs. 'I'm sorry . . . I thought—'

'No. It's fine. It's me. You know it's me.' Tears prick at the corner of her eyes. 'I want to . . . it's just, it's been so long . . . I—'

He leans in and kisses her gently. 'I shouldn't have tried—'

'Please,' she says, tears running freely now. 'Never give up on me.'

He grins. 'As if. Come on, babe. We'll get there. We always do. Now . . .' He props himself up on an elbow, mirroring her earlier position. 'If it wasn't my glorious body . . . what was it that you'd been thinking about?'

She wipes a hand across her cheek. 'I was thinking that maybe it was time for us to move to a bigger house?'

He sighs. 'Do you really think moving will fix things?'

'I'm not suggesting we run away. Just sometimes . . . I don't know. I just feel like we could do with a fresh start. Besides, there are practical reasons too.'

'I agree that the stair situation is not ideal . . . but she hasn't actually fallen down them, has she? Typical that it would be the playground that would prove the biggest hazard. It's funny how she's so careful in the house, but outside it seems like anything goes with that girl.' He laughs. 'But she's fine, isn't she? No harm done. She might be more careful now. In fact, I think it's good that it happened.'

'Good that our three-year-old fell out of a treehouse? What if she'd hit her head? What if—'

Nathan turns over and pushes himself out of the bed. 'I need to get to work.'

Conversation over.

Chrissie whips the duvet over her head and wishes, just for a moment, that she could disappear. She's always been a worrier, but since Holly's fall, the thought of the stairs is starting to haunt her. There's a gap between her and Nathan, too, and she needs to find a way to close it, before it's too late. With the work he does, she doesn't think he has time to have an affair – but it would be better for them all if she could sort things out before he considers it a possibility.

◆　◆　◆

'Don't forget the recycling,' Nathan calls, disappearing out of the front door. She is in the kitchen with Holly, watching her stir her four remaining Cheerios around the leftover milk.

'These are like the rings at the pool, Mummy. For people when they fall in and they can't swim.'

'So they are, sweetpea. Tell you what though, why don't you eat them all up? Wendy will be here in a minute.'

Wendy is running late, and there's no time to chat when she arrives. Chrissie kisses Holly quickly and waves them both away as they hurry down the drive. Then she picks up the recycling box and takes it down to the bottom of the drive.

She's doing a final check of the contents of the box when she hears the sound of glass chinking on glass, and turns around just in time to see her neighbour, Arthur, stand up. He'd been obscured by the fence, and she'd been rushing. Distracted. If she'd known he was there, she'd have waited inside a little longer.

Damn.

She swallows. 'Morning, Arthur.' She tries a half-smile. Things have been strained between them for a while now, and she's fed up faking a huge grin and getting a cold glare in return.

He looks at her intently, as if he is trying to decide whether to even speak at all.

*Typical.* Chrissie goes back to sorting out her cardboards and plastics, making sure nothing has been dropped into the box that shouldn't be there. She feels her cheeks burn. She hates confrontation, and she still has no idea why Arthur is being so hostile.

'Chrissie . . .' he says eventually. It's something between a statement and a question.

She stands up. 'Is there a problem, Arthur? Have we done something to upset you?'

He looks away. 'If you can keep the noise down a bit,' he says, then ambles back up his driveway.

'What noise?' she shouts behind him.

He disappears into his house. Then calls back out to her, 'And keep an eye on that little girl of yours', just loud enough for her to hear.

His front door bangs shut.

Chrissie swears under her breath, kicks the recycling box across the pavement. It bumps into the fence post and tips half on to its side. A scrunched-up piece of card falls out. She bends down to right the box, pushing it up against her fence, and picks up the card, straightening it out.

It's Joseph Marshall's business card. Had she put it in there? She remembers taking it out of her jeans pocket, laying it beside the bed. Maybe Nathan saw it and assumed it was rubbish. He is pretty sharp at picking up things that are left lying around, keeping the place tidy – but it wouldn't be the first time he'd thrown away something of hers without checking.

She's about to toss it back into the recycling, but then she glances back at her house, up at Holly's bedroom, with the multi-coloured stars stuck to the window, and changes her mind.

*Mrs Tate – have you ever experienced grief?*

She takes the card back inside the house, feeling the weight of Arthur's stare.

*Keep an eye on that little girl of yours . . .*

It's as if he was reading her mind. She can't push the dark thoughts out of her head. What if Holly had really hurt herself . . . what if she wasn't OK? What if she still isn't? Children can have delayed bleeds on the brain after head injuries too, can't they? Just like adults? You hear about it all the time – someone falls, thinks they're fine, then a few days later – bam! Gone.

She pushes the door closed, leans back against it. Stands there at the bottom of the stairs, staring up at them. Fearing them. Despising them. She's been thinking about them a lot recently. She doesn't know why. Holly is always careful walking up and down them, but as Nathan had pointed out, she's only careful *in* the house. Her launching herself out of the treehouse proved that. What else might happen to her when Chrissie isn't watching? She can't watch her 24-7. She can't smother her.

But she can't lose her either.

*Have you ever experienced grief?*

What if there really was some way to protect Holly? Nathan, too. Things might be a bit strained at the moment, but she knows she'd fall apart if she was to lose him.

She just can't bear the thought of losing anyone else.

She walks through to the kitchen and sits down. Stares at the crumpled business card. Then she takes out her phone, emails Joseph Marshall, and waits.

◆ ◆ ◆

She doesn't have to wait very long.

The kettle has only just boiled when the doorbell goes. She knows it's him. Knows he's been waiting for her to contact him.

53

Bonkers as the proposition sounds, what parent *wouldn't* be tempted to at least look into it? Actually placing the call, though – that's something else again. But after what happened to Holly, she was rattled. Out of sorts. She's probably looking for answers that aren't there, but still . . .

*What if I could ensure that you never had to experience that again?*
She opens the door.

'Good morning, Mrs Tate. I'm very glad that you got in touch.'

'Can I get you a drink? Some tea—'

'Tea would be lovely. English breakfast. Milk, no sugar.' He bends down and carefully unlaces his shoes, slipping them off. Then he stands, straight-backed, hands in front, clutching his briefcase.

'Please,' she says, 'come through to the kitchen. It's where I spend most of my time during the day. I work from home, so I'm usually in here. Next to the kettle.' She's rambling. Nervous, now that he is in the house. He could be anyone. She's not normally so flustered, but there's something about this man that fascinates and unnerves her. She turns to find that he's now sitting at her kitchen table, his briefcase open in front of him. He has a pleasant but quite neutral expression on his face.

She pours hot water into the teapot. 'Maybe you could start by telling me who recommended me, for this . . . service of yours.'

'Not just yet,' he says.

She glances across at him, but his face is giving nothing away. 'Right. OK. Look – do you have any ID? I really should've asked you this at the door. I don't know what I was thinking.' She takes a deep breath, trying to quell her sudden panic at letting this stranger into her house. 'You haven't actually said who you work for . . .'

He takes an ID card out of his briefcase and slides it across the table towards her. She picks it up, checks the photograph. It's most definitely him. It's such a perfect likeness that it could've been taken right there and then. His hair is perfectly parted, just as it is now. He's clean-shaven, and his white shirt is tight around his neck. Navy tie knotted perfectly. She peers at the small type.

'Ministry of Defence?' She looks at him. 'I'm not sure I understand.'

'It's complicated, Mrs Tate. I'm contracted to the MOD, yes. But I'm not involved in that side of things. Perhaps if you let me take you through it?'

She turns the card over. FOR VERIFICATION, PLEASE CALL: 0500 775 3245. 'Where's 0500? That's not a UK dialling code, is it?'

He shakes his head. 'It's a special code. Government use. We have several. They aren't generally available to the public.'

'But if I call this number, they'll verify who you are?'

'That's right. My employee ID number is on the front.'

She frowns. 'But I've never seen a card like this before. You could've made it yourself for all I know. That number might go to some scam call centre where I'll end up getting ripped off just by dialling . . .'

He smiles. 'Of course. You're right to be wary. If you don't want to call the number, you can look up the government website, try to get through to a switchboard. But I'll warn you now, you won't get very far. Departments, subdivisions . . . You know what it's like trying to get hold of someone at the council? Try that but with even more hoops to jump through.'

He's right, of course.

She places the card down on the table and goes back to making the tea. Puts the mugs on a tray, and reaches into the cupboard for a packet of biscuits.

'No need to go to any trouble for me,' he says.

She's stalling. Wondering what it is that's made her invite him in. Give him a platform. It's all very strange, what with this and the

Meet-4-Meat debacle. Not to mention Holly's tumble out of the treehouse, and her neighbour's very odd behaviour.

'Please,' he says. 'I know this must seem very unusual. But if you can just give me a few moments of your time, I can explain how it all works, and you can decide what to do . . . and then you can go back to work, doing whatever it is you were planning on doing today.' He takes a mug from the tray and takes a sip of tea.

'Go on.'

'I'll cut to the chase, Mrs Tate. You've been selected . . . *recommended* . . . to take part in an important research programme. What we're offering is the opportunity for you to protect your loved ones' – he pauses, takes another sip of tea – 'and, more importantly, protect *yourself* . . . from ever having to face the pain of grief again.'

Chrissie lifts her own mug, cups it in her hands, enjoying the warmth. 'Well,' she says, 'that sounds completely ridiculous.'

He nods. 'I agree. But we've been running this programme for almost thirty years now. It's updated and improved by every single person who joins. In fact, the success rates are close to a hundred per cent now. It's really quite astonishing.'

'That's all very impressive, but you still haven't told me what it actually is . . .'

'It's quite simple, Mrs Tate. You need to decide on who is most important to you. Who are the loved ones whose deaths would hurt you most?'

*This is madness*, she thinks. She needs this man out of her house. Yet his question drops a montage of memories into her vision. Her mother: smiling, laughing. Whipping up chocolate cake batter, holding out the spoon for her to lick. Dabbing her skinned knees with Dettol after she'd come off her bike. The sting. The hot milk and Bourbon Creams on the couch afterwards, snuggled under a blanket.

Tears prick at her eyes. 'My mother—'

'Your mother is already gone, isn't she, Mrs Tate?' His voice softens. 'Who are the most important people in your life *now*?'

She picks up her tea. 'Holly, of course. My daughter.' She drinks. 'My husband. Nathan.'

'Anyone else?'

Another memory comes to her, and she pushes it away.

'A friend, perhaps? If there are no other family members?'

She nods, glances away. Doesn't want to catch his eye. Briefly thinks, *Andy*, then . . . 'Wendy. She's like a sister to me.'

'Good.' He takes a piece of paper out of his briefcase. 'The first part is usually the easiest.'

'The first part?'

'Three loved ones . . . People only really struggle when they have more than one child.'

'So they'd just choose more than three, then?'

He shakes his head. Scribbles on the form. 'I'm afraid not. Only three can be selected.'

How lucky for her that she has no one else she needs to add to the list. No dilemma to face. What if she had two children? Obviously Wendy wouldn't make the cut. And if she had three? Would she choose them all, over her husband? For all the times she has wished that they had a bigger family, she's now more than grateful that she hasn't.

'But why three? What's the significance of that?'

He puts down his pen. There's an interesting logo on the side. She's trying to work out what it is, when he catches her looking and picks it up again, covering the design with his palm. 'Three is an important number. Three wise men. Three wishes. The power of three . . . The best of three. Three blind mice.' He pauses, cocks his head once more. 'Obviously it's the minimum number that can be tested for a truly scientific experiment.'

'Experiment?'

'Of sorts.'

'I still don't understand.'

'I'll explain it in more detail next time. It's a lot to process right now.' He takes out another piece of paper, scribbles something on the top. 'OK, and now I need the replacements.'

'Sorry, what?'

He holds his pen, stares into her eyes. 'You've chosen three people you want to be saved. Now you have to choose the three people you want to replace.'

An icy finger trails across the back of her neck. 'When you say, *replace* . . .'.

He sighs. Then speaks slowly, carefully, as if he is talking to a child. 'If you want to prevent the deaths of your loved ones, then you need to select the people you want to die instead.'

# Nine

## MICHAEL (SEPTEMBER 1980)

Michael places the tip of the scalpel on the mouse's small belly, and cuts. He makes one careful incision, and the stomach cavity spills open, as if unzipped. He used to be squeamish when carrying out the business-end of pathology investigations, but after opening thousands of mice, a few rats, and even a few rabbits – it has become second nature. The most distressing part of his job is dealing with the protesters outside the lab. It doesn't happen often, and they usually have some advance warning, but although most of the activists are peaceful, it's not unheard of for scientists to be attacked.

He sympathises with them, but for him, carrying out animal experiments is a part of his job that he can never see going away. There are hopes that maybe one day all testing might be carried out in vitro – generated cell structures instead of the real thing – but that's a long way off, and he doubts that it could ever fully replace animals. What people also fail to grasp is, if you were to stop testing on animals, drugs would be entering human test subjects with a far lower safety profile.

On his less patient days, he's been known to ask the activists if any of them are in receipt of prescription drugs – or even paracetamol for their headaches. Would they forego these things to save their beloved rodents?

He uses tweezers in one hand, and the scalpel in the other, to remove the mouse's heart. Then he carefully bisects the tiny organ and places it on a slide.

The lab doors swing open and Edward appears. 'Any progress?'

Michael glances at him out of the corner of his eye, as he puts the slide on to the microscope. 'What's with the suit?'

'Ah . . . Thought I told you? Important visitors coming today. They'll want a tour. Progress update. The usual.'

Michael slots the slide into place and turns to face Edward. 'Another one dead. That's the progress update. Fifteen since July . . . Sixteen if you're counting our unofficial Patient Zero. That one is an outlier, though. I'm really only interested in the five batches of three.'

Edward shoves his hands into his pockets. 'Any extension of the time between infusion and death, at least? Give me some kind of hope here.'

Michael picks up his notebook and flicks to the most recent page of findings. 'Well . . . the batch-to-batch averages are looking good. And looking at them individually, it's one hundred and twenty-two hours, for Number Fifteen.'

'That's over five days. What was the one before? Three days?'

Michael runs a finger down the page. 'Three and a half, actually. Eighty-four hours.' He flips the page and draws two perpendicular lines on the blank page. Then he flips back, then back again. Draws fifteen evenly spaced marks along the horizontal axis, then five marks on the vertical, which he labels in twenty-five-unit increments, up to one hundred and twenty-five. He starts marking dots on the graph, flipping back and forth until he has all fifteen measurements. Then he carefully draws a curve, connecting all the dots.

Edward leans in closer. 'So, excluding our little zero, who only lasted around six hours . . . we've got steady progression here, wouldn't you say? Ten hours to one hundred and twenty-two . . .'

Michael runs a finger along the curve. 'There are some plateaus, you can see.' He takes a red pen and draws three circles around the areas where the line is fairly steady. 'They correspond to the new batches of infusion.'

'So your virus is improving each time? The line never drops down, does it.'

'I was going to do this later, properly – on the machine . . . get a nice printout. But yes, even with my quick sketch – it is looking promising.'

'How soon before we make the leap into humans?'

Michael laughs. 'You are joking, I assume?'

Edward shrugs and takes a slide out of a box on the bench. 'Not really . . . I'm looking for a realistic projection. The investors will want to know.'

'Who are these investors anyway? When are you going to tell me?'

He glances up at the clock. 'Ask them yourself. They'll be here in ten minutes. Just enough time for you to tidy yourself up a bit and get all your notes together. I've booked the meeting room upstairs.'

*Unbelievable.* Michael shakes his head as Edward disappears back out of the lab, doors swishing closed behind him. He gathers his notes into a pile. Takes the slide back off the microscope and puts it in a box, marks it, and places it in the fridge with the others. He catches his reflection in the dull metal of the fridge and decides that he will just have to do as he is. He hasn't brought anything to change into, and he's quite sure the investors aren't coming to check out his aesthetic qualities.

The phone rings as he's on his way out, and he thinks about leaving it to ring. It's Saturday morning. He doesn't have to be here.

It keeps ringing.

Whoever it is clearly wants to talk to him . . . and he's never been any good at leaving a ringing phone unanswered.

'Hello?'

'It's me . . . Have you got a minute?'

'Sandy. I thought you were going shopping this morning? Meeting Evette for lunch?' A sudden thought pricks at him. 'Oh bugger, sorry . . . Is everything OK? It's not . . .'

'The baby is fine, as far as I know.'

He can hear the smile in her voice, and he feels the tension drain out of himself.

'We won't know for sure until the twelve-week scan . . . You're not getting all stressed, are you?'

'Of course not. Listen, I've got a meeting . . .'

'That's fine, I won't keep you. I was just wondering if you fancied chops for tea tonight. I walked past the butcher's on the way back from Bennett's – they've got a sale on, by the way. Curtains and bedlinens, and—'

'Chops would be great, darling. But I do have to go now.'

'Great . . . I'll pop back down the street . . .'

'Bye, love.'

He hangs up as she is saying her goodbyes. He's late now, but he doesn't care. Sometimes the simple things are the important things.

◆ ◆ ◆

They're waiting for him in the meeting room.

'Ah, here he is . . . Busy at the coalface, as usual.' Edward stands when he walks into the room and the others follow suit.

Two men and a woman. The first of the men, greying temples and a sparkle in his eyes, walks around the long, oval table to greet him.

'Dr Gordon. It's a pleasure to meet you at last. Edward's been singing your praises for some time.'

Michael is impressed by the man's strong handshake. Something his dad had always encouraged in himself. 'Nice to meet you, Dr—'

'Simon Knox. I'm not a doctor, though. I leave that to the experts.' He smiles, revealing slightly crooked teeth. This endears him to Michael even more. 'And these are my colleagues, Helen Tracey . . .'

'Pleased to meet you, Dr Gordon.' Her hand is small and bird-like, but her gaze is sharp.

'Michael, please,' he says.

'And I'm David Armstrong,' the other man says. He looks around Michael and Edward's age, somewhere in his late twenties. The youngest of the three, although it's difficult to put an age on the woman.

All three of them look 'official', somehow – and Michael can't gauge where they might be from. If they were from a pharmaceutical company he'd expect at least one of them to be medical.

'Please, let's sit,' Edward says. He pours them all water from a glass jug, sliding the tumblers across the shiny table.

Michael lays his pile of papers on the table. 'You'll have to excuse me. I haven't had time to prepare anything formal . . .'

Simon Knox waves this away. 'Don't worry about that, Michael. We're just here to get a feel for how things are going. Answer any questions you might have.'

Michael takes a sip of water, his mouth drying up all of a sudden. 'Actually,' he says, glancing across at Edward, who gives him a half-smile that seems to be partly encouraging – but knowing Edward, the other part is saying, *Don't come out with anything stupid* – 'maybe you can start by telling me a bit about who you are. The company you're working for?' Edward clears his throat. A warning. Michael ignores it. 'I'm afraid I've been rather busy with the experiments, lately. There hasn't been much of an opportunity for Edward to fill me in.'

A silence falls around them.

It's Helen Tracey who breaks it. 'We're with the government, Dr Gordon.'

Michael catches Simon shooting David a look. Edward gives him a hard stare that seems to say, *I told you this . . .*

*No, Edward. No, you did not.*

'Ah, of course,' Michael says. 'The health service. I must say, it's quite early days for you to be involved. We'll need funding, and several years of research before we can do anything practical with—'

'We're not with the health service, Michael,' Simon says, pleasantly.

'Oh?'

They smile at him in unison, but they don't offer anything more.

# Ten

## CHRISSIE (NOW)

How do you decide who you'd want to die?

She's barely slept. Nathan cooked dinner for them last night, bathed Holly, and put her to bed. He seemed to sense that she had something on her mind, and she'd been itching to tell him – but although Joseph Marshall hadn't said as much, she got the feeling that this was not something she was meant to discuss with anyone else.

This morning, she feels wired. Anxious. The three cups of coffee haven't helped. She'd thought again to tell Nathan about Joseph Marshall, but he'd been in a rush, hadn't even bothered with breakfast. She'll grab him later, make him listen. Try to make him understand how scared she is all the time.

*You've chosen three people you want to be saved. Now you have to choose the three people you want to replace.*

It's ridiculous, of course. Fantastical. Is it some sort of Faustian pact? Is Joseph Marshall the Devil?

She shakes her head. Recommences pacing back and forth between the kitchen, the hall, and the front room – a room she rarely goes into, because it feels strange and formal, for some reason. Nathan had chosen the sofa and the matching armchair and they are stiff-backed and the room is poky and unwelcoming. This is why she spends most of her time at the kitchen table, in the brightness and the warmth.

Wendy was early today, and she'd seemed a bit fraught, although Chrissie had put that down to her still being worried about Holly. But Chrissie had been distracted herself. Too tired . . . and she'd suggested Wendy take Holly to the café by the school for a hot chocolate before nursery. She'd thought for a moment about confiding in Wendy, but again, she held back. Something is stopping her from revealing the details of this 'insurance policy' to her, or anyone. She's scared they'll think she's losing her mind.

She's loading the dishwasher, trying to keep herself busy, when the doorbell goes. She waits for a while, contemplating ignoring it. The more she tosses it all around in her head, the more she thinks this Joseph Marshall business is some sort of prank, or a scam. She should know better than to carry on with it, and yet something inside her, some sort of instinct, is telling her to go ahead.

The sound of the knocker being rapped firmly on the door makes her jump.

'OK, OK, I'm coming,' she mutters.

He's there on the doorstep. Looking exactly the same as before. There's a light breeze today. The apple tree by the fence is swaying gently. But Joseph Marshall's hair stays firmly in place, and his suit is exactly the same degree of crumpled.

'Good morning, Mrs Tate. I failed to mention it last time, but that really is a lovely car you've got there. A classic Mini Cooper? Rarer and rarer these days.' She responds with a tight smile, and he follows her into the house, untying his laces and slipping off his shoes as before. 'If you don't mind me saying, you look a little tired today.'

She sits down at the kitchen table, not bothering to offer him a drink. 'I didn't sleep very well. I didn't sleep well the night before, either. My daughter fell. It was an accident, of course, but it was quite a worry . . . and then last night – after what you left me with – well, is it any surprise that it kept me awake?'

'Understandable, of course.' He unclips the fasteners on his briefcase and flips it open. He has more paperwork, and next to it, a small rectangular box, about the size of a cigarette packet. The packaging is black, unmarked. 'So . . . do you have your list?'

She makes a noise that is somewhere between a cough, a laugh and a snort. 'My kill list, you mean?'

He purses his lips. 'I wouldn't quite put it like that.'

'Well, of course you wouldn't.' She sighs. 'Have *you* done this? Compiled these lists. Are you in the programme?' She stares at him for a moment, but he doesn't react. 'On second thoughts, don't tell me.'

'Do you have the list, Mrs Tate? I assume you read the guidelines before choosing?'

He'd handed her a piece of paper as he left, last time. Told her to follow the instructions carefully.

'I will need to take the guidelines back from you as well. I assume you haven't told anyone about this?'

'You should've made that clear on the guidelines. What if I have?'

'You're right, I'm making assumptions here. How very remiss of me. Please accept my apologies.' He cocks his head to one side, and he reminds her of a little bird. A sparrow, perhaps. 'If you like, I can reiterate the main points.'

'It's fine. I get it. Three people you would be happy to use as replacements, should there come a time of your loved one's pre-mature death. Right? Three people that you know. Provide your reasons for selection.'

He nods. 'This is a double-pronged experiment, Mrs Tate.'

Prongs. A devilish image pops into her mind. Forked tongue, cloven hooves.

'It's both physiological and psychological. The physiological element is quite straightforward. You must be in close proximity

67

to your loved one at their moment of passing. You must make the decision to save them.'

'I'd say that was more psychological, actually.'

'Very true. The physiological part is that we can stop them passing. We can—'

'You can cheat death?'

'In a manner of speaking. We have a mechanism to prevent it. Reverse it. There's a timeframe, of course. There can't be any hesitation. Once the process starts, it must carry on through to its conclusion. It must reach the end.'

'All right, then. So what's the psychological part?'

'As you said, making the decision – that's psychological, of course. But the primary psychological assessment is around your choices – who you have chosen to save—'

'And who I have chosen to kill?'

'To reiterate, Mrs Tate – *you* don't need to kill anyone.'

She laughs properly this time. It sounds high-pitched, strangled. 'Well, I would hope not. So how do *you* kill them, then? Assuming it ever actually happens. I hope it's humane, at least.'

He has the grace to look down. He shuffles his papers in front of him, before raising his gaze to meet hers. 'From what I'm told, the passing will mimic a predetermined cause.'

'Predetermined cause? What do you mean by that?'

He shakes his head. 'I'm sorry, I'm not at liberty to discuss that part of the process with you. You'll just have to trust me when I say that I have coordinated many of these appointments over the years, and I wouldn't continue to do so if I didn't believe it was ethical and above board.'

'But . . .' She rubs her eyes, tiredness sweeping over her as the caffeine wears off. 'It sounds completely unethical. I don't even know who's in charge of this thing . . .'

'I'm sorry, Mrs Tate. I know this all might seem a little . . . irregular.'

'You could say that . . .'

'But you need to think about what matters to you most. About *who* matters to you most. You need to accept that this programme exists, and you can be a part of it. Or you can choose to stop things now – but you should be aware that if you do that, it's possible that you'll be monitored anyway. We can't risk any of this information getting into the wrong hands.'

She sighs. 'It's ridiculous, is what it is.' A memory pops into her mind just then – her parents – an accident. Her mother frantic, just like *she* was with Holly . . . The memory fades, disappears in a puff, just as she tries to grasp it.

*I'll do it. Just to get you out of my house. I'll do it.*

'OK,' she says.

'OK you're happy to be monitored, or OK you're going to join the programme and reap the benefits – should they be required?'

'Meaning . . .'

'Meaning, maybe you won't need to activate the process. Maybe you'll be lucky. Maybe your family will live a long and happy life.'

'That's a point. What happens if I die first?'

He looks down at his papers again. 'Perhaps you can just give me the list, and I can explain how this works.' He slides the unmarked box across the table towards her.

She starts to open it, and his hand darts towards her – his long bony fingers curl over hers, and she shudders. 'Not yet . . . First, the list.'

The room seems to shrink around her and she takes a deep breath. Lets it out. Puts her hands on the table. *Forgive me.* 'All right. First, I'd like to choose my neighbour. Arthur Leake.'

# Eleven

## CHRISSIE (NOW)

As soon as the words are out of her mouth, she wants to take them back. Joseph Marshall is already scribbling them on to his form.

'Is that L-E-A-K-E?' he says.

She nods.

'And it's the neighbour on your left, or your right?'

'Right,' she says. She sucks in a deep breath. No going back now.

'I'll need the reason behind your decision,' he says, looking up at her. 'It's part of the data required for analysis.'

She's done some data analysis in the past, as part of some client feedback. It's very hard to analyse free text. They'd be much better off with a multiple-choice menu:

(a) They did something very bad to me
(b) They did something bad to someone I love
(c) There's just something about them that annoys me
(d) I have no real justification for this but I need to answer
(e) Something else

She thinks through these scenarios and knows that none of the first four really fit. There are so many other possibilities. The answer, when it comes to why you don't like someone, is usually '(e) Something else'. She's not even sure it will make sense when she says it out loud. It doesn't seem enough, somehow, and yet she says it anyway.

'He's been weird and rude lately. He's said a few odd things. He's been giving my best friend dirty looks.'

Joseph Marshall cocks his head at her again, that little bird-like gaze. 'I'll be honest with you, Mrs Tate. This doesn't seem like a particularly strong justification.'

She feels tears pricking at her eyes. Of course it isn't. It's ridiculous. She looks down at her hands, clasped together in her lap. 'I don't want to do this. I don't want to condemn someone to death.'

'Everybody dies, Mrs Tate.'

A sharp pain slices across her skull. 'Of course they do! But that's not down to me, is it? It's not up to me to choose who, and when, and why—'

'Please calm down, Mrs Tate.'

'No, I won't calm down. You've come here, to my house . . . You've started sowing these seeds in my brain . . .'

'Those seeds were already there. All I've done is suggest to you that they may need to germinate.'

She slumps back into her chair.

'Fine,' she says. 'I'll do it. It's a load of nonsense anyway. But let's see what happens, shall we? Nothing, I suspect. Apart from you collecting and analysing data on me that will no doubt come back to bite me later on.'

He nods. 'You're making the right choice. I wouldn't have come here if I didn't think it was important for you to be aware of this programme. You're helping us do important work here, Mrs Tate.'

Another memory swims into her mind. *We're doing important work here. Never forget that.*

'Arthur Leake is old,' she says, laying her hands flat on the table. Refusing to catch his eye. 'He's old, and he's a busybody . . . and he's clearly got a problem with me, or with my family, so yes. Put him on the list.' She pauses. Closes her eyes. 'The second one you should put on there is Karen Cole.'

'Reason?'

'She's . . . She's not a nice person.'

He nods. 'I'm just going to accept that the reasoning behind your choices is going to be simple. It's your list, after all. Do you have an address?'

She shakes her head. 'She works at the local Co-op. She's always over-sharing her tedious life on Facebook. I'm sure you'll find her.' She pauses. 'I'm not sure about the third . . .'

'Take your time. Perhaps we could have some tea? I very much enjoyed the cup you made for me yesterday . . . and if you had any biscuits?'

She busies herself with the tea, grateful for the break. As the kettle boils, she wanders through to the front room, stares out of the window on to the street. It's quiet at this time of day. The row of neat terraced houses sits patiently, as if waiting for something to happen. The occasional car passes. A young man is being dragged along the pavement by an excitable, skinny dog. A pungent waft of marijuana smoke trickles in through the air filter on the top of the window, and she takes a deep breath. Not that it'll have any direct effect, but it calms her anyway.

Back in the kitchen, Joseph Marshall is flicking through a magazine. It makes him seem more human, somehow. Surely the Devil doesn't have time for celebrity gossip and last year's winter wardrobe?

'Forgive me,' he says, noticing her, as she opens the fridge door. 'I don't often get a chance to just sit and read.'

She glances across at him and notices that it's not the celebrity magazine that he's been reading, but something called *Science Today*. She doesn't recognise it. Must've been something that Nathan picked up somewhere. He places it neatly back on the pile and returns to his papers.

The small black box is still on the table.

'Maybe I should explain the technical details first, while you're still mulling over your options.' He picks up a chocolate digestive from the plate she's laid on the table and nibbles at it with small, sharp teeth. 'Open it, please.'

She slides out the insert, revealing a black, fabric-lined tray. In the middle is an oblong plastic device. It looks a bit like a fitness tracker. She lifts it out, inspects it. It has one long button, inset at the front. A small transparent bubble at the top. A light, maybe? She turns it back and forth. No other features. Not even screw holes on the back.

'It won't run out of battery, if that's what you were thinking.' He takes a sip of his tea.

She turns it back and forth again. Something stops her from pressing the button. She lays it back into the tray. *A little coffin . . . How apt.*

'What is it?'

'The way that it all works is very simple, Mrs Tate. Firstly, I recommend that you keep this device with you at all times. It works a bit like a pager – once the button is pressed, an amber light will flash at the top. That's the first activation. After that, things will be taken care of for you. You'll be told when to press it again. That's when it'll glow green, and the procedure will take place.'

'I don't understand—'

'Remember – this only works if you are in *close proximity* to your loved one at the time of their passing. You must act swiftly – if you delay too long, we can't guarantee that it will work – so the onus is on you. This is your responsibility. Their lives are quite literally in your hands.'

It's difficult to process, but she feels like she's being swept away by it all. As if she's in another reality. Life and death, in her hands. Except . . . it's not true. It can't be. If this power existed, then why would it be kept so clandestine? Surely this would be some huge scientific breakthrough?

'I still don't understand why someone has to die . . . Why can't you just use whatever this is to save people?'

'Yin and yang, Mrs Tate. An eye for an eye . . . The universe must remain in balance. Can you imagine the consequences if we just let everyone live? The world is already overcrowded. This way, we can carry out good work – we can right the wrongs, we can let the good live – and the bad will come to an untimely end . . . dying just as they were always meant to. Just sooner than expected.'

'You can't guarantee that . . . You can't account for one of the bad ones dying some *other* way . . . something other than what you think their bodies are predestined to do. An accident, for instance.' She shrugs. 'Where's your balance then?'

He steeples his hands and looks her straight in the eye. 'In the end, Mrs Tate – everyone dies from the same cause. How it happens is variable, might be unexpected. It might be sooner than they would have expected. It might be far later than anyone could imagine. But there is a simple, universal cause of death, Mrs Tate.' He pauses, gives her a strange smile. 'In the end, everyone's heart stops beating.'

They stare at each other, for what seems like a very long time. The room is silent, except for the low hum of the fridge. It's a quiet house, when she's in here alone. Joseph Marshall doesn't bring any noise. She's not entirely convinced that he is breathing.

'Fine,' she says, at last. 'My third choice is Michael Gordon. I don't know where he is, but I assume you'll be able to make contact with him, if you need to. He used to be a scientist. Maybe he still is. Something low-level and mundane in a health-service lab, or so he always said.'

Joseph Marshall gives her a knowing smile, as if he's been waiting for this all along. He glances down, writes the name on the form. Looks up, pen poised. 'Reason?'

She swallows. *No going back.* 'He killed my mother.'

# Twelve

## Michael (April 1981)

Michael sits by the bed, holding Sandra's hand. It's a rare moment of calm, in what has been several tense hours for them both. Her breathing is slow and steady, and she has her eyes closed. There is a hint of a smile on her face. He leans over and looks down at her, feels a huge surge of love mushrooming in his stomach. He moves in closer, ready to plant a gentle kiss on her lips.

The spell is broken when her eyes fly open and she projects a terrifying scream of pain, right into his face. He flinches, but before he can work out what he should do, Sandra turns her face away and addresses the nurse across the room. 'Get him the hell out of here! I can't stand this anymore. Please—'

She grips his hand so tightly that he thinks she might have broken the skin. But despite his own pain, he keeps hold of her hand. He knows that this is far worse for her – and despite her screams, he is not going to leave her.

The nurse hurries to them, her soft-soled shoes swishing gently on the floor. 'Perhaps you should take a break, Michael. Go and get yourself a cuppa. Tiring on you, being here all this time.' She lays a hand on his arm and guides him gently away from the bed.

He shakes his head. 'I'm fine. It's her you need to look after. Will it be much longer, do you think? She seems to be in pain again . . .'

'It's a fucking *contraction*, Michael,' Sandra screams at him from the bed. 'They *are* quite painful, as it happens, and they—'

The scream cuts off the rest of her sentence.

The nurse gives him a sympathetic smile. 'The doctor will be in soon. He'll be able to give you a better idea.'

Michael contemplates nipping out to find himself some water – the stuff in the jug by the bed is warm and stale – and maybe a quick break would be the best thing . . .

Another scream.

'It's coming, Michael . . . Oh, *jesusmaryandjoseph* . . .'

He rushes back to her side, takes her hand again. He has never heard her swear like this. Never seen her look like this . . . like she's possessed, or something. If he's honest, he's finding the whole thing completely terrifying.

The doctor appears, then. White coat flapping. He nods at Michael and gestures for him to move away from the bed. A nurse follows close behind. She has a different-coloured uniform, and he realises that she must be the midwife – had she been in already? It seems like they've been there for days, although it is really only hours – fourteen, in fact – since she shook him awake and told him to get in the car.

He'd been so impressed, then – her standing there in her new, soft tracksuit. Her little holdall all packed and ready, on the floor by her feet. Her eyes had been gleaming – with excitement, fear . . . perhaps a bit of wonder in there too. 'It's happening,' she'd said, quietly, as if even she, who had carried the baby in her belly for nine months, could scarcely believe that it was about to come out . . . and that they were about to be parents.

Things move quickly after that. He gets a second wind, from the flurry of activity. Doctor – midwife – nurse. Gas. Air. Swearing. Repeat.

Scream.

Push.

Scream.

Push.

Scream.

Silence.

And then . . . the cry.

It's at that point that Michael faints.

He comes to on a chair by the bed. *In* the bed, his wife sits, rosy-cheeked, damp-haired. She has a baby at her breast. A slightly squashed, pink-faced little thing, wrapped in a cream blanket.

'Do you want to meet your daughter?' Sandra says.

She has never been more beautiful.

Michael sits on the bed beside them both. He touches his daughter's soft cheek.

'Christina?' Sandra whispers. 'After my mother? I mean, the nurse said they've already had two Christinas today. One Susan, a John, a James and two Marks so far. So it's not exactly unique, but I do love it, don't you?'

Michael simply nods. 'I love you both,' he says. 'I love you both more than anything in this world . . . and I promise you now, I will never let anything happen to you.' He runs a hand over his face, surprised to find that it is wet.

Then the baby starts to wail.

He takes the opportunity to nip out for a break. He follows the network of corridors to reception and heads to the bank of payphones near the main entrance.

'Has my godchild entered the world?' Edward's voice booms down the phone.

'Goddaughter . . . Well, if Sandy agrees to that. She might need convincing. Christina is now approximately seventy-seven minutes old. She's beautiful, of course.'

'Babies aren't beautiful. They all look the same. Like scrunched-up old men.'

'I'm not sure you're the right choice for godfather, actually.'

'Of course I am. Who else is going to tell her about how the world really works?'

'Are you coming to the hospital?'

'How about we wet the baby's head first . . .'

Michael glances at his watch. He could do with a drink. Some decompression time. Hopefully Sandy will get some sleep now. The baby, too. And maybe it's better if Edward visits tomorrow – when Sandy's had time to get used to things.

'Eagle?' Edward presses.

'Give me twenty. We'll celebrate Christina's one-hundredth minute.'

Edward is waiting in the pub when he arrives. Two pints of bitter, two whisky chasers. Laid out neatly on the table. Edward is doing his best impression of the Cheshire Cat.

'Congratulations, Daddy Gordon. Who'd have thought it, eh?' He grabs Michael's hand and shakes it hard. Then he rummages about inside his jacket, pulls something out with a flourish. 'Ta da!'

'Oh . . . very nice,' Michael says. 'Cuban, I hope?'

'Only the best for you.' Edward hands him the cigar. 'I took the liberty of snipping it for you.'

Michael sticks it in his mouth, savouring the smooth, smoky taste. He doesn't smoke cigars, as a rule, but Edward likes them on special occasions – and this is most definitely one of those.

He takes it back out of his mouth, scrutinises it. 'You know, I actually prefer them unlit.'

Edward snorts, flicks his lighter. Michael puts the cigar back into his mouth, lets his friend light it for him. He sucks the smoke into his mouth, swirling it around for a moment, and remembering to hold it for just the right amount of time before letting it back out. He'd made the mistake of inhaling one of these fat ones before, and ended up in a five-minute coughing fit where he thought he might actually die. These things were supposed to be pleasurable? Give him a pint and a packet of dry roasted peanuts any day.

'Anyway . . . cheers,' Edward says, raising his whisky glass.

'Cheers,' Michael says. 'To Christina.' They chink glasses and he takes a sip. Feels it burn down his throat.

'I popped into the lab earlier.' Edward downs his drink and smacks his lips together, satisfied. 'Hoping you might have an update for me? I looked at your notes but it'd be simpler if you talked me through things. Our furry friends seem to be quite happy . . .'

Michael blinks, trying to clear his head. 'You want me to talk about it *now*?'

'Well, we're not going to sit here and discuss baby formula and nappies, are we?'

'No, but . . .'

'I was just wondering how close we were to human trials.'

Michael sighs. He takes a sip of his pint. 'We're still a long way off. You know that. I need to scale up the animal testing, first. Things are going well, but the oldest survivor of the treatment is only sixteen weeks old.' Sandy's smiling face flashes before him. She's sitting propped up in bed with a glass of warm milk, reading from one of her baby books: *At sixteen weeks your baby may be able to roll over . . . They may have cut their first tooth . . .*

Edward sighs. 'OK. But that's good, right? No signs of any problems?'

'They're being closely monitored.'

Edward is staring at him now. The noise of the pub seems to retreat to a distant buzz. Muffled voices, as if coming from underwater. It is just the two of them now. Edward's expression has darkened. 'I've been thinking . . .'

Michael swallows. He knows Edward's expressions. Can almost read his mind. Michael knows how determined he is to set up this deal with the Ministry of Defence, knows that they can't finalise anything until they move to the next stage. Edward wants the cash, but more than that, he wants to be part of something big. Michael still doesn't know what it is that the government wants from his viral vector, but he knows it's top secret, and it's something far removed from what Michael ever had in mind.

'Go on,' Michael says, holding Edward's gaze. He takes another sip of his pint.

'What if we were to test it on ourselves?'

Michael coughs, and the beer goes down the wrong way. He slaps his hands on the table, splutters, feels his lungs burn. Edward jumps out of his seat and leans across, slapping him hard on the back.

'You can't be serious?' Michael's voice comes out as a squeak. His throat feels like it has been scratched with long, angry fingernails.

'We wouldn't be the first scientists to try something like this,' Edward tries. His voice is a little quieter, less sure.

'Oh yes . . . I mean, you've got Dr Jekyll, for one,' Michael says. He shakes his head and pushes the table away so that he can slide out from behind it. He stands up. 'I need to get back to my wife . . . and my daughter.'

'All right, all right . . . Look, sit back down . . .'

Michael dismisses him with a wave. 'You stay, finish your drink. I'll tell Sandy you'll pop in to see her tomorrow.' He throws his jacket on and strides out of the pub. He is doing a good job of looking strong, confident. But inside he is shaking. He should've known that Edward would come up with something like this.

He's outside when he feels a hand on his shoulder.

'Come on, I'll walk with you.' Edward falls into step beside him. 'Forget what I said. I was just getting excited . . . I feel like we're so close.'

Michael glares at him. 'We *are* close. But we have to do it properly. Or else there's no point.'

'Yes. Of course. Yes.'

Michael is walking quickly, and Edward is scurrying along, struggling to keep up. He needs to stay in control, but Edward has always been so persuasive. He'd always spent more time drinking with the debating team than in the lab.

'We can *think* about moving into healthy volunteers by the end of the year,' Michael says. 'Assuming that the current specimens continue to thrive.'

'And we can talk to the university's research arm, get them involved in recruiting the human subjects?' Edward says. 'Or are there any other sources we can use? We'd start with three healthy males, right? Students are always after the cash . . . I assume we'll be giving them payment for their time?'

'I expect so.' Michael slows slightly. 'We'll need to have them in a residential unit, for monitoring. And yes, we need a minimum of three. One thing at a time though, OK?'

Edward sighs. 'You know what I'm like. I hate all the waiting. I just want to accelerate things a bit.'

'Well, I do admire your enthusiasm, but I'm afraid we can't.'

As they continue along the main road, heading back towards the hospital, they almost trip over a homeless man, sheltering in a bus stop – legs sticking out on to the pavement. Dirty black boots in mismatched laces.

'Spare any change?' he says. His voice is mechanical. Bored. He has a paper cup in front of him, containing a load of coppers and not much else.

'What's your name, buddy?' Edward asks him.

'It's Joseph,' he says, more animated now, sensing some interaction, perhaps. 'Please . . . Can you help me?'

Michael pauses, takes a handful of silver from his pocket and drops it into the cup, then he carries on. He's at the end of the road before he realises that Edward is no longer with him. He's crouched down at the bus stop, chatting animatedly to the tramp, who seems much more alert now. Not so bored. Something that Edward is saying has perked the man up.

Michael feels a shiver run through him, but it's not from the cold. Students are always after extra cash . . . but they're not the only poor desperate sods out there.

# Thirteen

## CHRISSIE (NOW)

Friday arrives and the morning routine is back to normal. Except for the churning inside Chrissie's head. What was she thinking, giving those names to Joseph Marshall? She's going to call him later, cancel the whole stupid thing. She should call the police, really. Report him for harassment or something. But given that they don't have time to deal with real crimes, are they really going to have resources to spend on this? Besides, if they spend a second checking her background, they'll write her off as mad.

If Nathan has noticed that she's distracted, he hasn't given any indication. Holly is Holly. But Wendy had at least asked if everything was OK.

'It will be,' Chrissie had said, shooing her and Holly out of the door, 'when we finally go on our mad night out.'

*Mad night out.* Would it be? Could it be? It's been so long; she feels like she's forgotten how to enjoy herself. Wendy is single, lives alone. She goes out all the time, Chrissie assumes. Why wouldn't she? Her figure is still tight and untouched by stretchmarks. Her natural honey-blonde hair is still glossy and thick. One of the things that Chrissie had hated the most about pregnancy was her hair seemingly starting to thin overnight, big clumps of it coming out in the shower. She'd stopped highlighting it too, and felt drab and mousey for the duration and some time afterwards. It was fine now, but there was a youthful look to Wendy that Chrissie felt she would never experience again.

The wardrobe doors are open; dresses, skirts, and far too many tops are spread across the bed. She'd forgotten about most of these clothes, managing to get by day to day in the same faded jeans and a constant rotation of mix & match basics from Gap. She pulls out a mustard blouse. Runs her hands over the fabric. She'd worn this to her last work's night out, plain black trousers and ankle boots by day, pencil skirt and knee-highs by night. Flicked gel-eyeliner and a smudge of red lipstick. She'd looked hot that evening, remembers catching a look at herself in one of the old Victorian pub's many mirrors. She remembers the exact moment when Andy's eyes had grown hungry. Their usual risqué banter crossing the line into full flirtation . . . and then more. She'd never imagined she'd be the type of woman who'd have a one-night stand with a colleague, but she'd been drifting away from Nathan for a while at that point. But it was just that one night. Who knows what might've happened if she'd let things carry on? The whole thing had sent her into a spin, and she'd needed a break from it all. *Anxiety*, the GP had told her. She just needed some time.

Time to reconnect with Nathan – and incredibly she had, for a while. They rekindled an intimacy that she'd thought they'd lost.

Chrissie was still signed off when she found herself pregnant; and when that unexpected event caused her anxiety to spiral into something more, the company had let her leave without ever setting foot in the place again. The images from that last night out are burned into her brain. The last time that she really felt like herself, before the pregnancy hormones messed her up even worse than she'd been before.

It brought her and Nathan closer, for a while. Gave them a focus. They'd had a tearful heart-to-heart one night, where Nathan had confessed that he'd been feeling detached for a while too . . . They'd agreed that this was what they'd needed, although they hadn't known at the time. And just for that moment – that careful, close moment – Chrissie had forgotten that her mother was dead, and would never get to meet her first grandchild.

Chrissie knew that grief was something that never leaves you. It starts sharp, painful – piercing your heart, while you exist as nothing but a primal force clinging to life while it stabs you, over and over again. Then it dulls, to a deep throb, somewhere at the back of your skull. Things return to normal, except that they're not. And finally it hangs around, a light, distant mist – mostly out of sight, until it drifts into your line of vision at the most unexpected times and grabs your heart once more – a short, smothering ache. Those who've never experienced it can never fully understand. Those who have share a sad, lonely bond – but sometimes, that can be a comfort.

Nathan has never really understood. His own parents are emotionally distant, choosing the sunny climes of Spain to the English rain. Choosing sangria and expat drama over time with their own son. Their lack of care for him seems to have hardened his emotions. It's hardly surprising. But it's not something he talks about, and that's why she's struggled to cling on to him throughout. Perhaps they need a holiday – just the two of them. Time to rekindle their relationship. Maybe Wendy could take care of Holly? It would only have to be for a few days.

Chrissie is pondering this when the phone rings. Another private number.

'Hello?' she says, tentatively.

'Chrissie?' The voice is slightly muffled, the line crackling. A bad connection, just like the other day. Long distance, perhaps?

'Yes . . . Who is this?'

'It's . . .' – more crackling – 'from Meet-4-Meat.'

'Who? I spoke to Colin Scott before, he—'

'Colin's away . . . We wanted to talk to you about the logo. You left a message saying you didn't want to continue working with us?'

Chrissie sighs. She's straining to hear every word. The voice sounds familiar, but she can't place it. 'I'm sorry, I didn't catch your name?'

'We'd very much like to keep working with you . . .' A screech of static.

Wincing, she takes the phone away from her ear, taps the icon to turn it on to loudspeaker, then lays it on the table.

'As I said in my message,' she says, 'I just don't think I can get this logo to work. And apart from that, I'm a little concerned about the whole thing. This is the third logo I've done for you in under two years . . .'

'You don't need the money?'

Chrissie pauses, confused. 'Why do you care about that?'

'If it's the name, perhaps you could come in and help us brainstorm another one . . . Another concept.' Crackle.

'Well, I'd have been happy to do that a few months ago, but to be honest I'm not sure I want to get involved any further . . .'

'We'd pay you well.'

She rolls up a pizza leaflet that's been shoved under the fruit bowl, flicks it across the room towards the recycling bin. She's getting irritated now. 'I know you would. I charge the going rate . . .'

'Please consider it, Christina.'

Her next words shrivel in her throat. She's never given them that name. *Christine* would be the more obvious deduction, wouldn't it? That voice, too. A memory, just on the edge of her subconscious. A chill crosses the back of her neck, like a soft, cold breath.

'No,' she manages, her voice barely a whisper. She ends the call.

Maybe Wendy was right: the restaurant and Joseph Marshall *are* connected. But how? And why? And what do they want from her?

No.

That would make no sense. It's a coincidence, that's all. Or she misheard . . . It was a terrible connection. She didn't even catch the caller's name. So why, then, did the voice make her feel so uneasy?

She pours herself a coffee, adds a generous glug of cooking brandy. Takes a sip, and waits for her hands to stop shaking. The warm buzz hits her, and she's about to take another sip when she hears the sound of the key in the lock. Is it that time already?

'Mummy!'

Holly appears, brandishing another roll of paper. Wendy steps in behind her, closing the door.

'Wow, look at your hair,' Chrissie says, grabbing Holly in for a hug. Her hair is loose, tangled wild like a bird's nest. She looks up at Wendy, whose hair is not much different.

'It's blowing a gale out there,' she says, kicking off her shoes. 'And, of course, missy decided she didn't want bunches today after all.'

Holly grins. 'We were playing dollies, and I was the dolly . . . and you can't brush hair when it's in bunches, can you?' She runs off into the living room and Wendy picks the roll of paper off the floor.

'Another painting,' Chrissie says, blowing out a puff of air.

'Bad day?' Wendy says, sniffing. She's close enough to smell the brandy.

'Want one?' Chrissie flicks the kettle on and takes the bottle out of the cupboard.

'Oh go on then.' A pause. 'Are you going to tell me what's up?'

Chrissie doesn't look at her. Doesn't want to tell her about the phone call. Can't tell her about Joseph.

'It's nothing,' she says. 'I'll live.' She pours a capful of brandy into Wendy's coffee then turns around to face her, making sure a smile is firmly in place. 'Tell you what . . . Why don't you go upstairs and choose me an outfit, from the pile of stuff I've dumped on the bed? I can't decide . . . It's been so long.'

'Anything you're getting rid of?' Wendy says, her voice hopeful.

'Be my guest.'

Wendy disappears up the stairs and Chrissie unrolls the painting. It's Holly again – in the roller skates – holding hands with a woman with yellow hair. Both of them have upturned mouths.

Finally . . .

She leaves her coffee behind, goes through to the living room, where Holly is curled up on the sofa, engrossed in *Peppa Pig*. 'Hey,' she says, 'this is a lovely painting that you did of me and you. Thank you.' She sits down on the sofa and pulls Holly in for a hug.

Holly doesn't look at her, still fully transfixed by the TV in that way that kids are. 'Wendy said you would like it.'

'Oh, did you show it to Wendy before?'

Holly turns around. 'Of course, Mummy. She told me to paint it for you. Said you were feeling lonely because the last one had all of us in it and you needed one to be special.'

Chrissie is confused. The last painting she did . . . Is that what she means? The one with the two women, one happy, one sad . . .

'You mean the one with Daddy in it?'

Holly gives her a theatrical sigh. 'Yes, Mummy. Daddy and you and me and Wendy.'

In the last painting, Daddy was holding hands with two women. One was happy, one was sad.

Which one was she?

She feels an odd sensation start to swirl around her. Fear? Paranoia? She's about to quiz her further, when Wendy's voice shouts down from upstairs.

89

'You've got All Saints and Hobbs in here . . . Seriously, what can I nick?'

Holly is sucking her thumb, content. Oblivious.

Chrissie blinks, tries to dislodge the strange thoughts. Too much going on. Overactive imagination, that's all. She rubs Holly's cheek. 'Hang on,' she shouts back, 'I'm coming up.'

# Fourteen

## CHRISSIE (NOW)

Chrissie drums her fingers on the steering wheel. So much for the traffic-calming measures. The street is busier than ever tonight. She takes a soft cloth from the side pocket on the door and wipes a sticky mark from the windscreen. She is desperate for this night out. She's had a relaxing Saturday pampering herself, and plenty of time to forget all her jumbled thoughts of the last few days. Nathan and Holly got back from their day out just as Wendy arrived, and Nathan had given them both appraising looks and told them to have a good time.

She feels more like her old self – make-up and heels and hair done properly. Who knows . . . Nathan might reap the benefits of her rejuvenation later on – if he's still awake, that is.

As they sit at the end of the driveway, waiting for the few cars to pass, Arthur appears at his front gate, bin bag in hand. He glances over at the car, and Chrissie gives him a hopeful smile. He shakes his head sadly, and a shiver runs up her bare arms. For a moment she regrets being rude to him the other day. He's just *old*, that's all. Too much time on his hands to overthink and criticise. Maybe *she* needs to make more of an effort. But then she remembers the list she gave to Joseph, and she shudders.

She shouldn't have chosen Arthur.

What was she thinking? There are plenty more deserving cases than him. Not that it matters. It's a load of nonsense anyway.

As she *finally* turns out of the driveway and on to the road, Wendy shifts suddenly in the passenger seat, swivelling around. She thrusts a hand upwards and gives Arthur the finger through the back window.

'For goodness' sake, Wendy.' She's pissed off now. It's not Wendy who has to live next to the man.

'Oh, come on, he's a miserable old goat.' She swivels back round and kicks her bag under the seat. 'Here, let's have some tunes.' She hits the button on the ancient car stereo then twists the volume dial as high as it will go.

The unmistakable opening bars of The Who's 'Substitute' blare through the speakers as they accelerate up the slipway and on to the main road. Thankfully there's little traffic now, and the houses lining the dual carriageway pass by in a blur.

Chrissie starts singing, and Wendy joins in, loud and out of tune. Chrissie smiles to herself, glad that they're doing this. Feeling relaxed for the first time in a long time, and they're not even on their night out yet. She hopes the station car park isn't too busy. The song ends, and Wendy hits pause.

'You know . . . most shoes *are* made of leather,' she says, sounding confused. 'I've never really understood what he was trying to say there.'

Chrissie laughs, keeping her eyes on the road as she reaches over to turn the music back on. There's a screeching whirr as the cassette rewinds back to the start of the song, and she jabs at it again, hitting 'play' this time. '*His* shoes *aren't* though. He's poor. That's what he's trying to say. He's a fake. He's not who you think he is—'

'Most people aren't,' Wendy says. The earlier lightness has faded from her voice. 'Most people will let you down, one way or another.'

'Jeez. Happy Girls' Night Out, eh? Miserable cow. We'll be at the station in a minute. Then you can find out what's in my bag . . .'

Wendy snakes an arm behind her and fumbles in the back footwell. 'Oh, *this* bag.' She sounds brighter now, at the sound of the bottles chinking, punctuating Roger Daltrey's vocals. 'Prosecco, I hope?'

'Of course. Plastic glasses and a bag of cheese puffs.'

Wendy cackles. 'Cheese-puff teeth are *just* the thing to attract the sexy barmen.'

Chrissie pulls into the station car park and slides into the perfect space near the entrance. She kills the engine and peers up at the departures board. 'Three minutes,' she says. 'Let's go!'

They find seats across from each other at a table, and Wendy immediately goes about popping the cork on the Prosecco.

Chrissie opens the snacks, and takes one out of the bag, inspecting it back and forth in her fingers like a jeweller assessing a precious gem.

'The thing about cheese-puff teeth,' she says, 'is that they really help sort the men from the boys. A man, for example, a good-quality specimen . . . will politely tell you that you have something in your teeth, and offer to mind your drink while you pop to the loo. When you return, there'll be a beermat over your drink, letting you know that he hasn't roofy'd you, and a bowl of nuts, suggesting that he knows you like snacks, but thinks nuts are more sophisticated . . .'

'Because of the piss on them,' they say in unison, laughing.

'Whereas . . .' Wendy picks up the story, 'a boy is more likely to snog you anyway, sticking his inexperienced tongue right in there in the hope of licking off the cheese dust . . .'

Chrissie howls with laughter. It's lucky there's no one else in their carriage.

'I've missed these chats,' she says. 'How come we never discuss cheese-puff teeth anymore?'

Wendy sighs and leans back in her seat. 'I've missed *you*, Chrissie. You've been missing for such a long time . . .'

Chrissie wants to reply, about how they see each other more than ever since Wendy's been taking Holly to nursery, bringing her back, helping out when she has to go off on an occasional over-nighter to meet a client – but she knows that's not what Wendy means. Chrissie knows she's not been herself for a very long time. But losing her mum . . . and as a consequence, her dad – in quick succession – has changed her in ways she never expected. This night out will be good for them. She takes a sip of her drink. 'You know what?' she says. 'Do we have to even bother going into town? The trolley-dolly will be here soon. Why don't we just get a couple more drinks and stay on here to chat? We can go back and forth a couple of times. We're guaranteed a seat.'

Wendy looks at her like she's mad, then bursts out laughing. 'That is a bloody genius idea. Why have we never thought of this before?'

'Do you think the guard will make us pay twice?' Chrissie says, popping a cheese puff in her mouth. It might be full of chemical flavourings and colours, but it tastes damn good.

'Not if I flash my tits,' Wendy says. They both fall about laughing.

The journey carries on like this into Waterloo, with them only pausing for breath when a young woman appears with a trolley of drinks and snacks and they take a few minutes to choose.

94

'I can't really drink any more than this Prosecco, Wends. But we can make sure you get super-pissed for the two of us.'

They sit there chatting, drinking, giggling. Watching as people get off the train in London, then a new set of people hurry on. It's early enough that it's not too packed, and no one tries to sit next to them – although they do attract a few sighs from people who're unimpressed with their noise. The guard gives them a cursory glance on his first trip through their carriage, a raised eyebrow on the second, and then finally, on the third, says, 'I assume you ladies will be getting off some time this evening.'

'One more go,' Wendy says to him, 'please, mister', like she's on a fairground ride. They hear him chuckling as he walks away.

On their final leg of their back-and-forth journey, heading from central London to their suburban station, Chrissie becomes a little melancholic.

'This has been so good for me, you know,' Chrissie says, 'for both of us.' She takes a sip of the Diet Coke she's bought for herself, conscious that she has to be sober enough to drive the car back from the station. 'You know what else . . . a night out might be just what me and Nathan need too.'

Wendy snorts. 'I wouldn't worry about him too much. He's not suffering from lack of nights out.'

An announcement comes out on the tannoy. This is the final stop. The train isn't doing any more trips back into town tonight.

'What do you mean by that?' Chrissie says.

The train pulls into the station.

'Oh, nothing,' Wendy says, gathering up the rubbish. 'Come on, we better get off before they come and throw us off. Do you think they stopped the train running just to make us leave?'

Chrissie laughs, but it feels a bit hollow. Wendy's remark has confused her, but she doesn't want to delve further. She doesn't want to spoil this night out.

Wendy tosses the rubbish bag and the empty bottles into the bin. 'I had fun tonight,' she says. 'Let's do that again.'

Chrissie is still subdued as she reverses out of the parking space, turns, and heads out on to the road to take Wendy home. She puts The Who cassette on again, trying to kick-start the mood, but before long, Wendy is dozing in the passenger seat, and Chrissie is trying to blast cold air from the vents on to her face to keep herself awake. She'd drunk half of that first bottle of Prosecco, then one more small bottle herself. Wendy had three more of the small ones, but Chrissie knows she's had too much as well. She'd got carried away in the moment, and although they've been out for a few hours, it's not long enough for her to have metabolised the alcohol. One hour per unit is what they always say on the adverts, isn't it? She's at least three hours from being safe.

She takes it slowly, until she's back on her own familiar streets. Wendy is still asleep, slumped against the window, snoring. Chrissie is right there with her. Even driving slowly, she has to keep blinking herself awake.

Two more streets to go.

She rounds the corner to the eyesore of a street that they're knocking down to make way for the new rail line. No one lives here now. She picks up the speed just a little. It's late now, and it's quiet, and she just wants to get home. Those concrete planters are up ahead. Those stupid things that are meant to stop people driving too fast along her street. Except she knows she can squeeze around them. Her car is tiny, and the kerb on the right is low.

Then from nowhere, something flashes on the road. Darts out in front of her. And she swerves hard. She hears a thud as Wendy's head knocks against the glass of the passenger window, and then Wendy's awake and she's shrieking, 'Chrissie, look out!'

The left side of the car smashes into the concrete planter. There's a screech and a sickening crunch and Chrissie's head flips forward before slamming back into the headrest. The windscreen shatters, showering her with glass. There's a strong smell of smoke, like someone's let off a firework right next to her. She's screaming. Then the noises stop. Her ears feel fuzzy. She tries to turn her head but it hurts. She blinks, and warm liquid obscures her vision. She reaches out, blindly, reaching for Wendy to the left of her. Realising that she hasn't heard a sound from her since Wendy yelled, telling her to look out, seeing what was going to happen before she did. Trying to warn her . . . too late.

'Wendy?'

The car is crumpled inwards; Wendy's side has taken the brunt. They're crushed up against a planter. It's tipped on its side. They've hit it hard. Wendy is slumped forward over the dashboard. Her seat belt is unfastened.

Chrissie feels as if her own head is floating away. Wants to go with it.

No.

She reaches an arm out again.

'Wendy?'

*Oh Jesus, no. This can't be happening.* She finds Wendy's arm, grabs it. Shakes it. But it falls limp, like a rag doll's. She manages to unclip her seat belt, and turn, just enough to see that Wendy is in a far worse state than she is.

'*Shit-shit-shit-shit-shit,*' she mutters. She stretches over, touching Wendy's face. It's mostly red, small pieces of glass embedded in her forehead. Blood runs down her shoulder. On the floor, both their handbags have fallen open, the contents strewn across the floor.

Chrissie takes in the scene of pure horror. Wendy's seat belt. Either she didn't clip it in, or it has come loose, but whichever one it is, it's not looking good.

'Wendy?'

Why is no one coming to help them? *Because no one lives in these houses, dummy.* They are empty shells, awaiting demolition.

*Shit.*

She shakes her friend's shoulder, very gently. No response. On the floor at Chrissie's feet, the small black pager sits among the items that have fallen from her handbag. Red light blinking. Next to it, her phone – the screensaver is a cute photo of Holly, partially obscured now by a crack that is snaking across the surface.

Wendy makes a strange gurgling sound in her throat. *Oh God . . . Is she dying?*

The pager. The blinking red light.

Wendy.

Chrissie has to make a choice.

Her whole body screams in pain as she leans forward as far as she can and picks up the pager and the phone. She stares at them both for a moment. Closes her eyes. Tries to slow her breathing, focus, trying to tune into the sound of sirens in the distance. Expecting to hear a knock on the window at any time . . . someone coming to help them.

But there is nothing. Only them. Only this choice.

Her choice.

She presses the button.

# Fifteen

## MICHAEL (MAY 1982)

Initially, Michael had refused to be involved in Edward's unethical testing regime. In some ways, the timing was good, with Christina being born – it meant that he had plenty of excuses not to be in the lab out of hours, and it was much simpler to remain in denial when he wasn't part of anything that was going on.

Well, not strictly true.

The government investors had returned, of course, and it was difficult to turn down their funding . . . and the special 'bonus' for Michael, for one simple reason: *he* would create the infusions. He told himself that at least if he made sure the drug was as safe as he could make it, then the chances of disaster were lower than if he were to walk away. Besides, how could he walk away? He was as determined as anyone to see the virus work to its full capacity. The possibilities – if he was able to create a fully stable cell-regeneration drug – were, quite simply, endless. Life-changing for him, as well as for everyone who would ever come to benefit from his work.

So walking away was not an option.

They wanted to bring in their own experts. Their own doctors and chemists and everyone else they could think of . . . and Michael is sure that, in time, that's what will happen anyway. He's not strong enough to fight this, if it works. But for now, at least, he has some semblance of control.

Because he is the only one who knows how to make the virus work.

He feels a bit like the makers of Coca-Cola, holding on to a secret recipe that money can never buy. But in truth, everyone has their price.

The testing is going on in a secret location – one that he doesn't have security clearance for, and for that he is glad. It helps with the denial. He provides the drug and he receives the results, and it's his job to decide what to do next. The only bit he doesn't see is what actually happens to the test subjects while they're at the residential clinic. Every time he makes up a new batch for a new subject, he quietly prays that this will be enough to get them the results they need to move on to the next phase.

The 'official' human trials.

The ones that will be documented, peer reviewed, and shared with the media, when they have a successful outcome. The ones that will form the basis of his scientific papers – his name as the primary author, the developer of an all-powerful drug with the potential to reverse cell death.

It's mouth-watering.

And the denial works well to allow him to forget about the four homeless men that have mysteriously vanished from the streets around the university in recent months.

The first one was the worst, of course, because Edward had taken control of that himself. He'd taken a sample of the infusion from the store, and he'd given the tramp – the one called Joseph – acute alcohol poisoning – which wasn't too difficult – and then tried to revive him.

Unsuccessfully.

Luckily for them all, the viral infusion is a brand-new entity, so not traceable via any toxicology screening. No one would have the first clue what to look for. Yes, if they were to do a full screen, they might be concerned about what had triggered the immune system to go into overdrive – but they would have no idea what caused it.

Michael had wanted to drive the man to the hospital, leave him outside A&E if necessary. It was too late to save him, but at least they could leave him in the right hands. But Edward and the investors had taken care of it all, and Michael had been too scared to ask too many questions.

Michael was kept in charge of the infusions after that, and he made recommendations as to how to put the subjects into a state of shock, in order to test it on them. The good news is that there are currently two subjects healthy and well, almost three weeks after the procedure. They continue to be monitored several times a day.

The other news is that Christina is walking. Thirteen months and she's already determined to make her mark. Michael is as proud of co-creating that baby as he would be of any other scientific development in the world. He'd do anything for his daughter, and his wife. He's more determined now than ever to develop this drug – because more than anything else, he wants to protect his own little family.

# Sixteen

## CHRISSIE (NOW)

Chrissie wakes up in the ambulance with a strong urge to vomit. Harsh strip lights above her, narrow bed below. A blanket has been pulled up to her neck, and she yanks it away from her face. She's too hot, but she moves too quickly and pain whines through her upper body.

'Wendy?' Her voice is a croak. She tries to sit up, but everything spins. She's vaguely aware of the undulations of the road beneath, the sensation of moving very fast. She sucks in a breath. The spinning slows slightly, and the nausea subsides.

'Try to stay still, you'll need to be checked over.'

She blinks, and a face comes into focus. A nurse in pale-blue scrubs, sitting on a small seat bolted to the side of the vehicle below her feet. Female, from the voice. She can't quite make out her features, everything is slightly blurred.

'But Wendy?'

'We've sedated her. We can't do any more right now. Try to rest.'

She closes her eyes. They've given her something too. Her head feels detached, swimmy. She has a vague memory of a face at the car window. Strong arms lifting her out. The sharp prick of a needle in her arm.

'Why's there no siren?' she says, but she can't focus anymore.

Best to go with it. Best to sleep.

◆  ◆  ◆

She wakes again in a stark, white room. She blinks. Everything is crisp, clean. There's a faint smell of antiseptic. Next to her, a glossy white table with a jug of water and a ridged plastic tumbler sitting on it.

Her head is still a little fuzzy, and it takes a few minutes for her to remember what happened. Work out why she is there.

*Wendy . . .*

She reaches for the tumbler and takes a long drink, gulping it, mouth drier than she'd realised. Water spills down her front, cool and refreshing as it trickles over her chest and under the gown she's been put in.

Attached to the white-metal bed rail is a cable with a red button on top. She presses it, and there is a single buzz . . . and then a light comes on to her left, above the door, through the glass pane at the top. A red light, flashing . . . One, two, three . . .

The door opens.

'Ah, you're awake. Good. We don't have much time.'

Female nurse in pale-blue scrubs – she sounds familiar. But Chrissie doesn't recognise her face.

'Were you in the ambulance? Where's Wendy?'

The nurse opens a white cabinet in the corner of the room and takes out a large grey handbag. Red strap, and a small yellow monkey hanging from a clip on the side.

'Hey, that's my—'

'Yes,' the nurse says, placing it on the bed and rummaging inside. 'Here.'

She holds a small, black device in her hand. An amber light is blinking slowly. It takes Chrissie a moment to work out what it is. It looks familiar. She blinks hard, shakes her head. Her head is still not quite there yet, like it's not really part of her. She takes it, stares at it in her hand, like it's a precious stone.

'What's—'

'You know what this is. You activated it earlier. That's why you're here.'

Chrissie shakes her head. 'No . . .' This isn't making sense. 'I'm in hospital . . . There was a crash. Wendy, my friend, she's—'

'She's still alive, Christina. But you don't have much time. Look – do you need me to get one of the doctors along to see you? To explain again?'

'Chrissie. It's *Chrissie*,' she says.

But it's there now. Lodged back in her head. The pager. She pressed the pager in the car. Instead of picking up her phone and dialling 999, she grabbed the pager and pressed the button . . . It was red then, and now she's activated it, and it's amber . . . and now there's no way out. She has to complete the process. It has to go green. Doesn't it?

'I'm . . . I think I should call my husband . . .'

The nurse sighs. 'You can do that if you like. Of course you can.' She rummages in her bag again, pulls out her phone. 'Here you go.'

Chrissie takes it. Confused. She's still holding the pager in her other hand. 'But, I—'

'If you call your husband, then I'm afraid Wendy will die. Your choice, of course. But I assume the details of the policy were explained to you in full. You activated the process. If you change your mind now, there's no guarantee that you'll be released from the programme.' She pauses, tips her head to the side, as if recalling something difficult. 'In fact, no one's been released since I started here . . . I'm not sure that clause still exists . . .'

Chrissie sits up too fast, her head spins again. She drops the pager on to the bed as if it has burned her. 'But this is ridiculous. It's not real . . . It can't actually be *real*?'

The nurse shakes her head. 'You signed the paperwork, Mrs Tate.' She flips up the little upside-down watch that's attached to her breast pocket. 'Twenty minutes to go. You're wasting time. Your friend needs you.'

'Let me see her then!' Chrissie drops the phone. She throws the covers off and pushes herself down the bed. Her neck screams with pain. Her phone and the pager fall off the bed, landing with a splintering crack on the floor.

'Please, Mrs Tate . . .'

The nurse puts hands on her shoulders, tries to restrain her. Chrissie struggles free, slides off the bed. Her feet land on the cold floor and she feels weak, like she can't take her own weight. Her legs crumple beneath her. She's dimly aware of the single buzz, then the flashing light above her door. She's slipping away again, but she knows she needs to stay awake.

Her phone is in pieces under the bed. Not sure if it's smashed, or just split apart, she reaches under for it, just as footsteps appear behind her. Voices. Someone grips her arm.

'Mrs Tate, please, let us help you. You need to get back into bed. We need to discuss your options. Your friend, Miss Brookes . . .'

Chrissie pulls away from the grip, slides herself further under the bed. The pager is just out of reach.

A face appears beneath the other side of the bed. 'Let us help you, Chrissie.'

The pain in Chrissie's neck has blossomed, shooting agonising spasms through her shoulders, down her arms. She inches forward, just a fraction more.

'Chrissie, please . . .'

She gets a finger on the edge of the pager, and somehow, miraculously, manages to flip it back towards herself until it's under her hand. She lets out a long groan of pain. Anger. Frustration.

A hand grips her ankle. Another finds the top of her arm. As they start to gently pull her out from under the bed, she closes her hand tight. Clutches the pager. Voices swirl around her.

'We need to hurry. She needs to activate now.'

'Seven and a half minutes . . . Come on. Let's get her out of there.'

'Can't one of us just press it?'

'Don't be ridiculous. Everything is monitored. You know that. It has to be her. She has to want to do it.'

They pull her out. Try to get her to sit up on the floor, but she feels like she is made of rubber. Her hands flop uselessly. She looks down at the pager in her palm.

'Wendy . . .' she says. 'I want . . . I . . .'

She grips the pager, seems to have no strength left at all. Her shaking finger finds the button. Watches the light. *Amber . . . amber . . .*

*Green.*

Then everything goes black.

# Seventeen

## Joseph (Now)

Joseph has a report to write. Just like scientific conferences, it's been a while. But despite everything, the basic tenets of it come back to him.

*Introduction*
*Methods*
*Discussion*
*Conclusion*

He writes the headings on the paper, then stares at it for a while, before screwing the paper into a ball and tossing it in the fire.

The fire is the nicest thing about this small, drab room. It might be the nicest thing about this small, drab house that he lives in. But it's what they gave him so he shouldn't complain. Besides, the heat from the fire helps with the pain in his joints, when he's in the midst of a flare.

He leans back in the threadbare armchair and sighs. He barely notices that he's scratching his arm. The rash is more widespread now, and the heat is making it worse. But it's either the itch or the pain, and right now the itch is less of a bother. He slides the wrist monitor further down his arm. It's become looser, lately, and he suspects he's losing weight. Between that, and the rash and the joint pain, and him having to keep a constant eye on his heart rate, he's getting a bit fed up with his ailing body. Hence the need to confirm the details of his experimental subjects sooner rather than later. He taps the monitor and checks the reading. Stable, for now.

Yet he is, in the absolute sense of the phrase, running out of time.

He starts again. This time, he draws a line down the middle of the page, then one across the top – a couple of lines down. At the top of the first column he writes *Christina Tate*. She'd insisted it was Chrissie, but *Christina* was stuck in his head, wedged in there tight, and there was no way she was getting out again. Of course, he couldn't confirm just yet that she was the Christina that he required.

At the top of the second column he writes *Dr Ris Anderson*. On paper, she's a much better candidate. A doctor herself, and in a similar research area – it would make a lot of sense if *she* was his Christina. The way she had been with him, too. Calm. Rational. Interested. Polar opposite to the skittishness of the Tate woman. He'd followed Dr Anderson home after the conference. She didn't join the other attendees for the evening drinks. She was sensible and studious. Reminded him a little of himself.

Yes, as far as things stand at the moment, Dr Anderson is the front runner.

The fire crackles and pops beside him as he writes. Outside, a siren screeches somewhere in the distance. Afterwards, silence again, but for the spit and crunch of the fire as the logs ripple amidst the flames.

In Christina Tate's column he writes *DAUGHTER* in capital letters, underlining it twice. She has a child. This is something to be aware of. This is something that makes him want Christina Tate to be the one. He's been watching the Tates for a while. Their daily 'family time' in that little park, having left their mobiles at home so they can engage with one another. He hadn't expected his phone call to work so well, but it had. Chrissie had run off to answer it while that husband of hers remained distracted after his *own* little phone call. Yes, he'd seen Nathan Tate take a call as he'd wandered away from his wife and daughter, to the quiet confines of the other side of the park. Seemed that Mr Tate had a phone that Chrissie knew nothing about.

He rips off the paper and scrunches it into a ball. Tosses it into the fire.

Starts again.

Draws two lines down the page. There. Yes. Three columns now. A line across the top, spaced a couple of lines down. In the first column he writes *Chrissie Tate*. He has to use the name she gave him. Has to remove that unconscious bias. In the second, he writes *Dr Ris Anderson*. Then under *Chrissie* he writes *daughter*, and under *Ris* he writes *scientist*. And then he continues, more words, more evidence. Line by line by line.

The third column remains blank, for now.

Joseph smiles to himself, mentally planning tomorrow's day out. He's looking forward to researching his third subject.

# Eighteen

## CHRISSIE (NOW)

A young male nurse who has smiled at her but never spoken pushes Chrissie along the corridor in a wheelchair and leaves it in place outside another private ward. The soft swish of his soles disappears back down the corridor behind her. Unlike in hers, there is a small curtainless window, enabling her to see inside. The room is just like her own: white, plain, functional. Wendy is lying in the bed, hooked up to machines. Her eyes are closed. Most of her face is obscured by bandages and dressings, but Chrissie can still see that it is her. Her heart flutters. *Oh, Wendy.* On the far side of the room, a blank-faced female nurse stands still and quiet, watching.

Chrissie pushes herself up. Her legs feel weak. She presses her hands to the glass, peers inside, taps her nails on the window gently, not wanting to make too much noise, but wanting her friend to see her.

The nurse catches her eye, shakes her head. Mouths, 'She's fine. She's asleep.'

Chrissie mouths, 'Can I come in? Can I see her?'

The nurse frowns. A moment later, she appears at the door, opens it just a crack. Says, 'It's best to leave her to rest now. She's had quite an ordeal. So have you, Mrs Tate. Why don't you see if you can go home now? Get into your own bed, away from this place. Wendy will have to stay a bit longer. We'll need to keep her in for observation.'

'But will she be OK? I don't understand . . .'

'Please, Mrs Tate.' Gentler. 'Christina. It's best that you go now. I can call someone. Get them to come back and collect you? They really shouldn't have brought you down . . .'

Chrissie shakes her head. 'No,' she says. 'I wanted to come. But I can walk back. I'm fine.'

She returns to the window, presses her hands against the glass once more.

*Please, Wendy. Please wake up. Please be OK. I don't understand any of this.*

Although there is no sound of a buzzer, a door opens at the end of the corridor, casting a beam of light. Soft footsteps next. The male nurse who'd wheeled her along to Wendy's room, smiling at her again.

'Come on now, Mrs Tate, let's get you back. Get you ready. If everything is all right, we'll be able to bring you home. All of this will be over soon enough.' He has a soft Irish lilt and it soothes her.

She sits back in the chair and lets him take her.

◆ ◆ ◆

She realises, as the ambulance parks outside her house, that Nathan has no idea where she has been or what has happened to her and Wendy.

'Do you need us to help you into the house?' says the female paramedic. The one who'd been with her in the first ambulance. The one who knows everything.

'No,' she says. 'I can do it. Please . . . Just go now. Thank you for what you've done.' The nurse helps her down the retractable metal step at the back, and when she is sure that Chrissie is not about to keel over, she nods, pulling the doors closed behind her. The ambulance pulls away, gone before she's halfway up her drive.

She's not sure what she was thanking them for. But Wendy is alive and that's all that matters right now. She pauses for a second, leaning a hand on the fence. A wave of dizziness washes over her. She's still pumped full of drugs. Her skull feels thick, as if it has been soaked in glue and newspaper. Papier mâché in place of her brain. The pain in her neck has subsided, but she knows it'll return as the painkillers wear off. She needs to be careful.

She sways, dropping her handbag on the doormat. The small yellow monkey swings back and forth under the strap. Nathan yanks the door open before she can even attempt to find the keys in the depths of her bag.

'Chrissie? What the hell? What happened to your face? Where's Wendy?' He glances down the driveway. 'Did you get a cab? Where's the car?'

She'd forgotten about the car. She assumes it's a write-off, but still. Doesn't she have to sort insurance, all those things? Has it been towed to a garage? Perhaps someone will be in touch. It doesn't matter right now. She falls into Nathan's arms. He is still talking, gibbering, too many questions. Her vision swims. When he feels the weight of her grabbing him, arms circling him, gripping him, he stops talking and holds her tight.

'Chrissie.' His face against hers. She can feel tears on her cheek. His or hers? 'Chrissie, what happened? Last thing I heard was your text saying you were on the way back. Why didn't you call me? I don't understand—'

'Neither do I.' Chrissie steps back, tries to stay upright. Tries to focus her eyes. 'We were so close to home. Two streets away . . . Those stupid concrete planters. Something ran out in front of me. I swerved . . .'

112

The colour drains from Nathan's face. His eyes widen. 'And Wendy? Where's Wendy?' He peers past her down the driveway again, as if expecting to see her friend casually wandering up from behind. His voice is frantic. He seems less concerned about her now, more about Wendy.

Well, of course he's concerned, she's one of their best friends, not just *her* friend. Not just the girl who looks after Holly when they need her to; not just one of Holly's pre-school teachers. She is much more than that. She's like a sister. She is part of the family. Chrissie's head feels like it might float away from her. Memories of times that the four of them have spent together. Interactions between Nathan and Wendy. Fun, playful. He loves her too.

'Oh God, Nathan . . . It was awful. But she's fine. I'm sure she's fine.' She hesitates. 'She's still in hospital.'

Nathan rubs his eyes, as if becoming aware of the time all of a sudden. Of his tiredness. Did the sound of the ambulance wake him? What time is it? The dark is still heavy in the sky. Silent. It feels like 3 a.m. 'Well, what shall we do? Can we get someone to look after Holly? We should go to the hospital. Has someone contacted her parents?'

Chrissie shakes her head. 'They're going to move her first. They're taking her somewhere different . . . not where I was.'

'What do you mean, not where you were? Where were you?'

She shakes her head.

'Where were you?'

'A clinic. It doesn't matter. We're both fine. We're both going to be fine. Look, please . . . Let's get inside, I need to sit down, the hospital said they'd call me when she wakes up. We can go and visit her in the morning.'

'No.' Nathan is pacing up and down, making fists, shaking his head. He is frantic. 'No. I've got meetings tomorrow. I can't go in tomorrow. I need to go now. We need to go now—'

'Nathan, please,' she pleads. 'Wendy is in hospital. She's getting the care she needs. I need you to look after *me* right now.' Something about what he's saying is confusing her. Tomorrow is Sunday. Why does he have meetings on a Sunday?

He stops pacing. Stares at her. Blinks. 'Sorry. Of course you do. It's the shock.'

'I know.'

'You must think I'm ridiculous. You're here . . . That's all that matters. Jesus.' He steps in and hugs her tightly again.

She will go tomorrow, to see Wendy. She won't be getting out immediately, will she? She's not even awake yet.

'Let's go to bed,' she says.

Nathan takes her hand and guides her gently up the stairs.

She lies in bed, staring at the ceiling. They've given her plenty of painkillers, and she feels numb. Disembodied. She hasn't looked in the mirror yet. Seen what a mess her face might be in. It can't be that bad. They wouldn't have let her go home if it was. If she needed any serious treatment.

She wishes she'd asked for something to help her sleep. How can she get through the night, thinking about Wendy?

Thinking about what she's done.

She lies there and stares, trying to switch off her thoughts. Trying to let sleep take her. Nathan is on his side, hugging into her, curled around her as if she's a child. Just like the other night after Holly fell, and he curled himself around her, cocooning her small body. Making her feel safe. After a while she hears the gentle sounds of his snores. His adrenalin has worn off, but she's too drugged up for that release.

She lies there, watching shadows dance across the room, staring at the moon as it peeks through the gap in the curtains. She drifts in and out of consciousness, but never fully sleeps. Can't switch off. Too much . . .

At first she thinks it's a dream, perhaps she *has* fallen asleep. The shadows have changed. A flashing blue light circles slowly around the room. *No.*

She climbs out of bed, opens the curtains a fraction more. There is an ambulance sitting outside. Back doors open. An eerie silence hovers over the street. She steps back, her heart thumping so hard she's worried that they will hear it. Listens to the sound of them rolling the trolley out on to the road.

She peers through the curtains again. Watches as they push the trolley up the driveway.

Next door's driveway.

She holds on to the curtain, grips it so tight that her knuckles burn white in the moonlight. There is a small *plink* as one of the curtain hooks flicks off, the fabric dropping down, still in her grip.

Arthur.

They have come to take Arthur.

*Oh God. What have I done?*

# PART 2

PART 2

SCIENCE TODAY: Monthly Round-Up

Date: September 15, 1982

Source: University of Cambridge, UK

Summary: Molecular biology's hot topic centres around viral vectors – think of them like microscopic delivery vans, introduced to transport key genetic material to its desired destination in the host – and news is just in about a two-man team working out of Cambridge, UK, who have succeeded in instigating cell regeneration via their own modified bacteriophage. Pre-clinical trials have been deemed a success, and early testing has started in healthy human volunteers. No further information at present, and the team have requested to remain anonymous at this stage while the programme is still in its early stages. Groundbreaking stuff! More when we have it . . .

# Nineteen

## Chrissie (Now)

Chrissie's mouth feels like it's been stuffed with cotton wool. Her head throbs, and for a moment, she can't work out where she is. She sits up too fast, and her vision swirls. Colours and shapes dancing before her eyes. The room smells stale, a faint whiff of antiseptic mixed with sweat.

'Nathan?'

It hurts when she speaks, and she doesn't think she has the strength to shout. She turns her head slowly, causing a sharp pain to shoot down her neck, and is relieved to find a glass of water and a blister pack of pills sitting there, waiting. A note scribbled on a yellow Post-it is stuck on to the base of the lamp.

*Took Holly to the park. Didn't want to wake you. X*

The water is warm and a bit metallic, but it soothes her throat. She stares at the pills – four missing. When did she have them? Is it even safe to have any right now?

She blinks. She wants a clear head. Even if it hurts.

As she passes the window, she notices that the curtain is hanging all wrong, and she remembers last night, pulling it off the rail . . . watching as they took Arthur away.

That did happen, didn't it? Or maybe it was a dream. She hopes it was. In fact, everything from the afternoon before, from choosing her clothes and walking down the stairs, is a bit of a blur.

She showers gently, careful not to turn too abruptly. Her neck feels tight. Strained. The shower wakes her up, but not in a nice, refreshing way. She'd tried not to look at herself in the mirror as she'd undressed, but she didn't need to look to see the bruises on her chest, and to feel the tenderness of the damaged skin as the jets of water hit her like needles.

As she steps out, the car crash comes back to her with a slam, and she has to grip on to the towel rail to stop herself from falling. The impact. Wendy's face. Gasping for breath, she lowers herself to the floor and wraps a towel around her body, pulling it tight and ignoring the pain in her ribs. The car crash was real – and Wendy was hurt . . . badly hurt.

*Oh God!*

The rest of it comes back in waves. The strange clinic. The instructions. But maybe that part wasn't real. Perhaps she'd banged her head and she was having some kind of episode. The ambulance outside, and the trolley being wheeled up next door's path – that bit wasn't real, was it? She'd had four of those tablets. Some kind of strong painkillers – probably super-strength co-codamol. She would've been delirious.

A text pings on her phone:

I've dropped Holly at Lila's. I'll pop in to see Wendy after my meeting – can you tell me which ward she's in? You up yet? Let me know if you're OK, please. Nx

She blinks. She doesn't know where Wendy is. All she knows is that it wasn't the usual hospital. She can't remember arriving or leaving. It's all such a blur. She scrolls down her text messages and sees something from a withheld number:

Your friend has been transferred to Northlands General, Ward 5.

She can't remember seeing this message. The timestamp says it came in at 04:15. She was out of it then. She copies and pastes it into Nathan's reply. Ends it with:

I'm fine. Bit groggy. See you later x

She pulls on jeans and a T-shirt, slips her feet into her favourite trainers – the ones with the laces that don't have to be laced. Drags her hair back into a ponytail. She wonders again why Nathan is working today. Wonders when the playdate with Lila was arranged. Yesterday, maybe? When Nathan and Holly went out for the day? She feels like something is wrong, but she pushes it from her mind. He's probably told her why. Some deadline or other. Something she hasn't paid attention to.

She has to do better. But first, she needs to go and find out what's happened to her neighbour.

Chrissie pulls the door closed behind her and heads down her path. Turns right, and walks up the identical path in the front garden next door.

She's halfway there when she changes her mind. As much as she wants to believe it was a drug-induced dream, she knows what she saw. She turns, and walks quickly back down the path, almost making it to the recycling bins at the bottom of the drive before she hears a voice calling her name.

'Chrissie? Is that you?'

She sucks in a breath, lets it out slowly. Then she turns around and takes a few steps along the path again, back towards her neighbours' front door.

The old woman is standing on the step. She looks smaller than Chrissie remembers. Shrunken in on herself, her clothes seemingly a size too big. The soft skin of her face has lost its rosy glow, and she looks grey and worn, her eyes rimmed red.

'Oh, sorry, Maureen. I was about to knock then I noticed the curtains were shut and I—'

'My mother always closed the curtains when she was in mourning.' The old woman's voice is flat. 'Lost two brothers first. Accidents at work. My dad was next.'

Chrissie feels a chill run over her, goosebumps rippling down her arms.

'What's happened, Maureen?' She's almost at the step now, and she can already see inside the house. She can feel the change in it before she even thinks about going inside. A stillness that was never there before. Something heavy, hanging low, but just out of sight.

Maureen turns away and heads back inside, leaving the door open. Chrissie follows her in, pulling the door closed behind her. 'It's not Arthur, is it? Is he ill?' She knows the answer. A hard ball of pain rolls around in her stomach. *Please be wrong. Please.*

'Arthur's gone.' Maureen slumps into an armchair, gripping the arms so tight that her knuckles glow white. All Chrissie can do is stare at her in horror.

'Gone? I—'

'Massive heart attack, they said. He wouldn't have known much about it. Although, I'm not sure I believe that part, myself.'

Chrissie takes a seat on the couch. Her whole body feels heavy, as if she is being pressed down by an invisible heavy weight. Like the atmosphere has changed in composition, and the gases that keep them all from crumpling inward, or floating off into space, have become unbalanced. She can't bring herself to speak.

'I thought I heard someone at the door. I'd say it woke me up, but I was restless anyway. Arthur was up at the toilet. Twice a night, lately. But then he'd always come back and fall straight into a deep sleep again.' Maureen sniffs, and takes a hankie out of the cuff of her cardigan to wipe her nose. 'Only last night, he didn't fall asleep straight away. I lay there for a while, watching him. But then I must've nodded off, and that was me for a good few hours. I always wake again before the morning . . .'

'And was there someone?' Chrissie leans forward in her seat, the movement making her neck twinge. 'At the door, I mean?'

Maureen shakes her head. 'I don't know. I don't think so. Well, anyway, he must've fallen asleep at some point, but he never woke up again.' She pushes the hankie back up her sleeve and puts her hands on the arms of the chair again. They start trembling. 'He'd only been up to the toilet once, you see. So I knew something was wrong. I switched on the bedside lamp, and I knew for sure. His face . . . There was something wrong with his face. It wasn't his sleep face. You know what I mean, don't you? It was a different face. Like someone had taken a mask of my Arthur, and laid it out over a shop mannequin.' She grips the sides of the chair again. 'I don't know what I'm going to do without him, Chrissie.'

Chrissie thinks she might throw up, but she manages to swallow back the sharp taste of bile as it tries to inch slowly up her throat.

'I'm so sorry, Maureen,' Chrissie manages. It seems so inadequate. 'He was a lovely man.' He *was* a lovely man. It had only been recently that they'd had problems, and now it's too late to put things right.

Maureen gives her a sad look. 'He always liked you, Chrissie. He was worried about you . . .' She pauses. Opens her mouth as if

125

to say something else, but decides against it. 'You take care of your little family now, you hear me? It's all over much quicker than you think.'

Worried about her? Why? But it's not the right time to ask. She leaves Maureen alone, and slips quietly out of the house, feeling guilty but relieved that the woman had been too wrapped up in her own situation to ask Chrissie about the bruises on her face.

# Twenty

## Michael (October 1982)

Michael lifts the mouse from its cage and cups it in his hands. The rodent sniffs at his fingers for a moment, then it stops, and its keen red eyes stare up at him. Michael has experimented on probably thousands of mice and rats while he's been at the university; he knows they are the best way to test the safety of new drugs. He knows that the mice don't really know what's going on, and he tries his best to ensure that they suffer no unnecessary pain. But sometimes, when he holds one in his hands, stroking the soft fur of its back – times like now, when the tiny, defenceless creature stares up at him question-ingly – he still feels a surge of guilt.

*Get a grip, Michael.*

But he likes this mouse. He's named it Percy, and he's watched it grow from a blind hairless pup into the happy little thing that it is now. He thinks of his daughter. Christina is eighteen months now and she is running amok. Her favourite activity is to scribble on the wallpaper with crayons. What would Percy be doing now, if he wasn't trapped in this cage, awaiting a fate that he can't escape, but mercifully, knows nothing of?

'Cute.' The voice comes from behind him, following the gentle swish of the lab doors swinging closed. He'd not heard them open.

It's a voice he's got used to these last few weeks. He drops the mouse back into the cage and closes the lid, flicking the lock into place.

'Morning, Anne. You're in early.'

Anne walks around to the other side of the cage. As usual, her hair is neat and glossy, swinging loose in a long bob style that has recently become popular. He wants to tell her that she should have it tied back, but from the moment they met, it was clear that Dr Anne Cater – the Ministry of Defence's chief scientific officer assigned to Project Lifeblood – was not someone that responded well to orders from those she considered her subordinates. A small, lean woman with sharp, watchful eyes – she was hard on Michael's case from the beginning, and he could see no reason for that to change. *She's here to help you*, they'd told him – but in truth, she was here to make sure he did exactly what he was supposed to.

'Thought I'd get my hands dirty today,' she says, with just a hint of a smile. 'What can I do?'

Michael takes a deep breath. 'Well . . . if you're going to be in here, you really need to be covered up. There are spare lab coats on the hook in my office. And' – he hesitates, sure that she will berate him – 'you really need to tie your hair back. Contamination, you know?'

She gives him a look that says she doesn't like being told what to do. After a moment of them staring one another out, she concedes defeat and marches off towards his office.

'No Edward today?' she calls out as she's walking.

Michael shakes his head. 'Nope. I'm not sure where he is, actually. Said he had a meeting . . . I assumed with you.'

She comes back towards him, lab coat on, fumbling with a band to tie her hair back into a small ponytail. 'Not with me.' She fixes him again with her steely gaze. 'So. What can I do?'

He walks across to the fridge and pulls open the heavy steel door. It makes a sucking sound as the seal breaks, then again as he

128

closes it, after taking out a small glass vial. When he comes back to the bench, she is tapping Percy's cage, and the mouse's tiny claws are scratching on the glass.

'Please,' he says, laying the vial on top of a cloth on the bench. 'Don't agitate him. The BALB/c strain are very prone to anxiety. I need him calm for this procedure.'

'Maybe we need to breed our own then. Make them more suitable for our needs.'

Michael sighs. 'These mice are exactly right for our needs. Their genetic make-up is exactly right for cardiovascular experiments.' *You should know that*, he thinks. *What kind of doctor are you, exactly?* She's never said much about her background to him, and he hasn't felt he could question her. But he doesn't really want her agitating his specimens. Not when they're at such a crucial stage. Especially when some of them have seemed overly distressed as it is – a finding that he's not keen to share with the team until he's explored whether there's really a pattern. 'Maybe you should just observe.'

She nods. 'Whatever you think, Dr Gordon.'

Michael tries to pretend she's not there. He's not used to working with an audience, but she's clearly not going anywhere, and he hasn't even got Edward to distract her. Where the hell is—Dammit. He remembers now. Edward has gone to the Phase I clinic to talk to the lead investigator about starting their first-in-man trials. Their first *official* first-in-man trials, that is. He's still extremely uncomfortable about the pre-testing that went on, but he knows he needs to keep his mouth shut.

He ignores her and carries on preparing the two things that he needs: the aerosol spray and the injectable solution.

He blows out a breath. Closes his eyes and counts to ten. Part of him is hoping that it will work this time, but a bigger part is hoping it won't. More than once, he's wondered if there could be a way of sabotaging the programme so that they could stop it and he could get back to doing the research he always planned to do – the research where he wanted to find cures for all diseases. Where he wanted to help modern medicine move to the next level. When he started his undergraduate degree, full of enthusiasm and hope, he never once imagined he'd become embroiled in a shady government top-secret experimental programme. It sounds ridiculous when he thinks about it. And this evil scientist cliché that's sitting in his lab isn't helping assuage any of his fears.

But there's no point in attempting failure. They'd only bring in someone else. And he doesn't want to think about what would happen to him, or to his family, if he doesn't toe the line.

Michael opens the lid of Percy's cage and reaches in to pick up the mouse in his cupped hands once more, giving him another gentle stroke. Watching his little nose sniffing at his fingers – possibly for the last time.

'Don't you pick them up by the tail anymore? That's what we always did . . . back in the day.'

'Makes them angry. We've got a better chance of a good result if we give him a bit more care.'

Cater raises an eyebrow, but she says nothing more.

'OK, Percy. You know the drill . . .'

He holds the mouse in one hand, squeezing it gently to ensure a firm grip. He can feel the beating of its little heart against his palm. With his other hand, he slides the spray-vial out of the holder. Without giving himself a chance to change his mind, he pumps down hard on the spray, and watches as the fine mist puffs into the rodent's unsuspecting face. It opens its mouth wide, baring its teeth. Then it falls limp in his hand.

'Marvellous.' Cater claps her hands. 'Very efficient. What are we calling this thing again?'

Michael is still holding the mouse in his hand. 'It's KS4582A, for the time being. Not very catchy, I know. But I'm sure you've got people to come up with something a bit more *on brand*.'

She gestures towards the syringe. 'So how soon until you inject it?'

Michael lays the mouse down on the bench. The creature looks peaceful, as if it is sleeping. But its heart definitely stopped. It's definitely dead. 'There's a window . . . but we haven't worked it out just yet. We've waited too long before, but we can't do it too soon. The process has to be sustainable, if you want to use it in practice.'

'And this time?'

He looks at his watch. 'Fifteen minutes.' Michael stands. 'Can I get you a cup of tea?'

'Black, no sugar.' She peers down at the mouse. 'Do you think it felt any pain? When you sprayed it?'

'When I induced a massive heart attack?' Michael walks over to his office and flicks on the kettle. *You saw his face, didn't you?* That expression of sheer horror. He drops teabags into two mugs. 'We can't know for sure.'

They sit together, drinking their tea in silence, until it is time. And when it is, he lifts the mouse again – its small body still warm – and gently pushes the needle into the back of its thigh, then slowly depresses the plunger.

Again, they sit together. Watching. Waiting. During the early experiments, it took a while to kick in. But as things progressed, it started to happen quicker. Sometimes it didn't happen at all. Other times, it happened, then it reversed almost immediately. He's been honing the solution for some time now. Altering the components. Playing around.

Playing God.

The mouse opens its eyes. It blinks, as if it has just woken from a deep sleep.

'Oh, how wonderful!' Anne leans across the bench. 'Well done, Percy,' she says, stroking his head. Percy flinches, turning towards her, then clamps his mouth around her finger.

'Oww, *shit* . . . You little bastard!' She yanks her hand away. 'That thing needs putting down.' Her calm demeanour has evaporated, and as Michael looks at her face, he can see the real Dr Cater inside. As he suspected, she is not here to help. She doesn't care if this mouse feels pain – just as she won't care if the healthy human volunteers feel it either. He needs to tell her about the behavioural issues he's noticed in a few of his subjects, but now is definitely not the time.

He knows that they plan to use ex-soldiers. Prisoners, too. Those determined to be of little use to society. Expendable.

The whole thing is completely unethical.

'You should probably get some antibiotics for that bite. Just in case.'

He places Percy back into his cage and closes the lid. He picks up his lab book and writes down the details. There's a flutter of excitement in him. He's brought Percy back to life. But for how long?

Anne pulls off her lab coat and dumps it on the bench, then marches out of the lab without another word.

At home, Sandy is watching TV, a tray with her empty dinner plate and cutlery on the floor at her feet. He sits down on the sofa beside her, not daring to interrupt. He wants to tell her about the lab. About Percy. It's a success, but it doesn't feel like one. He's scared about what it means. He stares at the TV. It's *Dallas*, and it seems like everyone is pretty pissed off with JR. He stands again, wants to leave her to it, but she lays a hand on his arm, grips gently.

'Hey you,' she says. 'How was your day?'

'Oh, it can wait. I don't want you to miss your show.'

She pulls him backward and he flops on to the sofa beside her. She squeezes his hand, then leans in to plant a soft kiss on his lips. 'Tell me,' she says.

Michael nods towards the TV. 'But what about JR?'

She kisses him again. 'You know it's Bobby I like. JR is nothing but a big meany. If it wasn't for all that money, I'm sure Sue Ellen would walk out the door.'

'The money, though . . .'

'You know I don't care about money.' She tilts her head to the side, frowns. 'I care about you though. You sure everything's going OK with this new project of yours?'

'Yes,' he wants to say. Then, 'No.' But he says neither of those things. 'I think Edward might be a megalomaniac and I'm certain the "investors" are up to no good.' He doesn't say that either. Instead he says, 'Is Christina asleep?'

Sandy nods. 'Don't you go waking her. Your dinner's in the oven.' She kisses him once more, then turns back to her TV show.

Michael creeps quietly upstairs, into Christina's room. He hears her soft, snuffling snores above the quiet melody of the nursery rhyme playing on the cassette player. He looks down at his daughter and feels that familiar surge of love. *It's all for her*, he thinks. Provide for her future. Nothing else matters.

He tiptoes out of the room and back downstairs and into the kitchen. The table is set for him, and he takes the warm plate out of the oven and removes the foil. The mouth-watering smell of shepherd's pie helps him forget about everything. At least for tonight.

# Twenty-One

## CHRISSIE (NOW)

Chrissie checks the time on her phone: 3 p.m. Wendy is late bringing Holly back from nursery. Maybe they went somewhere after. But that's OK. That gives Chrissie some time to get on with her work – no. No she can't. Shit! It's Sunday. Wendy is still in hospital. Nathan took Holly to nursery before he went to work, didn't he? No. That's not right. Why the hell is he at work? Her memories of early morning are still hazy, but she remembers now – Nathan left a note, and then later he texted her, didn't he? She scrolls through her messages. Not nursery. The park. He took her to the park, and then he took her to Lila's and then he said he'd pop in to visit Wendy after work. Maybe he meant on Monday after work? Maybe it is Monday – has she lost a day? Now she's not sure what he means . . .

She frowns, another piece of the memories from the aftermath of the accident coming back to her. Last night – Nathan's frantic reaction. His worry about Wendy. Overreaction? Or not . . . Wendy is a big part of their lives. She's like the sister she never had. It's understandable he'd be worried.

She checks the rest of her messages. One from an unknown number: telling her that her friend is in ward 5 at Northlands General. Her last message to Nathan was at 14:15. Not even an hour ago. She blinks. She has no recollection of sending it. Her head. She'd definitely hit her head. This sort of thing happens. Maybe she should get herself checked out. Her neck hurts too. A lot. She can't drive. In fact, where the hell is her car? She slides her finger across her phone screen and orders an Uber.

◆ ◆ ◆

The room is nothing like she remembers. Was she even here? Her memories are still hazy – coming back in small, confusing pieces like a jigsaw of a painting with far too much sky. The text message: Your friend has been transferred . . . Wendy is propped up with pillows, a large gauze dressing covering half of her forehead. She's holding the remote control in her hand, frowning as she stabs at the buttons. Chrissie pushes the door the rest of the way open with her foot, both hands full carrying skinny cappuccinos from the Costa at the hospital entrance. The door makes a swishing sound as it opens.

'This bloody thing is useless,' Wendy says, not looking up. 'Total waste of a fiver. I can't even—' She looks up and her face shifts from frustration to shock, her sentence dropping off unfinished. It's just a moment, and then her face lights up with a tired smile. 'Oh, babe . . . Are you OK? I've been asking about you all morning and they wouldn't tell me anything—'

'Shh. Drink this.' She holds out the cardboard cup. 'Are you allowed caffeine? Shit, I didn't think . . .'

Wendy grabs the drink before she can pull it away. 'Thank you. Oh my God, if I'd had one more of those dirty dishwater teas.' She takes a sip through the drinking hole, then drops her eyes back to the remote. 'I wasn't expecting you. I thought maybe . . .'

Chrissie sits down on the end of the bed and tosses her small handbag towards the chair. 'I'm fine. Seriously. My neck hurts. My head's a bit fuzzy, but other than that . . .' There's a jacket slung over the back of the chair. A canvas messenger bag on the floor next to it. Both items look familiar, but she can't quite place them. The pieces don't fit. Her head starts to throb again. A sharp pulse on her left temple, just above her eye. The lights are too bright in here.

'Are you sure you're OK?' Wendy says. 'Here, take some water.' She leans over to try and pour some from the plastic jug next to her bed, then collapses back against the pillows from the exertion. 'Maybe I should call someone?'

'It's fine. Really.' She's not fine. She's really not fine. But it's got nothing to do with her head. 'Wendy . . . Whose jacket is that?'

'It's, uh. Oh God, Chrissie.' She bucks forward, slamming her coffee on the table, crying out in pain. 'Call the nurse, please, I—'

Chrissie is about to pull the emergency cord when the door bursts open. 'Didn't think you should have caffeine so I got you a hot chocolate, and—'

Wendy stops groaning and falls back against the pillows again.

'Well,' Chrissie says. 'I thought I recognised that jacket.'

'I, uh . . . hey,' Nathan says. 'Thought I might bump into you here. My meeting finished early, so—'

Chrissie blinks. 'It's Sunday, Nathan. Why would you be at work? I was in an accident. I haven't lost the ability to work out what day it is. I've been going over this since you first said it. You never work on Sundays. Ever.'

'I told you I was going to pop in here . . .'

'Yes, but why?' The smell of the place clears her head with one sudden lurch, like a foggy windscreen being wiped clean. 'Wendy is surrounded by medical professionals. Why weren't *you* with *me*?'

He opens his mouth to speak, and Chrissie raises a hand. 'Don't lie, please. You owe me that at least.'

'I can explain.' Nathan puts the drinks down on the bedside cabinet. 'I—'

'It's not what you think,' Wendy says, quietly.

Chrissie starts to laugh, but it sounds hollow. 'You're a right pair of clichés, aren't you?' She glances from her husband to her best friend; at their pale, shocked faces. She almost feels sorry for them.

'You could've died.' Chrissie blows out a long, slow breath. *I fucking saved you.*

Because she did, didn't she?

It all makes sense now. It's been staring her in the face all along, but she just didn't want to see it.

*Poor Arthur. Oh no. No, no.* He knew about the two of them, didn't he? That was what Maureen was hinting at. He knew, and he was too embarrassed to tell her. And now he's dead, and her bitch of a best friend is still alive.

'So how come you arranged a playdate at Lila's?'

Nathan looks sheepish. 'I wasn't sure where else to take her. Wendy said Lila was her latest best friend, so . . .'

Chrissie picks up her bag and walks out of the room without another word. She swipes angrily at her phone, ordering another Uber, and adding in a stop at Lila's house to pick up Holly. She messages Lila's mum, Amanda, saying she's on her way and can Holly be ready to leave as they need to get back home.

She ignores the driver's attempts at small talk as he whizzes through the quiet streets, taking a longer route that will avoid any traffic. Stone facades and shop fronts blur past, but she's not paying them much attention. She's on her phone again, staring at her contacts – trying to decide if what she's considering would be the best or the worst thing she could do right now.

She could just send a message, play it cool. But she's not feeling cool. She's been in a car crash, her best friend almost died – and some weird thing she did might've saved her . . . unless it's all a load of rubbish, of course. But then what happened to Arthur? And how long has her husband been cheating on her?

Chrissie leans back in the seat and thinks about Holly's drawings – always for her daddy, never for her – and this new one, with the two women. It's obvious now that one of them was Wendy. It's clear that Holly has been there with the two of them – the two of them holding hands.

How could they do this?

Bad enough to betray her, but to drag Holly into it? To make her lie, because she's too young to understand what's going on? That's unforgivable.

The taxi stops at traffic lights and her finger hovers over a name in her contacts list. She takes a deep breath, and hits 'call'.

The voicemail kicks in straightaway.

'Hi, this is Andy's phone. You know what to do . . . Beeeeeeeep!' he says, before the automated beep sounds, and she has a split second to decide whether to leave a message or not.

'Hey, stranger. It's me. Um, Chrissie.' Her heart thumps in her chest, so loudly she's sure he'll hear it on the voicemail. *What am I doing?* 'I . . . I need a bit of help with something. I know it's been a while, but . . .' She stops, sucks in a breath. 'Call me when you get this, bye.' The phone beeps again and she ends the call, just as the taxi pulls into a neat little cul-de-sac, where Holly is standing next to Lila and Amanda at the end of a short driveway, waving her hand madly.

A surge of love floods through Chrissie, and for a moment, everything else disappears. This is the most important person in her life, and she won't let anyone hurt her.

# Twenty-Two

## Joseph (Now)

Joseph waits patiently at the school gates. Many children arrive in huge cars that look more suited to navigating the terrain of the wilderness, not the narrow streets of residential north London. When he was a child he walked to school with his friends. Funnily enough, he can't remember their names, and he has no real interest in where they might be now. They'll be grandfathers, no doubt. Maybe they do the school run sometimes, in one of these oversized cars. Or maybe they're already dead. He scratches at his arm. The rash seems to have flared up worse than usual – which, ironically, is probably a result of his search to find a cure for what ails him.

He watched another zombie movie last night. There is a never-ending supply of them. Movies, TV shows, books. People seem to be quite obsessed with the undead. He's more interested in the gradual disintegration of the flesh. It might be far-fetched, but that's what he feels like is happening to him. He's had the rash on his arm since university, but over the years, it has spread – and no amount of cream will soothe it. He's more tired, too, and then he has these bouts of . . . mania. He bought the heart-rate monitor to keep an eye on it himself. He's been tracking the pattern. When his HR goes up, his thoughts become jumbled. He becomes impulsive. Not himself. When it falls too low, he can't function properly anymore. He aims to keep it within a safe range, but it's highly erratic and getting worse by the day. He could go to see a GP and ask for tests, but it's unlikely that whatever they find will help him. All it will do is elicit questions about the huge gaps in his medical history – and those are not questions he's willing to answer.

He knows he's running out of time.

He checks the wrist monitor, which also serves as his watch. Almost time for school to go in. Has he already missed her? Despite his meandering thoughts, he's had his eyes fixed on the teachers' car park and the route to the gates for an hour. The teachers always arrive before the pupils, unless they are late. And from his previous stake-outs, he knows she is rarely late.

'Oi, mister – you a paedo?'

The voice comes from behind him, and is followed by a cacophony of childish laughter. He turns to face a boy with a gelled blond quiff, his hand on one strap of his backpack. He looks about eleven, maybe. Tall and skinny, with a smirk on his face. He's surrounded by a small group of hangers-on, who stare at Joseph with expressions ranging from indifference to rage. It would be interesting to study this bunch. See what becomes of them when puberty hits and all their hopes for the future start to unravel before their eyes.

'I'm waiting to see Miss Millar. Not that it's any of your business.' He's not going to pander to this rabble. They should learn to respect their elders.

'Oh my God – I don't think she'll want to hang out with *you!*' This from a short but fierce-looking girl with bright red hair in a side ponytail. She's brandishing the handles of her skipping ropes like a weapon.

Another child, a pale and pudgy boy, takes a step forward and opens his mouth to speak, but then stops, as a tall, thin woman in

140

a blue floral dress appears with a pile of workbooks and a curious expression.

'That's enough. The bell's about to go, is it not?'

The children mutter their *yes misses* under their breath and scurry off into the playground. Once safely through the gates, the blond boy turns and gives Joseph the finger.

The woman is staring at him now, her curious expression holding a hint of concern. 'Can I help you?'

'Joseph Marshall.' He extends a hand.

She doesn't shake it. 'Are you a relative?'

Joseph shakes his head. 'Not as such, no. I'm here to see you, as a matter of fact. It's Miss Millar, isn't it? Tina Millar?'

She bristles, then, at the use of her name. *How does he know me?* she's thinking. He can see it in her face. 'I'm afraid you'll have to make an appointment with the school secretary, Mr Marshall. I'm running late for reception class, and I—'

'I've booked an appointment for nine forty-five a.m. I was told you'd have time to see me before your ten-thirty class. Is that correct, Miss Millar? Only, if there's an issue with the time, I'm happy to reschedule for when suits. It really is quite important.'

The bell rings. A long, shrill blast.

'I really have to get inside. I'm late . . .'

'You carry on, Miss Millar. As I said, I'll see you at the allotted time.' He makes no effort to move. He has no intention of going anywhere. It's not too long to wait now, and there's a bench nearby. Once she's gone, he'll head there and continue with his notes. He already has some observations, based on this brief meeting. It was important that he saw her just now – caught her unawares. He likes to gauge the reactions, before he gets into the detail. He's been observing her for a few weeks now, and it's lovely to talk to her at last.

'Well, I—'

141

'You get off now, Miss Millar. I'll see you soon.'

She frowns, then readjusts the pile of folders in her arms. She scurries off across the playground, the last one to the door, behind a few stragglers who've run past her and up the steps into the safety of the school.

'I really am very sorry, Miss Millar,' he calls out, and she stops walking and turns back to face him.

'About what?'

The folders are slipping from her grasp, and her hair slips out from behind her ear as she scrabbles around trying to stop them from falling.

'About your fiancé, Miss Millar. Grief is a terrible thing.'

# Twenty-Three

## Chrissie (Now)

Despite not sleeping a wink, Chrissie feels wide awake. Not a *good* sort of awake. Not the awake you feel after a decent night's sleep. It feels like forever since she's had one of those. The pain in her neck is subsiding. Not whiplash then, thankfully. But it still hurts if she turns her head too quickly. She flicks the kettle on for the umpteenth time and sits down at the kitchen table. Her phone is plugged into the charger, and she resists looking at it again. She'd spent most of the night refreshing her messages and emails, checking that the ringer was on – but Andy hasn't returned her call or replied with a message.

She sighs. Is it really so surprising? She hasn't spoken to him for four years. She ignored all his attempts at communication – deciding back then that the only way to deal with things was to pretend they didn't exist. Her old life in the office, after-work drinks in the city – that's all gone now. Andy was part of that, so he's gone too.

*Get over it.*

She leaves her phone where it is, and sets about getting Holly's breakfast things. Then she heads upstairs to get her little girl out of bed.

Holly is sitting up, chattering away to Blue Bear and Dollyanna – her current favourite toys.

'Mummy!' She throws her arms out when she sees Chrissie standing in the doorway. 'Is Auntie Wendy here yet?'

*Oh God.* 'No, sweetie. Auntie Wendy's not coming today. I'm going to take you to nursery—'

'But Auntie Wendy does my hair in proper bunches, Mummy. Are you going to do my hair in proper bunches? Where's Daddy? Can I have Coco Pops?' Holly tosses her toys on the floor and climbs out of bed, rubbing her eyes. 'Will Daddy be meeting us at the swings, Mummy?'

'Maybe, sweetpea. If you're good, OK? Let's get dressed first.'

Holly nods solemnly. 'Well, OK, Mummy.'

She carries on with the morning routine on autopilot: washed, dressed, breakfast, snacks in backpack, out the door, walk to nursery. Holly chatters away throughout, oblivious to the lack of response. She barely registers the look of concern on Gilly the nursery manager's face when she lets go of Holly's hand, letting her run across the nursery's small playground towards her friends.

'How are you?' Gilly says, rushing over to greet her with a hug. 'Wendy called this morning to say she wouldn't be in. Told me what happened. Is she OK?' She looks her up and down. Frowns. 'Jesus, are *you* OK?'

Chrissie manages a brief nod. 'I'm fine. I just . . . I need to sort some things out at home. It's been a bit of a crazy few days—'

Gilly looks confused, then blinks it away, her face settling back into an expression of concern. 'I can see you're struggling, Chrissie.' She hesitates for a second. 'Perhaps I could ask Amanda if she can take Holly for the afternoon. Her and Lila are thick as thieves at the moment. I'm sure she won't mind.'

Chrissie nods, remembering that she hadn't even thanked Amanda yesterday for looking after Holly when Nathan had dumped her there. She'll get her some chocolates or something. She wants to take something round for Maureen too.

144

'Chrissie?'

She blinks, realising that Gilly had continued speaking but she has no idea what she's said. 'Sure, yes please. That would be great.' She takes Gilly's hand and squeezes it. 'Thank you.'

'I'll sort it. Take care, Chrissie,' Gilly says. She turns away and walks towards the nursery entrance, where all the little kids are lined up now, waiting to go in.

Chrissie stands for a moment longer, watching. Churning things over in her head. Wondering how the hell she's going to explain Nathan and Wendy to her daughter.

But first things first – she needs to get out of this ridiculous programme she's signed up for. She's already made one mistake with Wendy. She's not going to make another.

On the way home, she stops and sits down on a bench on the winding path through the park. Just sits there for a moment, taking deep breaths. The air smells of cut grass, and the light breeze brings a hint of basil from the herb garden nearby. They'd had a kids' day when they started it. She and Holly had planted thyme and dill, and Holly had stood there staring at it for a long time, her face scrunched into a frown.

'Why's it not growing big, Mummy?'

'Oh, it will, sweetpea. Just like you will. But also just like you, the seedlings need some food and drink and a few sleeps before they get bigger.'

Holly had frowned even more. 'How many sleeps until I'm big, Mummy?'

'Lots and lots . . . but not too many. Besides, it's not always the best being big. Being little is fun too.' She crouched down and pointed at the seedlings. 'Look – aren't they cute?'

Just then, a bright yellow kite had swooped down across the expanse of grass, a small boy with a bubble of curly hair running after it, laughing. Holly had let go of her hand and run off to try and catch it, and Nathan had jumped up from where he was sitting on the bench, scrolling through his phone. He ran after Holly and grabbed her around the waist and she'd giggled.

Happy memories.

But now Nathan has messed everything up. And as for Wendy . . . An angry tear slides down her cheek and she wipes it away, before tapping her phone again and calling Joseph once more.

'Hello,' she starts, then pauses, realising that it's his voicemail again. 'It's me. Chrissie Tate. I need to talk to you about . . .' She stops, smiles, as an old man shuffles past with a terrier in a tartan doggie-coat ambling along beside him. The man and the dog stare at her in unison. She swallows, then speaks into her phone again. 'I need to cancel my . . . order. I'm not satisfied with the service. Please can you call me back when you get this.'

She tosses her phone into her bag and walks quickly through the park, deciding that she will go to the Co-op and get something nice for her and Holly's tea. No more pizza takeaways. She's going to cook more, and listen more, and be the best mum she can be. The double doors are wedged open, a blast of cooled air hitting her as she walks in. Karen is bent over, refilling cartons of milk from a metal cage into one of the fridges. Chrissie thinks about ignoring her, but then feels bad. It won't matter soon, once she gets Joseph to cancel things – but she should never have put Karen on that list. OK, so she's a bit brash and her son is a handful, but does she really deserve to be on someone's death list?

'Afternoon, Karen,' she says, picking up a basket and stopping by the fridge.

Karen straightens and turns towards her, her face all smiles until she realises who it is. 'Oh, it's you,' she says. 'Don't think I didn't see you shove that squashed avocado back into the box the other day.' She sniffs, then turns away again, taking out more pints of milk from the cage.

'I'm sorry about that,' Chrissie says. 'I was having a bad day. How's Tommy?'

Karen turns back to her, eyes narrowed. 'Er, he's fine, thanks.' She looks like she's about to say something else, but then a voice over the tannoy calls her name, and she shrugs and hurries off towards the tills.

Chrissie smiles to herself. It's a start.

After filling her basket with chicken and vegetables and a couple of those fancy desserts in the little glass dishes, she heads to the checkouts – stopping at a display of chocolates to get something for Amanda. She picks up a box of Milk Tray and lays it on top of her basket. A memory hits her then: Maureen telling her that Arthur bought her a box every birthday and Christmas, no matter what other presents he gave her. It gives her a little jolt, thinking that Arthur will never be able to buy them for his wife again . . . and it's all her fault. She picks up another box. She'll drop them round after she's prepped the dinner. Before Holly comes home.

Karen is no longer at the tills, and Chrissie tries to make small talk with the teenager who has taken her place – he seems surprised that someone is talking to him, but he says something that makes her laugh. She's smiling when she leaves the shop. Nathan and Wendy are far from her thoughts. And when her phone rings, she snatches it out of her bag, her smile turning into a grin.

'Andy,' she says, 'I'm so glad you called back. I . . .' Her voice trails off as the phone beeps once, then dies.

# Twenty-Four

## MICHAEL (JANUARY 1983)

Edward is sitting on his chair with his feet up on his desk with Michael sitting opposite. The desk is much less cluttered than the one that he and Michael shared over at the lab, but there is still the undeniable Edward touch to the place. The radio, for one, set to the same channel that he'd always listened to when they'd shared a space. KC and the Sunshine Band are currently wailing about giving it up, and Michael smiles to himself for a moment, remembering Sandy and Christina dancing to the same song in the kitchen only the day before. Christina is twenty-one months now, and Sandy has taken to motherhood like a duck to water. He suspects she'll want another one soon.

Percy is five months – which is four months older than most mice in a research lab. He has a few friends now, too – although they can't share a cage, so they have to resort to baring their teeth at each other through the glass. Percy himself is fairly docile, preferring to run around on his wheel than engage with the other mice on the cages either side. But Michael had let one of the trainees look after the other two, and they were instructed by Anne – who'd insisted that holding them by the tail was perfectly acceptable.

The song comes to an end and Edward stops singing along. 'Back with us, Mikey?'

Michael blinks. 'Sorry. I was miles away. Thinking about what you said . . . and don't call me Mikey. "Mike", I'll take. But you hate it if anyone tries to shorten your name, "Eddie".'

Edward laughs, then slides his feet off the desk and back on to the floor. He sits up straight in his chair, pulling on his cuffs. 'Look, *Michael* – I told them from the start. We're in this together, you and me. We come as a package. Now you know I don't want to lose you. You're the one who kicked this whole thing off. But they are getting impatient. They want to move on to the full procedure—'

'I've already told you, we're not ready for that yet.'

'The mice are staying alive, right? Hey, "Stayin' Alive" – we should go to the cinema and watch that movie when it comes out. It looks fun.'

Michael rubs his hands together, one of his little tics when he's getting agitated. 'Movie? What are you talking about, Edward?'

'The John Travolta movie – you know, with the funky dancing and the Bee Gees . . . We watched *Saturday Night Fever* on video together at that party—'

Michael shakes his head. 'The procedure. Can we go back to that?' He starts pulling his fingers, one by one, waiting for the satisfying click. 'The mice are doing well, yes. I have fourteen of them under observation, all at different stages. Percy is the eldest, as you know . . .'

'Look, Mike – the Phase I trials are a rip-roaring success. Everyone is happy with the outcome. Twelve volunteers, safely awoken from a deep coma – so far, no adverse events – no serious ones, anyway. Sure, some of them feel a bit spaced out, but that's the same even if they'd been brought out using the standard medication. Your vector *works*, Mike. Have faith.'

Michael sighs. 'I do have faith. Lots of it, as it happens. But what I can't do is rush this. You saw what happened when we rushed the first part. Those men—'

'Those men were nobodies. Nobody knew them, nobody is missing them. They served their purpose, didn't they? They gave you some valuable data.' He says the last word while making air quotes with his fingers. Michael is rocked by the horror of his friend's attitude. It's at times like this that Michael wonders how he ever thought they could be partners. He can't even understand how they became friends. Their values and beliefs are from such opposing sides of the moral compass that they don't seem to exist in the same reality. Maybe those quantum physicists really are the ones with all the answers.

'Bottom line, Michael. Our bosses want to move to the next stage ASAP. They want to bypass the usual timeframes. Move to Phase II, on a larger sample of subjects – and also test the two compounds simultaneously.'

Michael crunches his knuckles so hard he's afraid he might actually have cracked one. 'I already told you, Edward. It's one thing killing a few mice. We're not ready to start killing people.'

Edward slams his hands on the desk, making Michael jump. 'We've already started, Michael. What is it that you don't get? They've made it clear – they're not going to keep funding this if we don't push on with getting the results they want. They have plenty of potential subjects lined up . . .' He pauses, then leans back in his chair. 'There's something else, too.'

'Indeed there is, Dr Langdale,' says Anne from the open doorway. Michael has no idea how long she's been lurking there. She walks into the office, that usual dark-eyed smirk on her face. 'Dr Gordon. So glad you came over today. We have something very exciting to share with you.' She raises her hands. 'Please, gentlemen. If you'd like to follow me?'

Michael throws Edward a look, but he won't meet Michael's eye. The two men stand and follow her out of the office and down the corridor. She slows her pace, until the three of them are walking side by side.

'I think you're going to *love* this, Michael. We took on board your concerns about long-term follow-up of the Phase I subjects, and you know . . . you're absolutely right. Of course you're right.' She stops at one of the many closed doors, punches a code into a keypad on the wall. The door springs open and they follow her inside.

It's one of the many observation wards in the clinic. Set up with four beds and not a lot else. On two of them, men in pale-grey tracksuits are sitting propped up against pillows. One is reading a battered-looking copy of the *Daily Mirror*. The other is grinning to himself as his hands work rapidly on a Rubik's Cube.

On the far side of the room, the two other men are sitting on chairs, attached to monitors. Next to them, a screen shows their heart rate. A nurse stands in the middle of the two, fiddling with a blood-pressure cuff. None of them pay any attention to their visitors.

'You see, Michael – as you rightly pointed out – we need to check the vital signs at regular intervals, for as long as it takes.' She pauses, and leans closer to him, whispering in his ear. 'And who knows, yet, how long that might be?'

Michael doesn't like her being this close. He pulls away, folding his arms. 'Right. So what's the solution? I told you I don't think we can discharge anyone without arranging regular check-ups. And how are we going to make sure they turn up when we ask them to? Presumably these men want to get back to their lives.'

'Does it look like these men have lives, Michael?'

Edward has walked over to the nurse and is having a whispered conversation with her. She's nodding and smiling. And she giggles, then covers her mouth when she realises that Michael is staring. Typical Edward.

'Go on then,' he says to Anne. 'What's this exciting thing? Some kind of portable vital-signs monitor? Their own personal nurse?'

'You'll see,' she says, walking past Edward to another locked door. She keys in another code.

This room contains another four beds, and another four men. But there are no heart-rate monitors or blood-pressure cuffs in this room. At the far end of the room there are four small screens. Sitting in front of them is one of the technicians, a red-haired woman that he's seen around but never spoken to.

'Melissa?' Anne says. 'Would you like to demonstrate our new toy to the doctors?'

The woman picks up a small plastic box and turns around to face them. She's beaming. 'This is so incredible. Sorry, you've probably seen something like this before, but for me, working here – on this . . . it's like something from *Star Trek*! I still can't quite believe it.' She senses the weight of Anne's stare and stops babbling.

She holds out the plastic box in her hand and Michael bends down to look at it more closely. It's not a box. It's some sort of chip. Something with many metal sensors and minuscule probes. The whole thing is about the size of the lid of a pen. 'This,' she says, her face still split into a grin, 'is the R42VSM.' She holds it out and lets Michael take it.

He turns it back and forth in his hands, trying to work out what it does, and failing. It looks electronic. Some sort of computer component. Computers are not really his thing. 'Very nice. What is it?'

Her face falls at his lack of enthusiasm.

Edward snatches the small device from her hand. 'Christ, Michael. You really are a miserable git today, aren't you?' He shakes his head. 'Put him out of his misery, Melissa – although I'm not sure that's actually possible right now.'

'It's a prototype of a biometric tracker, Dr Gordon. We've been working with a lab in America. A government—'

'Let me guess. FBI? CIA? I'm sure they're both developing plenty of top-secret things, like we are.'

'FBI, yes.' Anne takes the device. 'I'm sure you're familiar with the concept, Dr Gordon. It's been on the cards for some time now. Small biometric devices that can be worn on the body, that are programmed to track whatever it is you're interested in. The data are stored on the microprocessing chip, which is then accessed via plugging it into a small collection tool once a week to download everything. It can then be transmitted to the central hub, via a modem plugged into your telephone line.'

'And how is it fitted?' Michael asks, looking around the room. 'I assume these men are guinea pigging this one?'

Anne nods. 'We make a small incision behind the ear. It's barely noticeable, when the hair grows to cover it. Yes, there's the minor inconvenience of them having to plug in a cable once a week, via a small, hidden port – but our American colleagues assure us that this technology is coming on in leaps and bounds. They think they might have a wireless-transmittable device by the end of the year.'

Michael nods, but says nothing. There's no doubt that it is fascinating. Exciting, even. But it feels like science fiction, just as the technician said. He's not sure he's ready for this. It's the start of a technological breakthrough, he knows it, and he knows that the governments in all the major-player countries will be working on their own versions of this. He hates to think what China and Russia might already have in their arsenals.

He looks around at his colleagues, and he feels the buzz of excitement coming off them in waves. He wants to feel like them. He wants to be part of this. But at the moment, the only thing he feels is the ice-cold fingers of fear, creeping slowly across his neck.

# Twenty-Five

## CHRISSIE (NOW)

Back at home, Chrissie dumps the shopping on to the table and shoves her phone into the charger. She tries to switch it back on, but the empty battery flashes red then the screen goes black.

'Shit.'

She leaves it charging, then fires up her laptop to check her emails. While she's waiting, she grabs the cold items from the bag and opens the fridge. There's a bottle of wine in there, invitingly chilled. But it's a bit too early for wine, even after all the stress. She slams the door closed and switches the kettle on instead. She checks her phone again, and the battery light is still red.

The laptop is waiting for her, but the only new emails are junk – offers from online stores she can't remember signing up for and has never got round to unsubscribing from. She checks the junk and the deleted folders, just in case – but there is nothing of interest. Nothing from the restaurant, responding to her messages. Nothing from Joseph Marshall. Nothing from Nathan or Wendy either, but that's not surprising. Neither of them communicates with her via email anyway. And even if they did, the pair of them are clearly still too mortified to know what to say.

It's strange, because of all things, she'd have thought this betrayal would hurt more. But she feels disconnected from it, as if it is just part of the strange turn of events that started when Joseph Marshall came to her door – and maybe even the least important part.

She takes the other things out of the shopping bags and starts to put them away. She'll take Amanda's chocolates around later when she goes to collect Holly. She picks up the other box – Maureen's box – and thinks again about Arthur. It can still be a coincidence, can't it? She blinks away tears. It has to be.

Her phone beeps, and she snatches it up. The battery light has gone green – 5 per cent and charging. It's come back on. She drums her fingers on the worktop, waiting for it to finish rebooting. Takes a mug out and drops in a teabag. The phone beeps again and the screen lights up. Then the tinkling sounds and short vibrations of missed calls and messages start firing like missiles. Her hands shake as she scrolls through. WhatsApps from Wendy and Nathan. Four voicemails. Missed calls from an unknown number. She's dialling the voicemail when there's a sharp knock at the front door.

She freezes. She's too rattled for this. Her whole body is stiff with tension. The neck pain still flares when she moves the wrong way, and now a pulsing has started behind her left eye. She sucks in a deep breath, holds it, releases it slowly. Gently clenches her hands into fists and unclenches them, then does it again. Just a couple of the tips she learned from the therapist she saw briefly after her mum died. Just enough to calm her before she sparks off a full-blown panic attack.

She flings open the front door, expecting to see Joseph Marshall standing there. The words are already forming in her mouth: *You have to stop this. Everything has gone wrong since I signed up to your stupid programme.* But it's not Joseph Marshall.

She stands staring at the man on the doorstep, her confusion turning quickly to relief.

'Andy,' she says. 'Thank God you're here.' He has barely changed a bit. Same thick, dark hair, slightly too long, curling under his ears. Same piercing blue eyes. He's dressed casually in a tight-fitting sweater and she can see the shape of his biceps. Strong arms that she wants wrapped around her right now. The tears come then, and he takes a step towards her, guiding her, yet following her into the house and closing the door. He smells so good. Familiar, even after this break. She can't believe she's left it so long. He sits her down at the table, then folds up an open magazine and tosses it across the table towards the pile that sits there permanently – barely read.

'Let me make us some tea.'

Chrissie drops her head into her hands and stares down at the table through her tears. The floodgates have opened now and she can't seem to shut them off. She listens to the sounds of Andy attempting to make cups of tea in an unfamiliar kitchen, swearing under his breath.

'You really need to organise these cupboards, you know. Most people have their mugs at eye-level near the kettle. But of course that's where your casserole dishes are. Make a lot of casseroles, do you?' There's a smile in his voice.

She grabs the wad of kitchen roll that he has pushed in front of her, and blows her nose noisily. 'Remember that kitchen in the old Holborn office?' she says, her voice ragged and wet. 'Made no sense. You had to walk the length of it back and forward three times to get yourself what you needed to make a cup of tea.' She looks at him. 'I think I might've been subconsciously channelling the "office-kitchen" experience.'

'You've been channelling something, that's for sure.' He plonks two cups on the table and sits down.

Chrissie attempts to smile. 'God, I must look a right state.'

'You look beautiful. As always.'

'Liar.'

'I prefer "charmer".'

She laughs. 'Can't argue with that.' She picks up her mug and takes a sip. It's been four years, but he still knows how to make her tea. She grips the mug tightly and stares down at the murky liquid.

'So,' he says, gently laying a hand on her arm. 'Are you going to tell me what this is about?'

A thought pops into her head. 'How did you know where I live? I moved here just before I left work . . .'

He sips his drink. 'Deborah – office-manager slash gossip – is still as discreet as ever.'

'Thank God for that.' She pauses. 'I might send her a present.' Her eyes flick towards the boxes of chocolates on the worktop.

*Shit. Holly.* 'I need to collect Holly . . .'

Her phone pings again and she jumps up to grab it from the charger. It's a message from Amanda, Lila's mum:

OK to keep Holly here for a sleepover? The two of them are busy building a den. Is there anything she doesn't eat?

Chrissie lets out a long, slow breath. One less thing to worry about. She quickly texts back:

Lifesaver! More like what does she *not* eat! Thank you for this.

She drops the phone on the table. 'OK. I've got a reprieve.'

Andy takes another sip of his drink. 'What time is Nathan back?'

Chrissie starts laughing. A fake, hollow sound. 'I don't think he'll be back today. Although, I don't actually know where he is—'

'I think you better start at the beginning.' Andy pushes his mug away and goes over to the fridge. 'I think we should crack open this wine, don't you?'

'I don't even know where to start.' She picks up her phone again and scrolls through the messages. Several can we talk?s from both Nathan and Wendy. She imagines them sitting there together in the hospital ward, faces etched with concern: *Maybe you should ring her? No, maybe you should?*

Bastards.

Where is she going to start? The whole thing is ridiculous. She waits for Andy to come back with the glasses and the bottle. Watching him busying himself in her kitchen. He looks quite at home. *Stop it, Chrissie.* This is not the time. Part of the reason she's so angry, rather than upset with Nathan and Wendy, is because she's angry at herself. She's a hypocrite, she knows. But she stopped it before anything really happened. Before she'd blown up anyone's life.

He sits down, and gives her one of his smiles. One of his smiles that could've led to a lot more, if she'd let it. 'Well?'

'So, this weird thing happened . . .' She starts with Joseph Marshall turning up on her doorstep, leads into the car crash, the pager, seeing her neighbour being taken away. Finishes with the affair, and the fact that Holly clearly knew all about it, but only being three, going on four, had no idea what it all meant.

Andy blows out a breath. 'I mean, that last part is bad enough. But the rest of it . . . I'd like to say that all this save-your-loved-ones thing is bullshit, but it's some bloody coincidence about your neighbour.' He shakes his head. 'Jesus.' He takes a large gulp of wine, then he pulls her work folder across the table towards him. 'I'm amazed you're managing to work while all this is going on.'

She shakes her head, then takes a sip of wine. 'I'm not. I must've left that on the table on Friday. I'm not even doing that project anymore. Total waste of time.' She watches as he flicks it open and has a look at her drawings. 'I was going to call you about this, actually. Thought you might be able to help.'

He looks up. 'Four years, Chrissie. I've bloody missed you, you know?'

'I know.'

He looks back down at the folder. 'This stuff looks like it might need a full rethink, but I have a feeling there are more pressing issues at hand.' He pulls her laptop closer. 'So, first things first . . . I assume you've googled this Joseph character?'

'I had a quick look.'

Andy sighs. 'Chrissie—'

'I was going back to it! As I just explained to you, everything has gone a bit mental in the last few days . . .' She lets the sentence trail off. She feels like an idiot. Maybe if she'd done more digging at the beginning, none of this would've happened. But then Holly's fall had made her rethink things. It was almost as if the fall was *meant* to happen. But that was ridiculous. There's no way Joseph Marshall could have predicted that. Unless . . . no. Now *she* is being ridiculous. There's no way that Joseph Marshall had anything to do with Holly's fall, and as for the car crash – that was her own stupid fault, and it's bloody lucky she wasn't breathalysed.

Andy is rapping away at the keys and she has another brief flashback to the office, and him being told off by Deborah for being too loud at his keyboard.

'Basic searching is bringing up nothing.'

She watches over his shoulder as he opens up another search window and types in 'Joseph Marshall researcher government UK' then clicks on the first link that comes up. It's the government site that Joseph told her to look at, but there's a '404 page not found' error. Andy refreshes the page and it reverts to the homepage, then he starts typing in the search bar on the site. 'Joseph Marshall.'

The screen freezes.

Andy frowns. 'Did you look at this site before?' He refreshes it again.

'Yes . . . Well, no. I meant to.' She frowns. 'He told me to contact them to verify he was who he says he was.'

'And did you? Verify him, I mean?'

She shakes her head. 'He told me it would take me round in circles. That I would never get through on the phone either. You know what these websites are like.'

The website refreshes and a circle with a diagonal line appears in the middle of the screen. A message flashes up: *Unauthorised Access Denied.* Then the window shuts down.

'What the hell?' He types the web address into another window, but it just hangs. 'Have you got a pen?'

She thinks he sounds cross, but then remembers what he was like when he was researching at work. He goes into an intense concentration phase and all he can manage are barked commands. She used to take the piss out of him whenever they stopped for a tea break or lunch. He couldn't seem to work any other way.

She slides a notepad and a pen across the table towards him. It's not her pen. It's dark blue with a silver logo on it, and she can't recall seeing it before. But as Andy picks it up and starts scribbling on the notepad, it comes back to her.

'That pen . . .' She leans over and snatches it from Andy's hand. Turns it over in her fingers, inspecting the logo. 'This is *his* pen.'

Andy takes it back from her and peers at it. 'I don't recognise the logo – but that doesn't mean anything. It could've come from anywhere.'

'It was on his folder too. I'd forgotten – but I remember now. He sat there where you are. He took out his folder and his pen and he laid them out so neatly. Before he picked the pen up and wrote notes. I don't know what he was writing—'

Andy lays the pen on the table, then takes his phone out of his pocket and snaps a picture of it. He scrolls through, swiping and clicking, and after a moment, a box pops up on Chrissie's laptop asking if she wants to accept the file from his phone. He clicks on it, and the image pops up on the screen. Then he goes to a new browser window and opens up Reverse Image Search. He uploads the photo, then sits back.

Chrissie stands behind him, one hand on the back of his chair. Over by the kettle, her phone beeps and vibrates. She ignores it.

The image throws up a match.

'MG Holdings,' Andy says. He opens up yet another browser window. 'Does that name mean anything to you?'

She shakes her head, just as the website for MG Holdings appears on screen. Unless she's mistaken, she knows exactly where the building pictured on it is. She takes a deep breath. Wendy was right. There *is* something dodgy about her design client. She sighs. 'Is the address on there?'

Andy is already scrolling down the page. There's little information, other than the photograph of the building. The frontage is a bit different now, and the sign says something else entirely – but she can tell from the buildings on either side, plus the ornate carvings at the top. She'd always thought it was such a waste of something that was once so beautiful.

She sees the address the same time as he does, but it means nothing to him.

'That's the restaurant I've been working on the graphics for,' she says. 'The place that keeps changing its name. I went up there. It's all shut down.'

'Right then,' Andy says. 'I have no idea what is going on here – but it's time we found out.'

# Twenty-Six

## Joseph (Now)

Joseph sits down at his dining-room table. He has the curtains drawn, although it's not yet dark. He doesn't like to look outside. He prefers the soft glow from the standard lamp in the corner of the room, the soft green fabric giving the light a calming, muted tone. The lamp, along with the rest of his furniture and decor, is like something he remembers from his childhood home. His mother's taste. He can't remember choosing any of these things himself. Only vaguely remembers moving to this house. They chose it for him, moved everything in. Made sure that he wouldn't be bothered by neighbours, after the last house he'd been allocated in one of those nosy community areas where everyone wants to know everyone's business. He's not sure why they fitted it out to look like his mother's house instead of his own room in Darwin College that he'd quite happily lived in for several years. But there are lots of things that Joseph doesn't quite remember about the time after he was in hospital. He's grateful to have a job, and a home, and some semblance of a life. Not that it's been particularly joyful, and it certainly hasn't been easy.

He scratches absentmindedly at the raised welts on his left forearm. Then stops, when he feels the soft liquid feel of blood. He peers down at his arm in the muted light. It's getting worse now. Much worse. He noticed another patch of it on the back of his right calf, when he was taking his evening bath last night. When he'd first noticed the rash on his arm, he'd assumed it was some sort of eczema. Tried some of the thick emollient cream that the pharmacist from the clinic recommended. The doctor he'd been assigned at the clinic – Dr La Tour – told him it was nothing to concern himself about, so he's mostly kept it out of his thoughts.

Except that he knows it's getting worse.

He also knows that it is not eczema.

There are other symptoms, of course. The headaches. The visions. The times when he can't seem to wake up, and yet he feels like he is looking down on himself. But he tries not to think about those either.

He opens his lab notebook wide and spreads it flat. To the right, he has positioned his teacup – in a saucer, of course – and next to that, his teapot, with the knitted cosy on top, keeping it warm.

He picks up his pen.

Three columns, again. Dr Ris Anderson – Mrs Christina Tate – Miss Tina Millar.

Unfortunately, Miss Millar, the teacher, has not agreed to participate. Yet. He will have to deal with that soon.

On the sideboard to his left, the old Bakelite phone sits waiting patiently. The one piece of modern technology in his house sits next to it. An answering machine. His superiors insisted on it, as he'd eschewed their suggestions of both a mobile phone and a pager. He does not want this type of intrusion in his life. He struggles to contain his own thoughts. He doesn't need others pushing theirs on to him, making incessant demands. So they modified the old phone to connect to the answering machine, and he knows there's a message on there. The green light is blinking. He doesn't like the light flashing like that, finds it distracting. But he doesn't want to listen to the message. Not until he has made his notes. Besides – he already knows what the message says. He heard the caller leave it, while he was eating his lunch.

Christina Tate.

He taps his fingers on the table. The thought of her makes him scratch his arm again. He thought he'd spotted a small patch of a similar rash on her inner forearm as she passed him his tea. He'd wanted to ask her about it. But he'd been worried that it had been nothing, a different sort of rash. Nothing to link him to her after all. Besides, confirmation that she is the correct Christina won't stop him from having to recruit the others. He still requires three. That's how it works. He was told this right at the start of his career. Wasn't he? He's doubting himself more frequently now, but he has to push through. Press on. He glances at his wrist monitor. Too high! *Calm down*, he tells himself. He takes a deep breath, counts to three before letting it out. He's no intention of cutting corners now. He must stick to the plan.

*Select subjects.*

*Initiate the programme.*

*Observe.*

*Summarise results.*

It's no surprise that Ris-the-scientist was interested. She called him immediately after the conference. Quizzed him at length about the programme, and about the purpose of it. About why she'd been chosen. She asked to meet with his superiors, and he had to fob her off. It's good that she's interested. He suspects they would like to offer her a job. Except they won't, because they don't know the full details of his little plan. So far only Christina Tate has been recruited, and he logged her in the usual way. They don't appear to have noticed his search for the other Christinas, or if they do, they haven't said anything. But just like last time he went off-piste with

165

his research, it will come back to him eventually. He'd had a visit, that time. A warning. 'You're welcome to recruit subjects, Joseph,' they'd told him, 'but please leave the rest of it to us.' Busybodies. Some of them are young enough to be his children! Don't they know who he is? Don't they know how important he is in the programme? Because he is important. Isn't he? He checks his wrist monitor again. The reading is too high. Too many thoughts spinning. Once it slows, it will drop by at least one beat-per-minute. This is what he's observed so far. His resting HR is dropping, little by little. Eventually it will drop too far and he'll cease to function. Unless he can find a way to reverse it.

Dr Ris Anderson refused to tell him anything detailed about her background – insisting that if he was working for the government, he must already know all he needed to know. So he had to bluff, and accept that. When in fact, he didn't know nearly enough. Yes, he knew that she was one of the three Christinas born in that Cambridge hospital that day. But after that initial search, he'd mostly drawn a blank. He suspected that his superiors had put a block on the records. Removed all the links that he would require to identify the Christina that he needed. He often had a message on his answering machine, telling him he'd been flagged for attempting to access classified information. But they didn't stop him trying. They are always watching him. He's come to accept that.

He knows that he is a research subject himself.

He sighs. He can't put it off any longer.

He needs all three subjects recruited, or this just isn't going to work. He needs to be able to study all three of their reactions, and then he'll know. He has to be sure. The car crash had worked out well. It was a stroke of luck that Christina and her friend had been drinking. That Chrissie was distracted – just enough for the space between the concrete planters to become an issue. He'd waited at the end of the road for them to return from their night out – keeping track of them all the way via the small listening device he'd planted in Chrissie's car. Old cars often had dodgy locks. Easy to pick. Her Mini was no exception. The seat-belt clip was already loose. It didn't take much to loosen it further. He'd needed some help to move the planter – he knew he didn't have the strength. But he'd already been observing the gang of youths who scoured the streets at night, looking to cause mischief. They'd already tipped one over a few days before, making a proper mess of the road. He hadn't needed to pay them much to do it again. They'd looked at him like he was mad, but hadn't hesitated to take the money and only too gladly performed their task. He'd waited until Chrissie's car appeared at the bend, then he'd thrown the yellow football across the road. He'd chosen one with foil reflective sections, to make sure it would catch in the headlights as it rolled across the road. The car had swerved, as he'd hoped, and crashed into the planter. It was a gamble, making sure that only the passenger was hurt, but it was one he was willing to take.

He won't need a car crash for Tina Millar. She has a young nephew. Something similar to Holly Tate's fall should do the trick. Thinking of whom – it's time to move to Phase II there. To make sure Christina Tate is fully on board. Holly is such a beautiful, trusting little girl. He's been enjoying his chats with her at the nursery-school gates during playtimes.

He presses the button on his answering machine and listens to her message again. He will deal with it. Keep her in the programme. He returns to the table, pours tea into his cup. It's still hot. That tea cosy is really quite effective. He adds milk, and stirs. Yes, he will call her back. But not just yet.

# Twenty-Seven

## CHRISSIE (NOW)

'Come on, let's go. We can take my car.'

Chrissie blows out a breath. 'Maybe I should try calling Joseph Marshall again. He might not have got my last message—'

'What are you scared of?' Andy says. 'You want to sort this out, don't you? You've just said yourself that this is all mixed up with the work you've been doing. It's some kind of scam, obviously.' He stands up and takes his car keys out of his pocket. 'I just haven't worked out what they're actually trying to achieve yet.'

'But the accident . . . and Arthur—'

'Coincidence, that's all. There's no other explanation.'

Chrissie takes the mugs and pours the dregs down the sink. Then she turns back to face him. 'And the private ambulance? And that strange clinic? How do you explain all that?'

'You banged your head, right? They probably gave you some heavy-duty painkillers when you were admitted. You said yourself you were out of it the next day.'

'No!' She shakes her head, stopping when it triggers another spasm of pain in her neck. She feels the fizz of her blood pressure rising. A swirl of light-headedness. 'I've told you what happened.'

'Does Wendy remember anything about being transferred from another clinic? You visited her in the hospital, right? Surely she—'

'I didn't get much of a chance to talk to Wendy, remember? I kind of had the issue of her screwing my husband to deal with.'

Andy opens his mouth to speak, then clearly thinks better of it. He turns and heads towards the front door.

'I know what you're thinking,' she says to his retreating back. 'I'm a hypocrite.'

He opens the front door and looks over his shoulder at her. Says quietly, 'I wasn't thinking that. We stopped that before it had barely even started. It was once. That one night. It's past.' He pauses. 'What Nathan and Wendy have done to you is a huge betrayal. Obviously only you can decide what to do next – but let's at least get rid of all this *choose your substitutes* nonsense so you can focus on your family?'

She's putting her phone in her bag when it rings. Andy has already disappeared outside. 'Hang on,' she calls after him. She checks the caller ID, hoping it's Joseph – surprised when it's Amanda. The swirling in her head speeds up. *Holly.* Maybe she just wants to say hi. She always wants to talk when she's on a sleepover.

'Hi,' she says. 'Is everything all right?'

Amanda's voice is too high-pitched, too fast. The words are coming out in the wrong order. Sharp spikes of fear prickle down Chrissie's back. Amanda is the calm one. Amanda doesn't get flustered.

'Amanda, slow down. I can't understand what you're saying.' Chrissie staggers to the door, grips the frame. Andy is leaning against his car. He gives her a 'what's happening?' look. She shakes her head gently and he starts back towards her. The prickles of fear have grown tendrils. Her whole body is buzzing with adrenalin, and yet she feels numb.

The next instant, Andy is there beside her. She taps the phone on to loudspeaker so he can hear.

'It's Holly,' Amanda is saying, her voice tinny and shaken through the speaker. 'They were playing in the garden.' She pauses. A breathy whimper escapes her. 'She choked . . . I did all the right things, I swear . . . The ambulance is coming . . .'

The numbness abates, and the blood rushes through her once more. She doesn't need to hear any more, she needs to get there. Right now. She tosses the phone back into her bag, and pulls out the pager.

'Wait!' Andy grabs her wrist. 'Let's get round there first. Where is it?'

Chrissie pulls away, squeezes her hand around the pager, keeping it safe. 'You're right,' she says, calm now. Robotic. She recognises the feeling of shock. 'It won't work unless I'm with her. I need to be in *close proximity*.'

'No,' Andy says. 'Not just that. Think about what you're doing. You can't just press that . . .'

She marches down the driveway. 'You don't believe it works anyway. What harm can it do?'

She turns right at the end of the drive and breaks into a jog.

'Chrissie, come on. I'll drive us.'

She hears his footsteps as he starts running to catch up with her.

'It's only round the corner.' The sound of an ambulance siren floats towards them. She picks up the pace, still gripping the pager.

'Chrissie . . .' He's level with her now.

'What would you do if it was *your* child in danger?'

'I'd . . . I don't know. I haven't got a child.'

She turns to him as they run around the bend, just as the ambulance appears from the other direction, heading to Amanda's. She doesn't say anything more, but she tries to say it with her expression. She's too scared to voice it, in case it's true . . . in case it's not true. It'd been just the once for them, yes. But that's all it takes.

She watches his expression change as the possibility that Holly might be his finally clicks into place. She'd thought he might have considered this before, when she'd left work so suddenly, but if he has, he's chosen not to realise it until now.

He grabs her arm, making her stop. 'Oh my God, Chrissie . . .'

She says nothing, just stands there breathing heavily behind the ambulance, watching as two paramedics jump out, one of them carrying an equipment bag.

She presses the pager once to engage. Twice to confirm.

The paramedic without the bag reaches into his pocket, looks at something in his hand. Then he disappears back inside the ambulance and brings out another, smaller, bag. He fixes his eyes on Chrissie as he walks towards the house, where Amanda is standing outside, wringing her hands.

'Are you her mother?' he says.

Chrissie nods.

'She's inside,' Amanda says. 'I've laid her in the recovery position, made sure she was comfortable. I did a First Aid course—'

'Is she breathing?'

Amanda bursts into tears.

The paramedic with the first, larger bag runs into the house. The other one gives Chrissie the smallest of nods. Her stomach lurches. *He's one of them*, Chrissie realises. *This is real!*

# Twenty-Eight

## CHRISSIE (NOW)

Chrissie holds Holly's hand in the ambulance. It is small and warm and Chrissie feels an ache as she looks down at her. Andy sits on one of the seats at the back, on the other side of the door from the female paramedic, who hasn't bothered to introduce herself but whose name badge says she's called Lisa. Lisa hadn't been at all keen for Andy to come with them, but the other one, who's told her his name is Danny, had somehow made it happen – just as he clearly made something happen back at Amanda's house. Holly is sedated, but she's fine. That's what Danny told her. Chrissie had rushed into the house behind them, but he'd held her back.

'We'll take care of this,' Danny had said.

Andy had held on to Chrissie, then. Now he's just staring at her. In shock. But something else too. At some point, they will have to talk about *everything*. But not right now.

'Are you sure she's OK?' Chrissie says. 'She looks like she's sleeping, but—'

'She *is* sleeping. We brought her back. Don't worry.' Lisa looks away.

Chrissie feels like there is something she's not telling her, but Chrissie didn't see what happened. She didn't see what they did to bring her back. Was she actually gone? She's going to quiz the doctor when she gets to the clinic. Find out exactly what went on.

The ambulance stops, and a moment later, Danny opens the back door and activates the ramp. Lisa makes her way down from the seat at the back and jumps out. Chrissie sees her beckon Danny with a nod of her head. They have a heated, whispered conversation, continuing the one they'd started in the house. Lisa clearly isn't happy about something. Chrissie had caught only a burst from her in the house: 'What the hell are you *doing*?' Now she picks up another as Lisa hisses in Danny's ear: 'You said you were *out*.' Danny scowls, turns his back to her.

So Lisa's not part of it. And yet she has allowed Danny to drive the ambulance here.

Andy has stepped outside. 'Where are we?' he asks Lisa. 'I thought we were going to the hospital.'

Chrissie recognises the building. She thought it had vanished from her memory. Had started to think maybe it was all drug-induced hallucinations. But she recognises the clean, white facade, the potted bay trees at either side of the tall glass doors.

Lisa walks away towards the entrance. 'Don't even ask,' she tells Andy. 'Best out of it.'

He turns back to Chrissie, a questioning look on his face.

'Yes. This is where I was,' she says. 'I told you I wasn't making it up.'

Danny climbs back into the ambulance and unclips the restraints that hold Holly's trolley-bed in place. He peers down at her. Then gently lifts her eyelids, one by one, and shines a torch. He checks her pulse.

'All good. Let's get her inside and they can bring her round and check her over.'

'Did you . . . Did you give her something back at the house?' Chrissie's throat feels dry. 'Was she—'

He glances at Andy. Frowns. 'Don't worry about any of that. I did what was required.' He looks away from her again. Doesn't want to meet her eye.

Chrissie feels uneasy, like maybe something is not quite right with the process, that Danny and Lisa are not fully aligned – their bickering had raised some alarm bells. But she senses that there's no point in asking anything more. The only thing that matters now is that Holly is OK.

◆ ◆ ◆

Inside the clinic, Holly is whisked away and Chrissie and Andy are directed to a quiet room containing soft white sofas and potted rubber plants. There's a high-tech coffee machine in the corner. Chrissie starts to make them drinks.

'How the hell are you so calm right now?' Andy sits on one of the sofas, but his body is hunched forward. He looks tense.

Chrissie lets out a long, slow breath. 'She's fine. They've saved her.' She takes the pager out of her bag and holds it in her palm. 'I saved her.'

Andy shakes his head. 'None of this makes any sense. What did the pager have to do with anything? The ambulance was already there.'

'Yes. But when I pressed the pager, everything changed. Didn't you see? The paramedic, Danny – he had a pager too, and then he took a different bag into the house—'

'But how do you know he wasn't always taking that bag inside? He just forgot to pick it up . . .'

'And he nodded at me before he went in. Did you not see that either? He—'

'He was acknowledging you – after checking you were the mother – letting you know it was under control.'

Chrissie shoves a mug into the coffee machine and shakes her head. 'Then we got brought here – not to the hospital. Lisa wasn't happy about it. About any of it. The two of them had words. She asked him what he was doing. He broke protocol, I guess. Perhaps she's not part of it, but she knows about it. Whatever *it* all is.'

'Then why did she let him drive us here?'

'Danny clearly said something to make her comply. My guess is she's had to do this before. She knows this place. She does what she's told, but she doesn't like it. Whereas Danny – he knows. He's a part of it.'

'Part of what, Chrissie? Do you know how insane you sound right now?'

The door opens and a smiling male nurse comes in. Chrissie recognises him straight away. 'Mrs Tate?' he says. 'How lovely to see you again. Holly is in recovery now, if you'd like to come and see her.' The nurse glances at Andy and grins. 'And this will be Mr Tate? Delighted to meet you.'

Andy shakes his head. 'I'm just a friend.'

The nurse shoots Chrissie a look, and just the hint of a raised eyebrow, as though he's heard this line plenty of times before. 'Grand,' he says. 'Let's go and see how this little one is doing then. She's just coming out of sedation so she'll be a bit groggy, so don't mind much what she says.'

'She talks nonsense at the best of times.' Chrissie takes the mug out of the coffee machine and leaves it on the side.

'Wee lamb, she is.' The nurse holds the door open. 'Follow me.'

Holly is in a room just like the one she saw Wendy in. Chrissie blinks. The memories of this place are coming back thick and fast. She was in a room like this too. Screaming and scrabbling under the bed. Half-crazed with fear. She takes a breath and tries to push the memories away. This is not about then. This is about now.

Holly tries to sit up when she sees them.

175

'Mummy! Guess what happened to me? I was eating lots of gummy sweets in Lila's garden and they were really big! And I put two in my mouth and then three and then they wouldn't go into my tummy and I fell over and Lila's mummy was screaming and then—'

'Shh, Holly-berry – it's OK now. You can just have a little rest here, and then we can go home.' Chrissie leans over the bed and touches Holly's cheek.

Holly throws her arms around her neck and squeezes. 'I'm OK, Mummy. The nurses said I had an accident and then I told them I had another accident when I fell out of the treehouse and they laughed but I think they want to talk to you, Mummy.' She pauses then, whispers, 'I didn't tell them about the man.' She lets go and falls back against the pillows. 'Who's *this* man in here with us? Is he another doctor?'

Chrissie gestures at Andy and he walks closer to the bed. He gives Holly a big grin. 'I'm Mummy's friend, Andy. We used to work together – a long, long time ago, before you were even born.'

Chrissie wants to ask her more about the man and the gummy sweets, but suddenly she can't get a word in.

Holly looks from Andy to Chrissie, her face scrunched in confusion. 'Did you really do other things before I was even born? Were you not just waiting for me to be born so you could feed me and play with me and give me a bath and put me to bed all the time?'

Chrissie laughs. 'Yes, I was doing all of that, sweetpea – but I had to go to work too – in an office – because I was sad and lonely while I was waiting for you and I didn't know what to do with myself all day.'

Holly frowns. 'Did Daddy not want to play with you?' She sighs. 'Maybe he was playing with Auntie Wendy.'

Chrissie leans in and hugs her daughter again. She doesn't want to think about how she's going to explain Nathan and Wendy to her. She's ignored them both for as long as she can, but she's going to have to talk to Wendy at some point. Maybe if they transfer Holly to the hospital . . . Chrissie is stroking Holly's neck when she sees the fresh scar, just behind her ear. Only an inch long, with three neat little stitches. Something flutters in her stomach. She steps back, zoning out, as Holly starts chattering away to Andy. She puts a hand to her own ear, runs a finger underneath, feeling the tiny ridge of scar tissue there. Something that's always been there – as far as she's aware. It had been Nathan who'd pointed it out. Her memory takes her back to that first night together, when he'd been so soft and tender, running his fingers across every inch of her. *How did you get this, babe?* She had no idea.

'Did you have to operate?' she says to the nurse, snapping back to the present. He's been sitting quietly at Holly's bedside. 'I thought—'

'It might be best if you talk to Dr La Tour,' he says. He walks over to the door and presses an intercom button. 'Mrs Tate to see you, Dr La Tour.'

He arrives within moments, before Chrissie has a chance to think about anything else.

He places a hand on her elbow, leads her away from Holly's bed to the far side of the room. 'As you may remember, Mrs Tate – from when you were here with your friend Wendy . . .'

Chrissie winces.

Dr La Tour gestures for her to take a seat. 'There's a drug that we need to administer after the pager has been activated. It's completely safe, of course. But it's what gives us the edge, here. Scientifically speaking, on the programme that you're part of—'

'Right. And you had to give Holly this drug? When she stopped breathing?'

He shifts in his seat. 'The thing is, there's another component to it, Mrs Tate. We need to monitor the saved patients long term. To make sure there are no further issues.'

'Wait, what? What kind of issues?'

'As you know, this programme is confidential. And it's still in the testing phase – although, we've been running it for many years now—'

'Testing? You mean this isn't a licensed drug?' She swivels around, looking for help. Reassurance. But both Andy and the nurse are fully engaged with Holly, who is keeping them entertained with her chatter.

'Please don't worry about this, Mrs Tate. It's all above board. I just wanted to explain to you about the chip—'

'Chip? What are you talking about?' She blows out a breath. 'Can someone get me some water, please? It's so hot in here . . .'

Her favourite male nurse, who's been doing a good job of pretending not to listen to what Dr La Tour has been telling her, gets up from his seat and disappears out of the door.

'Sorry. Perhaps *chip* wasn't the right word to use, but I thought it would make it easier to understand. It's a microchip. About the size of those miniature SIM cards that you stick in your phone. It's a tiny biometric tracker. We use it to monitor vital signs remotely. It's only a tiny incision behind her ear, and it'll barely scar. Believe me, this kind of technology is widespread. It's being used for all manner of things now – and medical is one of the most useful, I think . . .'

The nurse returns with the water and Chrissie practically grabs it out of his hand. She gulps it down, then blows out another breath, trying to calm herself.

'You've microchipped my daughter? Without my permission? She's not a dog!'

'I'm afraid you gave your consent to all of this, when you agreed to join the programme.'

'Well, I want out of the programme. And I want Holly out of this clinic. I've no idea what's going on, but I intend to find out.' She stands up too quickly and her head swims. She's been getting flashes of dizziness since the accident. She lets Dr La Tour take her by the elbow and guide her back to her seat.

'A lot has happened in the last few days, Mrs Tate. I get that you're concerned. But I can assure you, by joining this programme, you've absolutely done the right thing. Our ambulance got to your friend's house just in time. I hate to think what would have happened if you hadn't pressed the pager.' He stands up, then lays a hand on her shoulder. 'We're moving Holly to Northlands. Your local hospital. Where everything will be just as you'd expect it to be. Try not to worry.'

She shrugs him off. She doesn't want his hand on her. She doesn't trust him.

She doesn't trust any of them.

# Twenty-Nine

## Michael (July 1984)

Michael has stopped trying to argue with Edward and their superiors. Instead, he's spent the last few months working tirelessly to try to ensure that the compounds work as expected. Percy is now twenty-three months old, and there are fifty-nine other mice in the lab, all at various stages. All with varying temperaments – which is something that Michael is a little concerned by, but whenever he mentions it to Edward, it falls on deaf ears. On the plus side, they've only lost six over the whole of the last year, and upon performing autopsies on them, they were all found to have other conditions that would have prevented them from living longer than the standard two months in the lab. All of the mice they lost came from the same batch. That supplier is no longer being used.

As requested by Dr Cater, they have been breeding their own mice. Melissa the technician had volunteered to oversee their care, as well as working on the biometric trackers, a new version of which turned up a few months ago, as promised. These trackers are even smaller than the first ones, and have an inbuilt wireless transmitter. His daily work is becoming somewhat futuristic. If it wasn't for Sandy and Christina at home keeping him grounded, with their fun little games and their dancing and singing along to the radio – the current favourite is 'Lucky Star' by Madonna – he would be entirely convinced that he was living in a parallel universe.

He's been asked to give a presentation to the top brass. He was instructed to ensure it was given in layman's terms, as most of them are not scientists. He's put together a set of slides, and as he waits nervously in the boardroom, he resolves to channel Edward's drive, optimism and, most importantly, perfectly spun bullshit. The attendees file into the room and sit down. He doesn't recognise most of them; certainly none of them in uniform. But he nods and smiles and pretends that he's not intimidated in the slightest.

Eventually, just as he's about to start, Edward walks in with Dr Cater and gives him a thumbs up from the back of the room.

'Good afternoon,' he starts, scanning the room. All eyes are on him. He clears his throat. 'My name is Dr Michael Gordon, and I was the researcher to pioneer the KS4582A viral vector in the biological research lab I shared with Dr Edward Langdale, who you'll find watching shyly from the back. He doesn't like to make a fuss.' A smattering of laughter, and another thumbs up from Edward.

Michael finds his stride. He lays out the details of the viral vector as best he can, using his analogy of microscopic taxi drivers that Anne Cater had been so pleased with. Then he moves on to the other compound – the one that worries him more. The T7843Y, or as they've been calling it in the lab – the kill spray.

The mouse experiments have helped him to hone the process and ensure that the correct quantities are used for humans. Administer the spray directly to the eyes. The exact time will vary according to body weight, but within minutes, the subject will suffer a cardiac arrest. Within thirty minutes, the subject must be injected with the KS4582A – aka Cellregenix.

Then, before they are fully awake – insert the biometric tracker, to allow remote monitoring of vital signs.

This part hasn't been done on the mice, as they are being observed closely in the lab. But for the human subjects, this will be a necessary step.

He looks down at the table in front of him, where he has placed the demonstration items. A vial of the kill spray, with the nozzle attached. A syringe filled with Cellregenix. One of the new trackers. Then he turns back around and slots the final slide into the projector. On the screen, it says 'Any questions?'

Several hands shoot up.

Anne stands up slowly, smoothing her skirt, then walks briskly to the front of the room. 'Thank you, Dr Gordon. That was most informative.' She addresses the room. 'We will not be taking questions at this time.'

A murmur of voices, chairs scraping on the floor. 'All very fascinating,' he hears one of the uniformed men mutter as they make their way out of the room. 'But what is it for?'

Michael waits at the front of the room. His earlier feeling of ease has left him, and he feels a prickling of dangerous energy in the room. It's now only him, Edward and Anne, plus Simon Knox, David Armstrong and Helen Tracey – the group of 'investors' that he'd originally been introduced to, back when Edward secured the so-called funding for what started out as a potential cellular age-reversal compound that Michael had been sure would be a Nobel-prizewinning medical breakthrough. The possibilities had been endless – for treatment of all kinds of disease.

But that's not what it's being developed for now.

'It's not time to reveal all, I'm afraid, Michael,' Anne says. 'Not to the wider team.' She gestures for him to sit. 'As you know, the aim of the development of Cellregenix is for us to protect our people. Our key people. Presidents, top officials, royalty. Our armed forces and security leaders. And of course, their families. We are living in difficult times. We are not immune to the threats presented from our Cold War cousins. Our Irish friends. And many more, that I'm sure I don't have to tell you that even I do not possess the clearance to divulge.'

'I understand that,' Michael says. He flicks a glance at Edward, who raises his eyebrows, but says nothing. Edward doesn't care about the implications here. He just wants to make money, and to be involved in something excitingly secret. 'You want to be able to . . . reverse the effects of any terrorist activities.'

Anne nods. 'At the very least.'

'But the T7843Y?'

'The kill spray? Yes, I can see why you're concerned about that. But I won't assume you're so naive that you have no idea what is done with potential enemies of the state.'

Michael shifts in his chair. 'I also understand that. And I understand that we can't trial the' – he pauses; he hates speaking the term aloud – 'the *kill* spray, without having a solution for reversing the effects – assuming it works.'

'Well, then,' Edward cuts in. 'What's the problem?'

'The problem is that you're taking serious risks here. With human subjects. What if the effects can't be reversed? What if Cellregenix can't kick-start the heart cells into life when they've been completely shut down? In the healthy-volunteer trials – if we can even call them that, because I'm still not entirely sure that those men knew what they were consenting to – in those trials, we didn't actually kill the subjects, they were in a deep, medically induced coma, and we could've brought them back with the standard drug for that. Methylphenidate is perfectly safe—'

'And did you have to use that drug?' Anne crosses her arms.

'Well, no. You know we didn't. Cellregenix worked perfectly every time. And so far, none of the subjects have experienced any long-term adverse events.' He feels heat rising in his cheeks.

Anne uncrosses her arms and leans over to lay a hand on one of his. 'Right. So we know it works. We have to take this next step, Michael. You know we do. Or else how are we ever going to be able to use your incredible compound?'

'I just think . . .' Michael pauses. He can't believe what he's going to say next, and yet, he's going to say it. In the corner of the room, the phone rings. He ignores it. 'I just think, that before we move into a full-blown trial, we need to test the process out on at least one individual. Ideally three, so that we have enough data to get true results. Averages and variance. One really isn't enough, but . . . if there was some way to test on one of the—'

'You mean the expendables?' Anne says. The phone rings again. 'We . . .' She pauses, clears her throat. 'We have not been authorised for any more activity of that sort.'

Michael's unaccustomed to seeing Anne look uncomfortable. He absorbs her discomfort. 'Well, I—'

'Oh for goodness' sake!' Edward stands up and stomps to the front of the room. 'I'll do it. I trust you, Michael. What's the bloody worst that could happen, eh?'

'What? Edward, no—'

But it's too late. Edward has picked up the spray and directed it at his own face. Before anyone can do anything to stop him, he sprays it fast, and firm. Two pumps into each eye.

Michael leaps out of his seat and rushes towards his friend. 'Quickly, please. You need to wash this out. This is not even the correct concentration. It has to be calculated according to body weight . . . Oh Jesus Christ, Edward – what the hell have you done?'

The rest of the room stares in horror as Edward staggers, his legs buckling beneath him. He tries to grab on to the table, but his hand slips and he falls to the floor before Michael can reach him. He lands with a hard thud on his back, and the breath is knocked out of him. Michael throws himself on the floor beside him, puts

184

his fingers to his neck. Then his head to his chest. He looks up at the others. 'No pulse. He's gone. I—'

Before he can say another word, Anne is on the floor beside him. With a small grunt, she jabs the syringe of Cellregenix straight into Edward's heart.

'No . . .' Michael tries to grab it away from her, but he's too slow.

She depresses the plunger.

'You don't understand,' he says, his voice breaking. 'It's not like adrenalin. It has a different mechanism of action – it can't be allowed to circulate too fast. It needs to go in a vein. The median cubital. It—'

Edward's chest heaves. But his eyes remain closed. Michael lets out a long, slow breath. Then he puts his fingers on Edward's neck. 'There's a pulse. It's faint. But it's there. We need to get him to the critical-care team.'

'Well, then,' Anne says. Not even a hint of a waver in her voice, despite what they have all just witnessed. Despite what she has just done. She claps her hands together quickly. 'Let's sort that out then, shall we?'

The phone rings again. No one answers it.

# Thirty

## CHRISSIE (NOW)

They sedate Holly again for the ambulance journey. Dr La Tour says it is standard procedure, and Chrissie no longer wants to argue with him. This is what they did with Wendy – and with herself, too, as she has no memory of being in the ambulance and being taken home. The first thing she remembers is being on her driveway, in the dark. And then Nathan. Nathan being more concerned about Wendy than about her.

How did she not see it?

Andy is quiet on the trip, the two of them sitting side by side. It's been a pretty overwhelming day, and he must be as spent as she is right now.

'Thank you.' She squeezes his hand. 'You've been amazing.'

He frowns. 'You really need to call Nathan.'

'I know. I will, as soon as she's settled in at the hospital. I couldn't call him to the clinic. For one, I don't know where it is, and two – how the hell would I explain it all to him? The priority right now is Holly.'

'OK.'

The ambulance stops and the doors open wide. Bright sunlight streams in, and they have to shield their eyes from the glare, taking time to adjust from the muted light inside the ambulance. She blinks. Rolls her shoulders, trying to release the tension she's holding there.

Danny the paramedic jumps inside and goes to Holly. He's carrying his small bag again. The one that is clearly not a standard-issue paramedic bag. Chrissie hears the zip being pulled open, but she can't see what he's doing. He leans over Holly and does something – and after a moment, Holly coughs.

He steps back, re-zipping the bag. 'Right as rain.'

'What did you just give her?'

'Just something to bring her out of the sedation.' He lays a hand on Chrissie's shoulder. 'Trust me – she's going to be fine.'

Andy leans forward in his seat. 'Why are you bringing her here anyway? Can't she just go home?'

'Best if she gets monitoring in the paediatric ward overnight. It's standard with children in the programme. Just need to make sure there aren't any unexpected side effects.'

'But why here? You brought Wendy here too. Why can't you monitor them in your own clinic, where you've got all the God-knows-what going on?'

Lisa, the other paramedic, appears at the back of the ambulance. 'Ready to roll?'

'Yep.' He preps Holly's trolley for moving. As he leans over the end of it, close to Chrissie, he whispers, 'I can't say anything more. I'm sorry. And you'd be best to keep quiet about it all too. I'm sure you've been briefed, but the fewer questions, the better, eh?' Then he stands up straight again and pushes the trolley towards the doors, where the other paramedic leans in to meet it.

Holly's head turns towards Chrissie as they wheel her past. 'Mummy? I had a really funny dream . . .'

Andy and Chrissie climb out of the ambulance and follow Holly and the paramedics inside. A doctor in blue scrubs meets them at the doors. 'I'm Dr Burlington,' he says. 'I'll be taking over Holly's care from now.' Chrissie nods and keeps walking. 'You've done absolutely the right thing,' the doctor says, quietly, so that only she can hear. Chrissie ignores him and walks faster, catching up with Holly. She's still groggy, coming in and out of sedation. Her eyes are closed, and her small hand goes to her ear. Her face scrunches into a frown as she rubs a hand behind her ear. Her eyes flicker for a moment, and then she drops her hand back down again as the doors swish open and they wheel her inside.

Chrissie takes a step away from the trolley. Holly has found her scar, and she will have plenty of questions about that later. Chrissie's hand goes to her own ear, and she runs a finger down the soft flesh behind. Is there something there? Or is she imagining it?

'Are you OK?' Andy is at her side, his face etched with concern.

She nods. 'You're right. I need to call Nathan. Can you go with Holly to the room? Text me to let me know where she is? She's still half-asleep. I'll be there when she wakes up properly.'

'Well, if you're sure . . .'

She already has the phone out of her bag, her finger hovering over Nathan's name in her call-list. Andy jogs to catch up with Holly and her small entourage, and the doors swish shut once more. She sighs. She really doesn't want to talk to Nathan. Not yet. She taps out a quick text message.

No doubt you're at the hospital anyway, so I'll keep this brief. Holly's had another accident. She's fine. Again. But you might want to head across to paediatrics, if you can tear yourself away.

She drops the phone back into her bag, then marches across the car park to the other wing. The one where Wendy is.

Chrissie hesitates outside the open door to Wendy's room. She can see her sitting up in bed, her eyes cast up towards the corner of the room. She swallows, then pushes the door open. Wendy turns towards her, face lit with a smile – as if she's just been laughing at something. The smile falters and she picks up the TV remote, fumbling with the buttons to turn the thing off.

'Pricey, that, I bet.' Chrissie tips her head towards the small TV. 'Or do you get a freebie, seeing as you cheated death?'

Wendy frowns. 'If it wasn't for you, I would be dead.'

Something flickers in Chrissie's stomach. Does she know? How could she know?

'Your quick action calling the ambulance,' Wendy continues, looking at her with a slightly quizzical expression.

*Keep calm, Chrissie.*

'I was on autopilot, I think. Just lucky I was still conscious, I guess. Or . . .' *Or what*, Chrissie thinks. *You'd be dead and I wouldn't know what a cheating cow you are?*

'You don't need to say anything else. I know how lucky we both are.'

Thankfully Wendy seems to have misinterpreted her. She's not going to correct it.

Chrissie's eyes scan the room. 'Is he here, then? No jacket today.'

Wendy shakes her head. 'I haven't seen Nathan since . . .'

'Since I walked in and caught you both out?'

'I don't want to fight. I'm sorry, Chrissie, for what it's worth.'

'How long?' Chrissie raises a palm. 'Actually, forget that. I'm not sure I really want to know.'

'It's over. I . . . We . . .'

'Don't say things you might regret later, Wendy. All I know for sure is that it's over between me and him. And me and you, for that matter. I just wanted to ask you about something.' She takes a step closer to the bed. Wendy flinches slightly, pulling away. 'Jesus, I'm not going to hurt you. I just wanted to see if . . .' She pauses, wondering if she's going half-mad. 'Have you got stitches behind your ear? Can I see?'

'What? How did you know that? They said I must've caught the side of my head on something when my head hit the dashboard, but I don't know what . . .' Her voice trails off. 'What is it, Chrissie? You're scaring me.'

'Just let me see. Please.'

Wendy folds her ear forward and turns to the side to let Chrissie see. 'They said it won't scar . . .'

The room spins suddenly. The light is too bright. Chrissie falls back, her legs catching on the edge of the seat of the standard-issue leather visitor's chair by the bed. She closes her eyes. Feels herself sink back into the seat. Hits her elbow on the wooden armrest and the pain jolts her, making her see stars. Vaguely, she's aware of Wendy calling to her, asking if she needs help, and then another voice. Her mother? A crunch. A screech. The searing pain in her arm and the sensation of flying, then falling. The cold, hard road, and the smell of engine fumes.

She tries to open her eyes, but it feels like they're glued shut.

Somewhere, far away. 'Christina . . . Christina, can you hear me?'

*Chrissie. It's Chrissie*, she says, but only inside her head.

'Christina . . . Oh my God, what did you do?'

A man's voice. 'She ran straight out in front of me. I didn't have a chance . . .'

'You were driving too fast.'

'The gate was open . . .'

'Don't try and blame me for this. The doorbell rang. I—'

Sobbing.

'Baby. Oh, baby, please. Open your eyes, honey. Come on . . .'
Then, to the man, 'Where are you going?'

Footsteps. More voices. More sobbing.

Her mum again, angry now. 'No . . . You can't take her . . . You don't know if it's going to work . . . Where the hell is Michael? I said no. I said we can never be part of this . . .'

'I'm OK,' young Chrissie says, but no one hears her. She's still asleep.

'Chrissie? Open your eyes. Can you hear me, Chrissie?'

'I'm OK,' Chrissie says now, back in the room. A nurse peering down at her.

'I think you must've fainted, love. Just sit there a minute and let me check you're OK.'

'Jesus, Chrissie . . .' Wendy has climbed out of the bed and is standing over her. She's trying to take her hand, but Chrissie is gripping hard on the wooden armrests.

She stares at Wendy, and at the nurse. What the hell just happened? She touches a hand behind her ear.

Hears her mother's voice, sees her staring at her in the mirror as she stands behind her, brushing her long hair. Tucking it behind one ear. 'Don't worry, baby. It won't scar. Daddy promised.'

Chrissie pushes herself to her feet. Blinks the images away. The memory of her mother is so strong, it hurts her chest. Crushes her heart.

'I have to go.'

'No, Chrissie. Wait . . .' Wendy lays a hand on her shoulder, but she shrugs it off.

'Get better soon,' Chrissie says, walking fast out of the door, before the tears pricking at her eyes have a chance to fall.

# Thirty-One

## JOSEPH (NOW)

Joseph takes a thick black pen and makes three diagonal score marks across each page of his notebook. His research has mostly been of little use. He'd wanted it to be the scientist – hoped that maybe she might understand, and that would make it all easier.

But deep down, he'd known from the start that it was Christina Tate.

He hadn't seen her since she was a toddler, but the features were the same. Michael's eyes. Michael's smile. She clearly didn't have Michael's mind though, or she would've worked it all out. He'd left things for her. Little clues. But she'd either ignored them, or they'd been too cryptic – but the pen with the logo meant it was easy enough to track him down, was it not? And the magazine . . .

She hadn't called the police though. He'd know. Because the other two had before he'd managed to get any further with recruiting them, and of course it had gone straight to the top, through the alert system. He'd had Dr La Tour on the phone, telling him to be very careful.

Then Melissa – telling him she couldn't help him anymore.

She'd been a useful ally over the years. The only one from the original lab who'd kept in touch, despite the risk to her own job by helping him out. She'd helped him with searches when he'd been blocked himself, and more importantly, she'd helped him with equipment. It was easy to make a few things disappear when you were part of a team setting up clinics all over the country.

Or perhaps they *had* allowed it – another part of their surveillance . . . *Watch the little mousey – see what it can do!* Maybe they'd allowed Michael to stay in contact with him too, and it was Michael who'd chosen not to. Joseph picks up the letter opener that he keeps in its velvet-lined case, his initials on the handle. He knows that it was Michael who had sent it, all those years ago. *One little reminder*, the note had said. *You were a good doctor.* Michael hadn't signed it, but he'd recognised the handwriting. Neat and precise, like Michael.

That traitorous bastard.

Michael could've stopped this. He could've let Edward live on. In some ways, it was pleasing to him that Michael had developed a ruthless streak – demanded a higher position. But somehow he knows that Michael hadn't done it for the same reasons Joseph had gotten involved. Michael was never driven by money. No. No doubt Michael was trying to get things back on track to carry on with his medical research that he was so precious about.

He turns the letter opener over in his hands.

A certain clarity is forming in Joseph's mind. The letter opener has triggered a memory that was long suppressed. His mother's smiling face on the day he'd graduated, the same day he'd found out he'd been accepted to study for a PhD.

'You'll be needing this soon, Doctor. I'm so proud of you, son.'

That's two things they've taken from him. Two tangible things. His title. His mother. He understands now why they gave him this house, decorated it like they did. This was as much as he was allowed from the past. The poor woman died thinking she had buried her only son.

But they took *his* life that day. They duped him. They'd told him he would be a hero! *It's safe*, they said. *You know you can trust your old friend Michael.*

Some friend.

All this time. All alone. Given the scraps of work and monitored constantly. All the while Michael is somewhere, living his life as he wants it to be. Michael and that lovely wife and daughter of his. His own goddaughter! And he'd never got to see her again after that day.

That awful day in the clinic.

He's suffered headaches, visions. Felt a constant pressure on his chest – anxiety and fear and confusion all bundled together in him as he tried to make sense of it all. They'd told him he had to move house – that it wasn't safe there anymore – and his brain had been too befuddled to question it. And then he'd acquiesced, because it was easier that way.

But no more.

Because Joseph knows exactly what he needs to do next.

He puts the letter opener back in its case, slips it into his jacket pocket. Then he walks through to the hall, takes the key from another pocket, and opens the door to his special room.

He's spent a long time getting it ready. He's so pleased that he's finally going to be able to use it.

# Thirty-Two

## MICHAEL (JULY 1984)

A doctor and two nurses from the critical-care team arrive within minutes, after Anne pages them from the boardroom. They go about their business wordlessly, efficiently. It's not the first time they've been called to an emergency in the clinic. If they are shocked to see Dr Edward Langdale lying on the floor, they do not show it.

Michael can't stop shaking.

'Come on,' Anne says, leading him by the arm. 'I think we could do with a drink.'

He shakes his head, although he lets her guide him. 'I need to get back over to the lab—'

'Tea with three sugars, then. I'll come with you.'

She drives them back to the lab in Michael's car. 'He'll be OK. He's in the best hands.'

'He died, Anne. That spray works. You can confirm that with your bosses.'

'Yes, he did. And then he came back. I know you said I injected him in the wrong place, but it worked, didn't it? He had a pulse . . .'

'He's in a coma. Who knows if he'll wake up again. We had this before, remember? With a couple of the—'

'Yes we did, and we lost them in the end. You don't have to remind me. But please – let's think positively here. The Cellregenix I administered today is a far cry from the compound we gave to those early test subjects.'

Michael laughs, but there's no humour in it. 'They weren't test subjects. They were vulnerable men who trusted us. And we repaid that trust by killing them.'

Anne turns into the car park without another word. He's sensed a softening in her, since what's happened to Edward. He's been harsh on her in the past – telling Sandy what a bloody-minded bitch she is, when, in fact, she's perhaps just a woman trying to do her best in a male-dominated world. She's been given a position of responsibility, and she doesn't want to let anyone down. She might present a hard shell, but she's softer inside than even she might care to admit.

In the lab, Michael heads straight to the phone to call the clinic and get an update on Edward. There's a note wedged underneath from Melissa, who has been in the lab dealing with a new batch of mice. He frowns.

> *Tried to call you at the clinic but no answer. You need to call Sandy. Says it's urgent.*

His heart thumps.

He's dialling the number when Anne comes in behind him. She flicks on the kettle, but then she catches sight of his face.

'Michael? What's happened? You're as white as a sheet.'

'It's Sandy. I don't know what's happened. There's a note here saying to call her urgently.' He misdials and the operator pipes up – *this number is not recognised, please try again* – and he swears under his breath. *Shit. Shit!* 'Can you call about Edward? Use his phone, it's on another line.'

'Yes, yes, of course. Don't worry about that now.'

Michael redials and this time he gets through. Sandy is frantic. 'Slow down, slow down,' he tells her, but he feels the panic rising in a wave across his chest. His throat constricts. 'Is it Christina? Tell me what's happened . . .' His hands are shaking so much he thinks he might drop the phone. He fumbles with it, puts it on to speaker and lays the handset on its side.

'She just ran out, Michael. She just ran out! One minute she was there behind me, and then the doorbell went and when I got there, there was no one there, and I stepped out to have a look, and then she was out – she just ran out. She'd been desperate to get out all day, and I'd been too busy . . .' Sandy stops speaking and dissolves into sobs.

He blows out a small breath. 'She can't have gone far, Sandy. She's probably hiding . . .'

'No, no, she's not lost, Michael. She got hit. A car hit her. She ran straight out of the gate, and the car – it didn't have time to stop. It all happened in a flash. I tried to grab her but you know what she's like. How fast she is – she was straight out . . .'

'Jesus, Sandy – where is she now? Is she in an ambulance? Is she . . .' He can't bring himself to say it.

'She's outside. She's alive, but it doesn't look good, Michael. She took quite a hit. I need to go back. The ambulance is coming . . .'

'Sandy, this is Dr Anne Cater. Don't let them take her. I'm sending someone to get her right now . . .'

Michael looks up at Anne, who is standing over his desk – those steely eyes fixed on him once more. 'What the hell are—'

'Trust me, Michael. She's better off here. You know she is.'

Anne shoots back over to Edward's desk and picks up his phone. He hears her making the arrangements.

Michael swallows back tears. His mind flits back to Edward lying on the floor, and when he closes his eyes, he imagines it's

Christina, lying on the road. If only they'd gone for a higher fence, with a higher gate – she wouldn't have been able to reach it.

He talks again to his wife. 'Sandy? Go and stay with her.'

Anne is back at his side, lays a hand on his arm. 'We're sending an ambulance from the clinic, Mrs Gordon. They'll take care of things—'

'Wait, no – what?' Sandy's voice hardens. 'You're not taking her in there. You're not giving her—'

'Go and wait with her, Sandy,' Michael says. 'It's our best chance.' He hangs up the phone and looks at Anne again. 'I hope you're right about this.'

'Michael . . . Don't you understand? This is what this whole programme is for.'

◆ ◆ ◆

Michael and Anne arrive at the clinic at the same time as the ambulance. They take Christina into the critical-care room with minutes to spare. He looks down at the battered, bloodied body of his daughter, and he knows he has no choice. He already has the syringe prepared. Sandy is in the corner, sobbing, being comforted by a nurse. He knows she doesn't want him to do this. He doesn't want to do this. Anne has implored him, but he's still not sure if it's really safe.

'Can someone give me an update on Dr Langdale, please?'

Anne fires daggers at him, then quickly rearranges her expression into one of concern. 'Michael, we can deal with Edward later. You have your daughter to think of now.'

He glances up at the clock. Five minutes until it's thirty since it happened. Will it still work if he waits? Her pulse is weak and thready, but it's there – maybe she'll come back by herself. He needs to know that Edward is OK before he subjects his daughter to the same fate.

'I need an update, please.'

'Mr Langdale is stable,' one of the nurses tells him. 'Stats are good. He's still under, but his pupils are responsive and he's passed all of our tests.'

Michael takes a deep breath and gently inserts the syringe into his daughter's median cubital vein, in the crook of her elbow. It has to be angled just right, the fluid released at a steady rate. There's a moment where no one in the room dares take a breath, as they wait to see if the drug will work.

Then Christina's body jolts slightly, as if it has been given the resus paddles. And then she opens her eyes wide. Then her mouth falls open and she screams, a long, shrill sound that threatens to shatter glass.

Sandy is up, and at the side of the operating table, and she's screaming too, and crying, and she's grabbed hold of Christina and the two of them are sobbing and shaking and suddenly there's this electrical buzz in the room, a ball of energy fizzing around, as everyone who's witnessed this takes it in.

'Baby,' he says, leaning over to her, murmuring into the huddle of his wife and child, who are no longer crying, but rocking gently. 'It's OK now. Everything is going to be OK.' He peels Sandy away and helps her to sit down. 'The nurses need to check her over. I need some air.'

He leaves them to it, and walks out of the lab.

'Where are you going?' Anne has followed close behind him, her heels clicking on the linoleum floor. 'That was quite something. I told you it would work.'

His voice is cool. 'She could've died. She still might. I should've let Sandy call an ambulance, deal with it the proper way. She's already told me she wants no part in this.'

Anne hesitates. 'You're invested now though, Michael. I wanted to make sure you were on board.'

'*Invested?*' Shaking his head in slow wonder, he produces an empty laugh. 'Consider me on board, Anne.' He punches the keypad and walks into Edward's room.

Edward is lying on the bed, hooked up to monitors. A steady beep.

'He's breathing on his own,' Anne says. 'We brought him back.'

Michael ignores her. He walks across to the bed, takes the syringe out of his pocket, then before Anne can object, he stabs it expertly into Edward's vein, in exactly the same place as he administered it to his daughter.

'Michael, what are you doing, he's already been injected once—'

After a few moments, where no one seems to breathe, Edward's eyes fly open, and then his mouth – that same glass-breaking scream that came out of Christina. Then his face slackens, and he falls silent. Blinks. He peers at Michael. 'Where am I?' His voice is different. Thin, reedy. His face looks different too. His eyes, dull – as if the light behind them has been dimmed.

'He's already got a tracker,' Anne says. 'I suggest you put one into your daughter, too. As you said – we need to monitor them.'

Michael nods. He lays a hand on Edward's shoulder. 'Just you rest, my friend. You're a bit of a miracle, you know. Took a couple of attempts, but you're now officially the first person to receive the kill spray, and be brought back by Cellregenix.'

'Patient Zero,' Anne says. 'Congratulations, Michael.'

Michael looks down at his friend. There are dark rings under his eyes, and when Michael waves his pen back and forth, Edward's eyes follow, but slowly. Michael doesn't want to think what damage might have been caused to him by the unknown dose of the spray, and the double dose of Cellregenix. What the hell had Edward been thinking, spraying that stuff on himself like that? Had he really been so desperate to get the programme underway? To get the results that Anne wanted? Michael had taken a risk with the second injection, but with Edward still unconscious after the first administration from Anne, he'd felt like he had no choice. He has no idea if Edward will recover from this. But all they can do now is watch . . . and wait.

Anne is smiling, which is rare, and makes Michael uneasy. 'Time for a drink now, surely?' she says.

He shakes his head. 'I'm going back to my daughter. We treated her before her heart stopped, so I'm hoping she'll recover well, just like the others. But I'm telling you now – if she doesn't . . .' He lets his sentence trail off. He doesn't need a response.

# Thirty-Three

## CHRISSIE (NOW)

Holly is sitting up in bed, chattering away to Andy. Chrissie's heart lurches at the sight of them.

'Mummy!' Holly shrieks when she sees her come in. 'Where have you been? I woke up and you weren't here but it's OK because Andy was here and he's nice.' She throws her arms out, and Chrissie rushes to her, hugging her tight.

'I'm so sorry, sweetpea. I thought you were going to sleep for a lot longer! I went to see Auntie Wendy, and she says she hopes you feel better soon.' Holly seems happy enough with this, already flitting her attention back to Andy, and the nurse who's sitting in the corner, observing with a bemused smile on her face. No doubt she's wondering why Holly has been left alone with 'Mummy's friend' and why her dad hasn't turned up yet. Chrissie lets out a breath, calming herself. Holly is fine. Wendy is fine – but the memory she'd flashed back to when she'd seen Wendy's scar from the tracker has given her a jolt.

'Andy, can you step outside with me for a minute?'

He turns, giving her a questioning look.

'Mummy! You can't go away again, you only just got here!'

'It's OK, honey,' the nurse says. 'Mummy will be back in just a minute. Maybe she's going to find Daddy?' She throws Chrissie a look.

Andy follows her outside. 'What's up? She only woke up a few minutes ago. You asked me to keep an eye on her . . .'

Chrissie shakes her head. 'Not here.' She starts walking quickly down the corridor, to the open vestibule at the end near the lifts, where there are some chairs and magazines and a slightly battered-looking coffee machine. 'I know I did. And thank you for that. I just wanted to ask you something.' She pauses, lifting up the hair away from her ear. 'Show you something, in fact.'

'OK . . .' He takes a step towards her. 'What am I looking for?'

'A scar. Behind my ear. It will be really faded by now . . . I had this flashback when I was with Wendy. I—'

He frowns. 'Just a tiny thing. You'd never see it unless you were looking. It's almost aligned with the fold at the back of your ear, but yes . . .' He steps back and she lets go of her hair, letting it fall. 'There's definitely something there.' He pushes a lock of hair behind her ear. His voice is soft. His warm breath brushes her cheek.

Chrissie blinks and breathes in the smell of him. He is still standing close. Gazing at her, with those melting eyes. That night comes back to her. That one night, where they'd—

The ping of the lift arriving yanks her back into the present. The doors slide open and Nathan steps out. He stops dead, as his face cycles quickly in three distinct changes, from a nervous frown to eye-widening shock, and finally, to brow-creasing anger. Nathan has only met Andy once before, at one of her work's Christmas parties, but he'd taken an instant dislike to him, accusing Chrissie of spending too much time with him that evening, leaving Nathan to fend for himself. Any time she'd mentioned him after that had made Nathan annoyed. Always making little digs about the two of them. Thinking about it now, he was probably looking for signals that matched his own transgressions.

'*You?*' Nathan barks. 'Why am I not surprised?'

The other lift-travellers step out and around him, faces tinged with curiosity and embarrassment.

'Nathan—' Andy begins.

Chrissie raises a palm towards her husband. 'Before you say another word, number one – this is absolutely *not* what you think. Number two – you have absolutely no room to talk, and three – Holly is fine. No thanks to you.'

'No thanks to me? You were the one who told me you didn't want me at home. You're the one who dumped her at Amanda's instead of looking after her yourself . . .'

Chrissie feels heat rising in her cheeks. She didn't want this confrontation, but here it is. 'Will you listen to yourself? The reason you weren't at home is because *you* decided that screwing my best friend was more important than trying to sort things out with *me*, and—'

'Guys, please?' Andy steps in and stands between the two of them, raising palms to both. 'We're all here because of Holly. Let's deal with the rest later on, shall we?'

Nathan's nostrils flare, but he says nothing more. Chrissie stands there, staring at him. Balling her hands into fists, then stretching out her fingers, hearing the gentle snap as the bones realign.

'Why don't you go in there and see her by yourself for a bit?' Chrissie tries to sound gentle. Keep the anger at bay. 'She'd like that.'

Nathan's eyes flit to Andy, then back to her. He looks like he has more to say, but decides against it. 'I can't stay long. I've got an important meeting in two hours. It's a conference call, but I can't dial in from here.'

'Fine. I'll be back up in half an hour. OK?'

'OK.'

She waits until she hears Holly's happy shriek as her dad walks into her private room. Then she turns back to Andy. 'Let's go for a coffee.' She stabs the button on the lift, and they wait for a moment in awkward silence until it arrives.

◆　◆　◆

The hospital's branch of Costa Coffee is tucked away in the bowels of the building. It's windowless, brightly lit and chaotic, but she manages to find a seat in a corner, piling up dirty cups and plates on to a tray and dumping it beside another on the wooden station where they keep the sugars and napkins. She wipes the table with a squirt of hand-gel from the bottle she keeps in her bag, and a wad of napkins. Andy returns with a tray, then lifts the mugs on to the table, followed by a huge slab of cake.

'It's coffee and walnut. The other stuff looked a bit past its best. Thought a sugar hit was required.'

'Are those hot chocolates?'

He nods. 'Double-sugar hit. When did you last eat?'

She laughs mirthlessly. 'I have no idea.'

Andy cuts the cake in half. 'So, I did some googling while Holly was asleep.'

'Was she asleep the whole time? Was she OK? I feel awful that I ran off like that, but I had to talk to Wendy.'

'She was in and out. Delirious. She's fine, Chrissie. Try not to worry.' He cuts a piece of cake with his fork, and chews. 'So this scar . . . ?'

'I was hit by a car. I'm sure of it. Unless I'm having some sort of false memory. Either way, I'd forgotten about it. Then when I saw Holly's scar, I remembered something.'

'People often repress memories. Traumatic or otherwise. It's a way to protect yourself from the pain.' He takes another bite. 'So, what do you remember?'

'I remember my mum brushing my hair. Telling me it wouldn't scar. Saying that my dad had promised. But I don't know why she seemed so sad about it. It was nothing. You couldn't see it then and you can't see it now, unless you really look closely. Sorry, you were telling me something . . . you were googling?'

'I was doing a bit of research while Holly dozed. On MG Holdings. Their main business category is listed as medical research. Nothing to do with restaurants.'

Chrissie stares at him, trying to take it in. She can't work out how Meet-4-Meat is connected to Joseph Marshall, and what it might mean. It's all too much. Right now, she needs to focus on Holly.

'I should get back. Thanks for the drink. And the cake. Probably saved me from a sugar crash.'

'I'll call you later, OK? I want to help you get to the bottom of this.'

Chrissie nods. She picks up her bag.

'I'm not sure how I'm going to sort this all out with Nathan. I'm still so angry with him, but . . .' She looks away. Can't meet his eye. 'I don't want her to grow up without a dad in her life. She needs that stability. Mine was great. Until . . .' Does she really want to get into this now? She's been thinking about her dad a lot lately. Thinking about her mum, too. And now this scar – and the memory of that, not fully formed.

Maybe it's time to find out the truth of what really happened to her mum.

# Thirty-Four

## MICHAEL (SEPTEMBER 1984)

Michael strolls into the lab late. Well past eleven. Edward is at his desk, working. 'Hey, how's it going?' Michael says, dropping a pile of foolscap folders on to his desk. He'd taken his lab notes home overnight in an attempt to get them into some semblance of order. He's usually the most orderly person he knows, but the last few months have been unusual, to say the least. And now that he doesn't even have his friend to bounce ideas off, he's felt a bit adrift.

'Good morning, Michael.' Edward glances up at the clock and frowns. 'You're really rather late. I've fed all of the mice and made sure that Percy had an extra treat – I gave him a piece of carrot that I had left over from last night's dinner. I think he liked it.'

Michael sits down and stares across the room at his officemate. Edward is a shadow of his former self. Physically, he's completely different – as if he has aged ten years in a matter of weeks. But more than that, he seems smaller, more delicate. His hair is longer than usual, and it flops listlessly into his eyes. He's stopped wearing the smart suits he'd taken to turning up in since the MOD came on board – instead, he appears to have replaced his wardrobe with sale-item polyester numbers that look at least a size too big for his shrunken frame.

More than that though, he is just no longer the same person. In some ways, he's become more methodical, less slapdash than he was before – which should be a good thing, and yet somehow, it isn't. He no longer takes risks, or seeks joy, and in fact the worst thing is that he seems completely devoid of humour.

He's been back at work for two weeks, after spending two weeks in the clinic, recuperating – being prodded and poked and monitored 24-7.

But something happened to Edward that day in the board-room, when he self-administered that spray. And despite him surviving, and waking up from the coma, after the second shot of Cellregenix – Michael fears that the old Edward is gone forever.

'I'm heading over to The Eagle for lunch in a bit,' Michael tries. Edward used to enjoy their weekly Friday lunch out. He'd enjoy winding up the students, who were crammed in there for the weekly special. He'd have too many beers, and come back to the office anyway. It was quite lucky that he was generally too distracted to do any actual lab work. He'd probably have set this place on fire.

'No thank you, Michael. I made sandwiches.' He doesn't look up. 'I'm finishing writing up my notes about the mice's behaviour. I thought you'd want me to carry on.'

Michael sighs. 'Sure, that's great. Carry on.' He's seen the notes already, although there will surely be an extra half-page per mouse today. The notes are a detailed report, far too detailed. But Edward's content, and maybe that's what he needs to be doing right now, while he's still in recovery.

The old Edward would have scribbled things like 'calm', 'agitated', or even 'feisty little bugger'. Michael smiles to himself, thinking about some of Edward's previous habits. It's a wonder he passed his degree, never mind his PhD – but then he always was good at pulling it out of the bag when required.

'I'll see you later then.'

208

Edward is writing calmly, neatly into his lab book. He doesn't look up.

Michael invites Anne for lunch instead.

◆　◆　◆

'This is very kind of you,' she says, once they are seated at Michael's usual corner table, in the back part of The Eagle pub, known as the RAF Bar. The walls are adorned with wartime memorabilia, and the ceiling is etched with marks where the WWII airmen burned their names and squadron numbers into the ceiling. Anne doesn't seem to have noticed the decor, and while he'd normally point it out and explain the history, he feels like it would be lost on this woman. She's too cold to care about the more human aspects of history. 'I don't generally go to pubs during the day,' she says, shrugging off her jacket and pushing it along the cushioned bench-seat that he's kindly let her sit on, taking the hard wooden chair opposite for himself. 'In fact, I don't go very often at all.' She picks up the menu and runs her finger down it, studying the selection.

Michael takes a sip of his pint of bitter. He wouldn't normally drink alcohol at lunch – sticking to Coke while Edward would work his way through a couple of 'shandies' that had barely been threatened with lemonade – but he needs a bit of courage for this. He studies Anne as she studies the menu. There are only seven items on there, and Michael tends to have the same thing every week – fish and chips. He senses from her intense evaluation of the dishes that she's actually a little nervous. They have never been alone together outside of the lab or the clinic.

She looks up and gives him a brief smile. 'I think I'll have the steak and kidney pudding. Not very diet-friendly, but . . . well, it is Friday.'

Michael smiles back. 'Good choice.' Might do her good, too. There's barely a pick on her. He gestures to the waitress and orders their food.

It's Anne's turn to sip her drink – she'd gone for a small gin and tonic.

'To be honest, Anne, this isn't purely a social outing.'

'Oh?' She puts the drink down and raises one of her expertly groomed eyebrows.

'I wanted to talk to you about Edward.'

She purses her lips. Looks away, as if she is deciding what to say next. 'We talk about him in the daily clinic briefings. We're monitoring his stats. Everything is as expected, is it not?'

'Hardly.' He takes a long drink. 'It's not going to show up on his vital-signs measurements, but please don't pretend you don't know what I'm talking about.'

Anne fixes him with her gaze. 'Why don't you assume that I don't.'

He sighs. 'Fine. We'll play it your way.' He takes another long drink, then gestures to the waitress to bring them another round. Anne doesn't object. 'Edward has gone through some changes since' – he pauses, deciding how to word it – 'the *incident*.'

'Go on.'

'You really want me to spell this out, don't you?'

'You're the expert on these compounds, Michael.'

'But I'm not a medical doctor. Surely the doctors in the clinic have had some thoughts.'

She drains her drink, just as the waitress lays the new ones on the table and lifts the empties. 'Food'll be with you in a minute. Kitchen's been hit today.'

Anne smiles at the waitress, then turns back to Michael.

'I'd like to hear *your* thoughts.'

'You can't have missed the physical changes. He barely even looks like himself.' Michael picks up a beermat and starts to shred it. 'He's not the *same*, Anne. You've known him for long enough. You know what he's like . . . or rather, what he *was* like. Would you have been persuaded to invest in Cellregenix if today's Edward had turned up at that first meeting? Would you have been swayed by his charm – his drive . . . his vision?'

Anne lets out a long, slow breath. 'We've noticed the changes, yes. We had been hoping that things would improve. But I sense from what you're saying that they haven't?'

'He's like a completely different person. I can't see how he can continue to head this programme.' Michael closes his eyes. *There, I've said it.*

'We've already considered this, Michael. We had hoped to leave it a little longer, but now that you've brought it up, I think we need to move forward with a decision.'

The waitress appears again, two plates in her hands. She lays them on the table. 'Watch it now, they're hot. Can I get you anything else?'

Michael stares down at the food. 'This is fine. Thank you.'

When the waitress has left, he looks at Anne again. 'What kind of decision?' He'd told Sandy about all of this just last night. He'd told her that while he didn't really want to move into more of a project-management role on the project, it would make sense for him to do it – as he and Edward are the two who really know most about all of it. Of course this means the Ministry of Defence will have to give him next-level security clearance – the same as Edward has now – and he'll have to attend a lot more meetings. It's not ideal, but it's preferable to having someone from the outside coming in. He doesn't want to have to start explaining all of the science to a newcomer. Sandy wasn't happy about it. She's still angry about Christina's treatment. She was deeply concerned about it all being experimental, and what the long-term effects could be – which is hardly surprising, given that Michael was the one who'd taught her about research and how you need to monitor things over time. He'd tried to reassure her, but things between them have been more than a little strained. Even the extra money and the chance of a bigger house hasn't swayed her.

'We're going to remove Edward as the lead on this,' Anne says as she spears a chip. 'I'm sure you've already worked that out.'

'I'm happy to move into that role,' he says, chewing on a piece of fish, 'but I want to still be involved in the research side. It's my compound, I can't—'

'That's only part of it, Michael. And as much as we'd love to have you move into that role, it's not quite that simple. We need to work out how to deal with Edward first, and how he fits into the organisation.' She pauses, and cuts into her pudding. It collapses, oozing thick gravy and chunks of meat on to the plate. 'If, in fact, he fits in at all.'

Michael lays his knife and fork on his plate. 'What do you mean?'

'Michael – your friend is a liability now. We can't have this project compromised.'

Michael moves the cutlery into the centre of his plate. He's barely touched his food, but his stomach is no longer fit to handle it.

Anne takes a sip of her drink. 'The way we see it is simple. We can move him on to ancillary duties – and we will have to monitor him closely. Very closely. Or . . . and believe me, I don't really want to do this . . . he could just disappear.'

Michael swallows back bile, the small lunch that he'd managed threatening to make a reappearance. He lowers his voice. 'You mean you want to *kill* him?'

212

'No need to look quite so shocked. I know about those early experiments on the tramps, you know.'

'That was all Edward's doing . . .'

'Precisely. So, in any event, we think it's best that we make the world think that he is no longer with us. I have a team who are arranging a fake funeral, an obituary, you know what I mean.' She waves a hand dismissively, then dives back into her food. 'This is really good.'

He stares at her, horrified. Any good thoughts he'd had about her briefly are gone. Her, and whoever it is that she works for. What the hell is he signing up for here?

'And if you don't *actually* kill him? What "ancillary duties" do you have in mind for him? How will that work?'

'Well, we give him a new identity. We pay for him to live out his remaining years comfortably. We can make him feel like he is part of the programme, even though, officially, he won't be. The brilliant Dr Edward Langdale will die tragically young, and be much lauded for his efforts on your fictional compound – the one that you've worked on for years, but sadly, failed with . . . no one will think badly of you, Michael. You can officially work on something else, or you can "retire" and just continue to work with us. We'll make sure you and your lovely family are well looked after.'

'And what will happen to Edward? Who will he become?'

'Oh, that's the neat part of all this. It'll tie things up nicely.' She drains her drink and waves a hand at the waitress, signalling for the bill. 'We'll give him the identity of that first tramp he brought in. He was never identified, you know—'

Michael shakes his head. He would never forget that man's name. 'You mean Joseph Marshall? You're going to give him that poor man's name?'

'A fitting substitute, don't you think? After all, that's what he is. We can't let *everyone* stay alive now, can we?' Anne takes a ten-pound note out of her bag and leaves it on the table. 'Take the rest of the day off, Michael. Go home and spend some time with that young daughter of yours – I do hope she's still thriving after her own cutting-edge treatment. Come Monday, you're going to be a busy, busy boy.'

He opens his mouth to speak, closes it again. She vanishes out of the pub, leaving a blast of cool air in her wake.

*Joseph Marshall.*

Poor Edward. Poor *him*. He can't believe what he's got involved with. He'd made the compound to do something good! He bunches his hands into fists, then rubs them into his eyes, trying his hardest to force back the tears.

*Oh God. What have I done?*

# PART 3

PART 3

# Thirty-Five

## CHRISSIE (NOW)

It's strange being back in the house with Holly and no Nathan. But after the almost altercation at the hospital, they'd both agreed it was better if he stayed away. Luckily, his work has a small apartment that they sometimes use for clients from overseas. And fortunately, it's currently available and his boss has let him use it without asking too many probing questions.

'Is it time for nursery now?' Holly said, the minute they walked through the door.

'Not today, sweetpea. We're going to have a little bit of time at home first, OK? Remember the doctor told you to be a good girl and to make sure you didn't go running about too much – just for a little while?'

Holly nodded. 'OK.' She disappeared through to the living room and Chrissie followed. Her little girl climbed up on to the sofa and curled up, sticking her thumb in her mouth. She'd stopped sucking her thumb about six months ago, but maybe it was just a little bit of comfort that she needed right now. Chrissie took the soft blanket from the back of the sofa and laid it over Holly, then switched the TV on and flicked through to the saved programmes.

'*Dora the Explorer*,' Holly said, quietly. Thumb still in her mouth.

She hadn't watched that show for months either. But Chrissie wasn't going to try and read anything into any of it. Holly looked exhausted. Dark circles under her eyes. It's all been too much for her. Too much for Chrissie, too.

For a long moment now, she's been just gazing at her daughter as she sits curled up and contented. And for that moment, she forgets about everything that's going on.

But then she remembers.

The knock on the door. Holly's tumble from the treehouse. The car crash. Arthur. Nathan and Wendy. Holly choking.

Andy.

She sighs and opens the fridge. She takes out a cold can of Diet Coke and pops it open, taking a long drink – enjoying the burn of the cold, harsh bubbles on her throat. She sets the can down on the worktop.

*What the hell am I going to do?*

The two boxes of chocolates are still sitting there next to the biscuit tin. She never got around to taking Maureen's to her. And she forgot all about the box for Amanda. God – she needs to go and see Amanda. Reassure her that Holly is fine. The poor woman has been texting and calling for updates, but she's been too wrapped up in herself to reply properly. She keeps thinking that she's going to wake up and find out this has all been some crazy dream – a Bobby-Ewing-appearing-in-the-shower moment. Her mum had loved watching *Dallas*. It was the highlight of her week. Chrissie remembers sitting beside her on the sofa watching it, not really understanding anything, but loving the glamour of it – struggling to believe that people lived like this in a big ranch house far away on the other side of the world.

It's funny the memories that she's been having of her mum lately. Things were bad for Chrissie, back when she was pregnant with Holly; and then afterwards, when she found herself with a tiny human to look after and no one to help her do it. No one to teach her the best way to put on a nappy, or get a Babygro over a little head without causing screaming. How to tell if it's a hungry cry, or a pained cry from colic. Nathan's mum hadn't been interested. They'd come over when Holly was born, but only stayed a couple of weeks then buggered off back to Spain. It was no surprise, really. But Chrissie had hoped, just briefly, that his parents might've stepped in a bit more, in the absence of her own.

At least Holly's parents love her – Chrissie knows that will always be true. She knows that both she and Nathan would die for Holly, if that was what it took. It's just their own relationship that never really got back on track. And she can't even really blame the postnatal depression. Their closeness was gone before she even got pregnant.

She leaves Holly in front of the TV and pops upstairs to get changed. Her clothes seem to reek of hospitals – something astringent yet stale, and her own sweat underneath. She jumps into the shower just long enough to rinse the stickiness off her skin, then throws on a clean pair of jeans and her favourite soft jumper. She takes socks from the drawer but doesn't put them on, deciding that she's left Holly alone for long enough. She hurries down the stairs, but a couple of steps down, she stumbles slightly, slapping a hand on to the wall to stop herself falling.

'What the . . . ?'

A piece of the stair carpet is ripped and frayed, one of the hard nylon fibres catching on her little toe. It's just luck that she got caught in it right now. Luck that it was her and not Holly. If Holly had tripped . . .

Her mind goes back to Holly's accident in the park. The phone ringing, dragging her away. All very convenient timing. A prickle of fear runs down her back. The sound of Holly's cartoon drifts up from the living room.

She feels sick.

She needs Andy to come back. They need to keep searching for what's behind all this. Joseph Marshall might not be answering his phone, but she's sure that he hasn't gone away. He's just waiting for the right time to carry out the next part of his plan – whatever that might be.

She hurries down the stairs and into the kitchen. Her hands are shaking. She picks up the Coke and drains the rest, then pops her head into the living room. Holly hasn't moved. She's still under the blanket, thumb still in mouth. 'You OK there, Holly-bee? Do you want a snack?'

'I'm OK, Mummy.'

Her phone buzzes in her pocket and she whips it out. 'Andy – thank God. Listen, I think Marshall caused that first accident, with Holly in the treehouse. Maybe my car accident too. I think he's making all of this happen.'

'Slow down,' Andy says, his voice calm. 'We'll deal with that. I'm trying to find out more. I need to come round and show you some stuff I found online. Is that OK? Is Holly OK?'

'Holly's fine. She's— Oh God.'

'What? Has something else happened?'

Chrissie feels the Coke burning up her gullet. She thinks she might choke. Swallows it back, and tries to breathe. 'The list . . .' she manages.

'What do you—'

'My second substitute, Andy. Remember? Because despite all this madness, I'd actually forgotten. My stupid, stupid second choice because I couldn't think of anyone else and she'd pissed me off that day—'

'Chrissie, what are you talking about?'

'Karen Cole. She was the second on my list. Holly's fine . . . So that means—'

'No. No, they wouldn't have. Not now, surely?'

'Why not?' She grabs her car keys and rushes through to the living room. 'Come on, Holly, we need to go out to the shop. Mummy forgot to buy some things for dinner.'

'But we can have pizza?' Holly says hopefully.

'No pizza, honey. Come on. Let's get your shoes on.'

Andy's voice comes loudly through the phone that she's left on the kitchen table. 'Chrissie, where are you going? Tell me what's happening . . .'

'We're going to the Co-op.' She pushes Holly's foot into her left shoe, then snatches up her house keys and speaks closely into the phone. 'We need to see if Karen Cole is OK.'

'What do . . . Oh,' Andy says. 'Oh shit. I'll meet you there.'

# Thirty-Six

## MICHAEL (OCTOBER 1984)

It's typical of Edward to leave a confidential memo sticking out of a pile of papers on his desk. Well, typical of the old Edward – who no longer exists.

Edward has been granted some leave while everything is put in place regarding his new identity and his new role within the organisation. Michael shouldn't be shocked that Anne and her cronies went ahead with the plan to fake Edward's death and bring him back as Joseph Marshall, and yet he still is. He'd hoped that Anne might've seen some sense. Shown some humanity. But it wasn't to be. No doubt it wasn't her making the final decision, but the worse thing about it was – she had probably been the one to suggest it to her superiors.

The memo on Edward's desk had arrived the day of his accident – that's what they're calling what Edward did to himself. Michael had seen him shove the memo into the pile, and given that Edward received confidential memos on a fairly regular basis, Michael hadn't questioned him. He'd given up on that long ago, when it was made clear that he was not to be made privy to this sort of information. He was just supposed to be the researcher.

Just! After all the work he'd put into it. Sandy had told him to walk away when it became obvious what his role was, but he hadn't listened. And then Christina had her accident, and he'd ignored Sandy again.

Things are falling apart around his ears, and he doesn't know how to fix them.

He pulls the brown foolscap envelope out of the pile. It's addressed to Edward, and marked with a red CONFIDENTIAL stamp, but other than that, it's just an envelope. Not exactly high security, considering what they're up to in this place. Then again, perhaps they weren't aware of how slapdash Edward's filing system was.

Michael picks up the letter opener from Edward's desk.

OK, so he shouldn't be opening this envelope. He knows that. He's been tasked with sorting out Edward's desk, incinerating his papers, and throwing everything else in the bin. He will do that, of course. But they're not going to know if he takes a peek at the contents of the envelope before he chucks it in the fire.

He slides the letter opener along the seal. The opener's handle has Edward's initials on it, and Michael suspects it was a present from his mother. He'll keep hold of this. Pass it on to Edward when he can. He should be allowed some sort of link to his old life, surely?

There are two sheets of paper inside. Again, the top of the first is stamped with that same stamp – and another one beneath NOT FOR DISSEMINATION OUTSIDE CORE TEAM. So Edward was in the core team? He really was high up the food chain. Michael hadn't been particularly interested at the start, too focused on his research. But now . . .

He pulls the paper out of the envelope and starts to read.

*Team,*

> *As you are no doubt aware, trials of Cellregenix have been*
> *extremely successful. We've come far since those early days,*
> *and we are now confident that the formulation is stable.*
> *We do not yet have the full formulation details – batches*
> *made by our new team have as yet proved unstable, thus*
> *we are still relying on the batches made for us by Dr*
> *Gordon – but we have seen some progress on this and hope*
> *to have further information soon . . .*

Further information soon? Progress? There's been no progress as far
as he is concerned. He has the recipe, they want it. Anne has asked
him several times, but until they agree to give him the privileges he
deserves, he's keeping it. He's still working on it – although they
don't know that. He's made further progress with the cell regeneration and the on/off switch for proliferation actions that he'd originally set out to achieve – but he won't make the mistake of sharing
his findings with Edward this time – or anyone else, for that matter.

He picks up the letter and continues to read:

> *As you also may be aware, we have decided not to go*
> *ahead with combined trials of kill spray and Cellregenix,*
> *as it is not in our operational interests to pursue this line.*
> *kill spray (T7843Y) is fully operational, and has been*
> *allocated with immediate effect to the anti-terrorism*
> *division, but we do have a different use for it ourselves.*
> *We are pleased to announce the details of our new pro-*
> *gramme – Project Three . . .*

So they'd already decided not to use it, before Edward trialled it on
himself? What was the point of the presentation that day, then? Did

they know that Edward was going to do what he did? Was Edward just hoping for some theatrics? Trying to make a name for himself somehow? Did he actually *want* them to keep using the kill spray?

He reads on:

> *Project Three is based on the basic scientific tenets of research. Three experimental subjects is the minimum number required to obtain basic results, showing the average and variability. It is also a number steeped in history – a powerful number in numerology, and a powerful number in science. And it will be a powerful number in this programme.*

'What the hell?' Michael mutters. This is bullshit, not science. This memo is clearly not meant for the research team, but to inform others in the programme. Those making decisions on who should be allowed to benefit? He reads on:

> *We must protect the future of our country. The people who run it, the people who advise on the policies that we must implement to keep us all safe. We need these people, and we must reward them for the work they do.*
>
> *We know that Cellregenix can bring someone back from the brink of death. This project will allow our powerful elite to have some security in their lives – for themselves and for their loved ones. We will allow them to choose three people close to them to benefit from this programme. This will remain classified at the highest level.*
>
> *Furthermore, in the interest of balance – we will allow them to choose three 'substitutes'. This is to ensure that*

*we do not tamper with the ongoing mortality rates of
the country. We must preserve the status quo, while also
ensuring that the privileges are awarded to the people
who require them.*

*By using this approach, it also allows our behavioural
sciences unit to monitor the participants and to gather
data on moralistic approaches to . . .*

Michael stops reading and drops the paper on to the desk in disgust. Is this some kind of joke? All this stuff about 'three' and keeping balance in the universe. Someone in power has gone insane. He notes the name who has signed this off. Not someone he's heard of, but presumably someone Edward had been familiar with.

*Substitutes . . .*

That was the word that Anne had used in relation to Edward. What kind of government department is this, that people can be discarded so easily? How is it scientific to add a moral choice into this? Who on earth decided on the 'rule of three'? How does anyone go about making those choices? As for the trackers . . . vital signs, and who knows what else – being captured continuously and uploaded to a database somewhere, where so-called scientists and programme leaders with their own dubious moral codes can analyse and interpret in any way they see fit?

He shudders. This whole thing is so wrong on so many levels. But there's not a thing he can do about it. Who is he supposed to tell? The police? A secret division of the MOD must surely trump the lowly police. Besides, who would even believe him? It's like something from a sci-fi movie.

He slides the paper back into the envelope.

What now? He can't very well tell anyone that he's read it. He slips it in between a pile of old notes that he already has pegged for the incinerator, then he hoists up the whole lot and hurries out of the office. He wants this stuff burned. He wants no part of this.

But he knows that when Anne and her cronies come knocking, asking him again to give up the formula and his years of research notes, that he will give them what they want.

As long as they put him in charge.

Because he needs to infiltrate the system, and change it into something better. Something more in line with his original goals. It might take him a while, but he'll do it. He's on the inside now. He's already one step closer.

# Thirty-Seven

## CHRISSIE (NOW)

'Holly, please . . .' Chrissie ushers her out of the front door but she is still only wearing one shoe.

'I don't wanna go, I wanna stay here!' Holly stamps her one trainered foot.

Chrissie looks down at her face, sees the tiredness behind her eyes. She doesn't want to drag her out, but what can she do? Holly is sniffling now, starting to cry.

'Oh, God – of course. Just wait here for one second, sweetie, will you?' Chrissie bolts back inside as Holly slumps down on to the front doorstep, hugging her knees to her chest.

She flies back out in seconds, slamming the door behind her. It doesn't stay shut, and she has to bang it harder to get the lock to click. She has the box of chocolates in her hand, and she grabs Holly's other hand and half carries, half drags her down the path. 'Walk, Holly. Please . . .'

'Are the chocolates for me, Mummy?'

Chrissie sighs, glad that she's stopped crying. 'We're taking them next door to Maureen, and we're going to see if she wants to play with you for a little while, OK?'

'Can I have the chocolates at Maureen's?'

'Maybe, sweetie . . .' She knocks on Maureen's door.

After what seems like an age, the door opens and the old woman peers out. She seems to have shrunk since Chrissie last saw her, and she feels another pang of guilt for what she did. She will never be able to make up for this.

She's about to speak, but then the old woman's face lights up when she sees Holly, who is clutching the chocolates with both hands. She's still only wearing one shoe. Chrissie is holding the other by the laces.

'Well, those look like some lovely chocolates there, young Holly. Would you like to bring them inside and we can sit by the fire and eat them together?'

Chrissie holds out Holly's shoe. 'Would you mind watching her for a bit?'

Maureen smiles and takes it from her. 'After that, you can go out and play in the back garden – we've got a new bird feeder, you know.'

Chrissie sighs with relief. 'Thank you. I won't be long, I promise.'

'Don't worry, dear. You know I'm happy to look after her any-time.' She opens the door further and Holly scampers inside.

Chrissie thanks the woman again, then heads off, walking as fast as she can, towards the Co-op.

◆ ◆ ◆

Andy is waiting for her outside. 'Hey,' he says. 'Take a breath. Did you run here?'

She shakes her head. Her face is hot, her legs burning. It wasn't quite a run but it wasn't far off, and it's the first exercise she's had for a while. Once this is all over, she really needs to get in shape.

'Karen,' she manages, through panting breaths. 'Is she here?'

'I don't know. I was waiting for you.'

She shakes her head, still too breathless to talk normally. She marches into the shop and goes straight to the counter.

'Is Karen here?'

'Hey, I'm being served right now. Wait your turn.' A stern-faced young man in a suit, holding a bag-for-life, glares at her.

'Sorry, I—'

'Can I help you, madam?' A short, dark-haired woman has appeared before her wearing a shift manager's badge, but her name is not Karen, it's Caroline.

Chrissie's heart, already pumping hard from her walk, flutters in her chest. She feels Andy's hand in hers. The warmth of him as he leans in close to her.

He clears his throat. 'We were hoping to speak to Karen . . .'

'She's out the back. Her shift's just finished. Can I help?' Caroline says, her tone suggesting she doesn't really want to help but she'd quite like to know what's so urgent.

'Ah, of course,' Andy says. 'Got our times mixed up. We'll catch her outside . . .' He pulls Chrissie's hand gently, trying to guide her out of the shop.

'No.' Chrissie pulls away from him and marches through the 'Staff Only' door.

'Excuse me, you can't go in there,' Caroline says, following fast.

But Chrissie has already burst into the space that is stacked with trolleys and boxes. At the back, next to the open door, there's a plastic table and two chairs; next to it, a small unit with a sink and kettle. Next to that, a row of hooks – some with coats hanging there, some with overalls.

And next to that, a bemused look on her face, is Karen. She's got one arm in her denim jacket, and she stays like that, unsure what to do next.

'Oh thank God.' Chrissie's body slumps as the tension leaves. 'I thought you were—'

'You're not allowed guests through here, Karen. You know that.' Caroline has caught up with her. 'In fact, if I'm not mistaken, it was you who decided to enforce this rule.' She crosses her arms.

Chrissie starts to shake.

'What's this about?' Karen says, her voice wary. 'Has something happened to Tommy? His dad was picking him up today, and—'

'Tommy is fine.' Chrissie shakes her head. 'I'm sorry, Karen. I got the wrong end of the stick.'

Karen and Caroline look at each other. Karen shrugs. 'Okaaaay.'

'Let's get you home,' Andy says. He guides Chrissie out of the open back door, into the car park. She drops her hands to her knees, tries to take in a few lungfuls of air. After a moment, she lets Andy take her elbow and guide her to his car.

◆  ◆  ◆

Back at home, Chrissie allows Andy to fuss over her for a bit. She's exhausted. Every little thing is another source of stress – but at least Karen was fine. No doubt she'll dig for more information the next time she sees her, or she might just start a rumour among the nursery mums that Chrissie is losing her mind. God, she'll have a field day when she finds out about Nathan and Wendy. She'll be wondering about Andy too. Chrissie spotted the interested look she gave him, her eyes flicking down and up the height of him while Chrissie was close to having a panic attack among the boxes of crisps.

Well, so what. She might be an irritating gossip, but Chrissie is glad she's still alive. Though that does raise a serious question.

'Why do you think they didn't kill her?'

Andy has come through to the living room with a tray of tea and biscuits. Under his arm, he's carrying his laptop. He manages to set the tray down on the coffee table without dropping the Mac, which is quite impressive. He sits on the sofa, leaving the middle seat between them free, then flips the screen up.

'I have a theory about that,' he says. He picks up a chocolate digestive and munches it in two bites.

Chrissie waits for him to carry on.

He moves a bit closer to her, then turns the computer around so that they can both see the screen. 'I've been doing quite a bit of digging.'

She wriggles a bit closer to him.

'It's all linked to that holding company. Your meat-logo client. MG Holdings. I did a full company search and I got the names of the directors. Pretty standard stuff.'

'Still no word from Joseph, you know.'

Andy nods. 'Never mind him right now.' He taps on his keyboard. 'Nothing much came up for most of the directors – well, nothing that seemed relevant. But this one . . .' He clicks on another tab and a page opens, showing a grinning man in a white coat, standing next to some gleaming laboratory equipment. 'His name is . . . Chrissie, are you OK? Are you going to faint or something? You're white as a sheet.'

Chrissie pushes herself back into the couch, hard. Violently, almost. 'I should've known. I should've *known*.' She punches the sofa next to him, making the computer jump.

'You know who this is? This . . . Dr Michael Gordon?'

'Of course I do.' She lets out a cry of frustration, then goes silent, before speaking again, quietly this time. 'My maiden name is Gordon.'

'I don't—'

She points at the screen. 'That, Andy, is my extremely estranged father.'

His eyes go wide. 'Your dad? I thought . . . I assumed . . .'

'You thought he was dead? I wish he was. I've acted like he is for so long, I actually started to believe it.'

'I don't understand. What did he do?'

Chrissie shakes her head. 'Not now. Please. Let me see that.'

She takes the Mac from his hands and scrolls down the page. More pictures of him, older ones – when he was young and fresh-faced. More grins. Others with him. Most, she doesn't recognise. But there's one face she's looking for. Someone she hasn't seen for a very long time – even longer than since she last saw her dad.

Another dad, of sorts. Her godfather. Edward. Not that he was much use to her. He died when she was a toddler, but her dad had talked about him a lot. Told her what a great man he was. She scrolls further, starting to think she's wrong.

Knowing she's not.

'Chrissie, what are you looking for?'

She holds a hand up. Keeps scrolling. Finally, there he is. Him and her dad together. 1983. They're both holding a lab mouse in each hand, laughing. The caption says 'Post-doctoral scientists Dr Michael Gordon and Dr Edward Langdale, celebrating their first success in the development of a new compound, Cellregenix – source: *Science Today*.'

Dr Edward Langdale.

Barely recognisable now. Not dead, after all. Aged? Sure. More than normal? Possibly. It's all starting to slot into place.

'Chrissie? The source. That's the magazine on your table, right? I saw it the first time I was here. Wondered why you had it . . .'

Chrissie nods. More pieces slot into place. 'I know who Joseph Marshall is,' she says. 'And I think I know what he wants.'

233

# Thirty-Eight

## MICHAEL (JANUARY 1985)

Michael and Sandy are having a late breakfast at the Wimpy in the high street. A bit of a treat, and, with things being strained between them lately, much needed. There's a play area in the corner of the restaurant, filled with plastic-covered foam shapes, some building bricks and a sad-looking rocking horse. It's a bit pathetic, but Christina loves it. She's happily playing with another little girl of about her age, her kids' portion of sausage and beans largely ignored.

Michael smiles. 'She's such a good kid, isn't she?'

Sandy lays her cutlery on her plate and picks up a triangle of toast, nibbling it like one of his lab mice eating a chunk of carrot. She doesn't answer him. She's been distant since Christina's accident, and the aftermath. The decisions made by Michael that she should've been consulted on. She had never wanted to get involved in the Cellregenix programme. Hadn't consented to Christina being given the drug. She'd been so supportive of his career until the MOD had come along and ruined it. He gets why she's pissed off with him. He just doesn't know how to fix it.

He tries again. 'You know, things have really improved between me and Dr Cater since I insisted they push me higher up into the programme. At first I thought they really did just want me to shut up and give them my notes.' He pauses, taking a slurp of tea. 'But it seems they wanted me to fight for this promotion – if that's what they're calling it. I suppose it is, technically. The extra money certainly points that way.' He puts his mug back on the table.

Sandy sighs. 'All sounds great for you, doesn't it, Mr Bigshot? But what if something goes wrong?' She glances over at Christina, who is giggling now, in the corner of the play area, with her new friend. 'What if she's not OK? It might all seem fine now, but what happened to Edward—'

'What happened to Edward is *not* the same.'

'Might as well be. You don't know. Not yet. You told me yourself how risky all this is . . .'

'Sandy' – he lays a hand over hers – 'you know what I'm trying to do here. This is my life's work. Ever since my dad died, it's all I've wanted—'

'You wanted to find a cure for cancer, Michael. Now *that*, I understand. *That* is something honourable. Something that will save millions. But this' – she shakes her head – 'I don't even know what this is. You won't even *tell* me what this is.'

It's Michael's turn to sigh. 'You know I can't tell you any more about it. That's the price I've had to pay for getting further involved. Besides, it's better that you don't know. Just know that my part in it is still the same. *I'm* still the same. I want to help people. I was scared for Christina. Terrified. I'd do the same for you, you know.'

'I don't *want* you to do the same for me.'

He stares at her, and she pulls her hand out from under his. 'You don't want to be saved? If you were going to die too soon . . . you wouldn't want to be saved? Get that second chance to carry on?'

'You're messing with fate, Michael. No good can come of it.' She looks away from him and stares out of the window. Fat drops of rain are hitting the glass. The heavens opening just as Sandy has mentioned fate.

He doesn't believe in any of that. He's a scientist. He remembers his mother weeping when his dad got sick, praying for him. Begging the vicar to do something about it. *It's not fair. Why us?*

But cancer isn't fair. It doesn't discriminate. His mother could've said all the prayers she wanted, bathed his dad in holy water every day. Given all her savings to the Church. Given up her worldly possessions. But none of it would've helped. His dad had been strong and fit, but he'd worked in smoky factories full of grease and machinery. Who knows what that environment does to the body. To the lungs. No one yet knows what causes a normal cell to go into overdrive. To start dividing itself again and again. Proliferation is a necessary function of cells, but when it's out of control, it results in a cluster. A lump.

A tumour.

And then it takes root elsewhere. Malignantly slithering through the body, switching on the same defect in organ after organ, until the body can't fight back anymore. It withers and fades and, eventually, it shuts down.

He'd watched that happen to his dad. And he'd shunned his mother's dependence on faith, instead burying himself in his books – trying to learn all he could about cancer. Passing his exams with flying colours, getting into Cambridge.

And now this programme – this research, with unlimited funds. But with a catch, of course. He still hopes that he can convince the MOD to move away from what they are doing. To refocus their efforts on things that matter. His cell-regeneration compound is meant to complement harsh cancer therapies. Switch the cells

236

back on after chemotherapy has destroyed them – but only the good cells. Not those dark, damaged things that torture and kill without reason.

Because there is no reason. He can't for a moment think of a reason why cancer is needed. It doesn't have any benefits. He can't see any way to harness anything positive from the cell action that it creates.

'Michael? Did you hear what I said?'

Sandy's voice is too loud for the small restaurant, and he senses a change in the atmosphere. People halting their conversations to listen to theirs. In the corner, a child starts to cry. Michael twists round in his seat. Glares at a woman who is staring over at them, plastic fork paused halfway towards her lips, a soggy chip dangling from it.

The normal sounds resume. The child stops crying.

Sandy is staring at him.

'I'm sorry,' he says. 'What did you say?'

'I said, I'm leaving you, Michael. I'm taking Christina, and we'll go and stay with my mum and dad for a bit. They'll be glad to spend time with her—'

'Sorry, what?'

'I think you heard me, Michael. I can't do this anymore. You spend all your time at that lab. And I don't like this project . . . this programme that you're involved in. It's . . . unnatural.'

'Sandy, you encouraged me to get more involved. You said—'

'I said you needed to stand up for yourself. I said Edward was taking all your credit.' She pauses, pushes her plate away. 'How *is* Edward? You don't really mention him anymore. Not since . . .'

'Edward's not doing great. But we're looking after him. He—'

'And Christina? Is she going to end up "not doing great" too? Is it only a matter of time?' Her voice has risen in pitch and volume, and the clatter of cutlery and chatter has halted again.

'Sandy, please,' he hisses, 'you're making a scene. I've told you – everything is going well now. I'm changing things. The compound is really working. Not one other person is sick. Edward is a different thing, he's—'

'Edward was your friend, Michael.' She's lowered her voice and picked up her handbag. 'He's Christina's godfather, for goodness' sake. Not that I think he should be anywhere near her right now. Not until we know that she's definitely OK . . . and you find out what exactly is wrong with him.' She stands up and projects her voice across the room. 'Christina – time to go.'

Michael can feel the weight of the stares from everyone in the restaurant, but he doesn't turn around. Christina appears at the table, her cheeks flushed, a big grin on her face.

'I made a new friend!'

Sandy takes her daughter's hand. 'That's lovely, darling. You can tell me all about it on the way to Granny's, OK?'

'Oh hooray, we're going to Granny's!' She turns to Michael, who hasn't moved. Frowns. 'Daddy, are you coming to Granny's too?'

Michael swallows back a lump in his throat. 'Not just now, honey. You go with Mummy and have a lovely time, OK? You tell Granny to save me a piece of that yummy chocolate cake she always makes with you. OK?'

Christina leans across and throws her arms around his neck, giving him a wet kiss on the cheek. Then Sandy pulls her away, and he watches as the two of them walk out of the door.

The rain has stopped now, the sun casting a bright glow on the glistening pavement. He stares down at his plate, at the half-eaten cheeseburger and cold, soggy chips.

'I was only trying to protect you both.'

'What's that, sir?' A teenager in an apron is taking his plate off the table.

Michael gives him a brief smile. Shakes his head. 'It doesn't matter.'

But it does. It's the only thing that does.

# Thirty-Nine

## CHRISSIE (NOW)

Chrissie is pacing back and forth in the kitchen. Her mind is whirring. 'He knew all along who I was. All that weird formality. Calling me Mrs Tate.' She shakes her head. 'I need to go and collect Holly.' She tosses the magazine on to the table.

Andy follows her through to the hall. He has his laptop in his hand, still open. 'Can you back up a bit here, because you're not making any sense.'

Back in the kitchen, she stops pacing. 'This is all about my dad. I should've worked it out.'

'Worked what out?' Andy puts his laptop on the kitchen table, then opens the magazine and starts flicking through. 'What am I looking for here, Chrissie? Help me out, please?'

She marches over and snatches the magazine from his hand. She rifles through the pages. Stops. Lays it flat on the table and prods it hard with a finger. 'This.' Then she grabs his laptop and scrolls down the page she was on before. 'And this.'

Andy looks from the magazine to the web page and back again, his face scrunched in confusion.

'Your dad, OK. And his partner – Dr Edward Langdale.' He looks up at her. 'I'm still missing the connection . . .'

'Edward Langdale died in 1985. Some accident at the lab that was hushed up. My mum knew, for sure, but she wouldn't tell me. I didn't really know him. I was too young. He wasn't much of an active godfather. I always felt so sad for my dad, losing his friend like that. Like he'd lost such a big part of his life that he couldn't replace. He never seemed happy after that. He got a new job, some big promotion, and he was just never around. And then my mum said we were going to stay with my grandparents, and that was that.'

'You must've still seen him, though. Did they get back together?'

She shakes her head. 'No. She would never tell me why. Even when I was older and more able to understand, she would never tell me why. She only ever said that he was a good man and that he loved us both, but that they couldn't live together anymore.'

'Did you ask him?'

'Yep. He wouldn't tell me either. Then as time went on, I stopped asking. And I saw him less and less. There was some sort of barrier there.'

'And that's why you haven't spoken all this time? You just . . . drifted apart?'

'No!' she snaps. 'That is *not* why.'

'OK. Look, why don't you tell me how this is connected to Joseph? We can talk more about your dad later.'

'I wish I didn't have to talk about him at all. But the thing is – I think that he lied to me. About Edward. I don't think he died at all.' She leans over the table and spins the magazine around. Points at the man standing next to her dad. '*That* is Joseph Marshall. He left this magazine for me to find, didn't he?'

'I—'

Andy's question is cut off by the sound of knocking at the front door.

Chrissie hurries through to answer it. 'That'll be Maureen bringing Holly back. We'll need to discuss this later, we can—' The sentence dies in her mouth as she yanks open the front door. The smile she'd prepared falls flat. She blinks. Takes a breath. 'Oh, hi.' She pulls the door open wider. 'Why didn't you use your key?'

Nathan steps inside, Wendy close behind. She has a large dressing on the side of her forehead, but other than that, she looks well. She's smiling nervously.

'Hi, Chrissie,' she says.

Chrissie ignores her and addresses Nathan again. 'Maybe you should give me that key, actually. For now. It'll be a bit confusing for everyone if you just come and go as you please.'

Nathan doesn't say anything, but she catches a look that passes between her husband and her former best friend. *Stay calm*, it says. She swallows the rest of her words. There's no point having a row. There are bigger things to worry about right now.

Andy is standing by the table when she walks back into the kitchen. 'Nathan,' he says, by way of greeting. 'I was just going—'

'No you weren't,' Chrissie snaps. Then she stops herself, sucks in a deep breath. 'Why don't you go through to the living room? All of you. I'll make us some coffees.'

'Can I help?' Wendy tries.

Chrissie shakes her head. 'It's fine. Andy – this is Wendy. Wendy – Andy. He's a friend from work. Well, from when I used to have a proper job, that is. He's been helping me with some stuff.'

The air bristles with tension as Nathan takes a step closer to Andy. 'What kind of stuff?'

Andy steps back. 'Chrissie needs a bit of support right now, mate. I—'

'I'm not your mate.'

242

'Oh for heaven's sake!' Chrissie pushes herself between the two of them, shoves a hand on both of their chests. 'Go and sit down, please. There's stuff we need to discuss.'

There's a pulsing in Nathan's cheek as he adjusts his jaw, deciding not to say anything else at this point. She'd seen the flash of anger in Andy's eyes too. They are both capable of eruption. She knows this. But she doesn't want them fighting right now. There are things to be sorted. Discussed. She needs to tell them everything. Nathan leaves the kitchen, and after a brief shared glance with Chrissie, Andy follows him.

'Where's Holly?' Wendy says.

Chrissie turns. She'd forgotten she was there. 'She's next door. With Maureen. I think Maureen's happy to have the distraction. I told you about Arthur, didn't I?'

Wendy cocks her head to one side. 'No?'

'He died. Massive heart attack. It was while you were in hospital.' She turns away, takes mugs out of the cupboard. 'So much has happened since then . . .'

Wendy absentmindedly pushes a strand of hair behind her ear, her finger lingering there for a moment. She catches Chrissie's eye. 'Oh God, that's terrible. Poor Maureen. I feel really bad now, flicking him the bird as we drove off that day.' She looks away. 'And Holly? How is she?'

'She's fine. Considering.'

'That's great.' She gathers a breath. 'Listen. The doctor told me I'm on some sort of long-term clinical trial now. With this device monitoring my heart rate and blood pressure and whatnot. It's good, I think. Apparently they had to give me some experimental drug. I . . . I was wondering if they'd given Holly the same. You were asking about the device?'

Chrissie spoons coffee into a cafetière. 'Which doctor was this?'

243

'I can't remember his name, to be honest. He came that day you were there. After you left. Made me sign a couple of forms. Said they'd be in contact to arrange some payment, too. All a bit weird, though, right? I mean, aren't you supposed to consent to being given experimental drugs and put on clinical trials? I watched a programme about this after that big disaster that happened when all those people nearly died after their bodies reacted to the trial drug, and—'

Chrissie pushes the plunger down to the bottom of the pot. 'I consented for you. You would've died otherwise.'

The kitchen falls silent around them. Nathan's and Andy's raised voices drift through from the living room. Sounds like they're fighting for a moment, and then the shout of 'offside' confirms that they're actually watching football.

'Men,' Chrissie says. She puts the pot on a tray, adds the mugs and the sugar bowl.

Wendy takes milk out of the fridge and pours some into a jug. 'Thank you,' she says.

Chrissie picks up the tray. 'For what?'

'For saving my life.' She pauses. 'I'm so sorry, Chrissie, about . . .'

'We need to find a way to make this work. For Holly. She's all that matters right now. There's some stuff going on, and I need to explain it all to you. Later . . . Well, maybe then I'll find time to be angry with you again about Nathan. But right now, there's some stuff that you need to know.'

'OK.'

She's just laid the tray on the coffee table when the door goes again. 'I'll get it.' She heads back through to answer the door again, hoping that this time it is Maureen with Holly, and not the other option that she's been dreading – Joseph Marshall. She's not sure what she's going to say to him now that she knows the truth of who he is. She's still not sure what's going on, but this 'experimental drug' and the monitoring device is all part of it – and both Wendy and Holly are part of it now. But thankfully, Karen is not. She might not particularly like the woman, but it had been a mistake to add her to the list.

She pauses behind the front door. She doesn't sense that Holly is out there. She'd hear her. She'd be knocking again, calling 'Mummy, Mummy' in her usual little-girl way.

Also, Maureen wouldn't be bringing her back. She'd told the old woman that she would pick Holly up later.

A prickling sensation flits across her neck, down her back, down her arms. Like the day when Joseph first knocked on her door and she'd tried to hide away from him upstairs. Sure that if she opened it she'd be opening the door to another life. That nothing was going to be the same again.

Her hand hovers over the handle.

If it is Joseph, she's going to be calm, tell him to take her off this programme and explain exactly what Holly and Wendy have been given, and why. But his lack of contact, and the fact that Karen is not dead, has made her wonder if something has happened to Joseph. If maybe the programme has been cancelled automatically. Maybe it's all over, and all she has to deal with now is her messed-up marriage . . . and maybe Arthur really did have a heart attack.

She takes a deep breath and yanks the door wide open.

Her Mini is sitting on the driveway, patched up and re-sprayed. 'What the . . . ?'

A tall, slim man in a long, dark overcoat is standing behind it, hands in pockets. He's wearing a charcoal tweed trilby, wisps of greying hair poking out from under the rim. He's facing away from her. Perhaps getting ready to leave, as he's been standing there for a few moments now. Then he turns, and her mouth drops open.

They stare at each other for a moment. Then the man smiles, and his face crinkles as his eyes light up. *Her* eyes. 'I brought your mum's car back, Christina. That was quite a battering you gave it . . .'

'Hello, Dad.' She takes a step back, letting him in.

# Forty

## Michael (January 1995)

It's been ten years since Michael became the head of Project Lifeblood. Anne had suggested drinks after work, and he's looking forward to it. He's found himself warming to her more over the years. The initial power imbalance hadn't worked, for either of them – but since Edward 'died' things had changed. She'd respected him for standing up to her, for pushing changes on her to make the project more scientifically valid. But he still feels bad about his friend.

When Edward was officially given his new identity, they took him off to work in a different clinic. They'd begun with that small one in Cambridge, not far from the lab that it had all started in. But now they have branches all over the country.

Not that the public know anything about them, of course.

They're hidden in plain sight. Taking spaces forgotten and unused. Dingy basements and old warehouses. Places with businesses operating above them, or in front of them, all through a holding company to deal with the finances, keeping them unlinked to the Ministry of Defence. Knowing what he knows, Michael is sure that this is not the only shady, secret programme operating across the UK. The MOD have unlimited funds for this, it seems. Because the stakes are so high.

He'd been given a tour of Porton Down, shortly after he'd passed the security clearance level to take over the running of things. He was fascinated by what was taking place there, the research that had been going on over the years – but he was also sure that he wasn't hearing the half of it. Given that in his programme they'd been happy to use the homeless as their unwitting volunteers, it wasn't much of a stretch to think that there were plenty of ex-servicemen doing the same at the government's official biological weapons research facility. And there would be levels of clearance that he would never achieve, and would never want to.

Sometimes, he's quite sure, it's better not to know.

His Cellregenix-based programme is as ethical as he can make it, considering what they are doing with it. He scrolls down through the list of participants in the database. There are 500 under active supervision via the trackers. One hundred more who've not yet been 'activated'. The stats are good. The participants are stable.

Except for Joseph.

Something went very wrong inside his body when he was given the extra dose. Despite not being allowed contact with him, Michael is sent monthly blood samples from him, part of Joseph's employment and benefits. He gets a house, a job, anything he needs. As long as he draws a sample of blood once a month and sends it to the lab.

Joseph's cells are degenerating. But for every cell that dies, another one proliferates into a small cluster. He has a rare form of blood cancer, but one that won't spread to other organs. One that has never been recognised in any other human.

Michael has managed to recreate the condition in mice, by giving them the same cocktail of drugs that Edward had. But so far, the mice have died before he could follow the effects long term.

Joseph is dying, but slowly. At the moment, he doesn't know – officially, at least. No doubt he has worked out that something is wrong with him. The stats from his tracker have shown an erratic heart rate too. Anne has made it clear that they are to follow his progress without letting him know. In some ways, he is Patient Zero. A recipient of the first successful batch of Cellregenix – and only one other patient received an infusion from that batch.

Michael's own daughter.

It was hard when Sandy left him, taking Christina away. But he knows that she is happy and healthy – and safe. Sandy refused to allow monthly blood draws, but he has the data from her vital-signs tracker, and he is allowed blood twice a year – after agreeing to pay her GP a lot of money to tell her she had a disorder that required long-term medication and regular blood tests. The medication she collects is something harmless that she will never think to question, and there is an alert on the system that if she changes GP, the instruction will follow.

Her cells are fine. Over ten years on, and she is as healthy as ever. No signs of the proliferating quirk that Edward/Joseph has. And as long as things remain like this, Michael has no need to tell her anything about it.

She's become interested in his work, of late, and he feels bad lying to her – telling her that it's not very interesting; trying to steer her away from a career in science, when actually there is nothing he'd like more than to have her involved and to teach her everything he knows. But she's nearly fourteen now. She'll soon be fed up spending every second Saturday with her dad. There will be make-up and boyfriends and heartbreak to deal with.

The last part, he knows plenty about himself.

He's remained friendly with Sandy. Neither of them so far have had anything other than a casual relationship with anyone else, and he'd take her back in a second. But she doesn't want him, and that's something he has to accept. He lost her trust the day he saved his daughter, and there's not a thing he can do to win it back.

The doors to the lab swing open behind him, and he blinks back into the present. The harsh strip lights buzz above him. The mechanical hum of the fridges comes back into focus. 'I'm just finishing this. Give me five minutes.'

'Michael.'

The voice is not Anne's, as he'd expected. He looks up. 'Sandy? What are you doing here?' He smiles, delighted at seeing her. *She remembered.* 'You remembered?'

She frowns. 'Remembered what?'

'Ten years, of course . . . We're going out to celebrate. Come with us.'

He can't read her expression. 'No, Michael. That's not why I'm here.'

His stomach lurches. 'What's happened? Is it Christina? Is she . . . ?' His mind goes back to that day – that life-changing day. Her accident. Him overriding Sandy's wishes not to take her to the clinic. But he'd saved her . . . Nothing can happen to her now. It is impossible. Her cells are perfect. He'd tested them many times now. Perfect regeneration properties. Basically, she can't die of anything other than old age.

'It's not Christina,' Sandy says. 'It's me. I've found a lump.'

# Forty-One

## Chrissie (Now)

Chrissie balls her hands into fists, feeling her nails cut into the flesh. She needs to hold it together. 'It's this way,' she says, heading back through to the living room where everyone in her life right now – except the most important person, of course – sits. 'Everyone – this is my dad.'

Michael steps into the room. 'I realise this is probably a bit of a shock.'

Wendy's mouth is hanging open. Nathan looks angry.

'Hello, Dr Gordon.' Andy's expression is neutral. 'You've saved us the job of trying to track you down.'

Michael nods. 'Are you the one who searched for MG Holdings? It flagged up on our system.'

'I thought it might.'

Nathan stands up, his cheeks colouring. 'Is someone going to tell me what the hell is going on here?'

'Do you mind if we open the window?' Wendy says. 'I'm getting really hot.' She gets up off the sofa and goes over to the wide window that overlooks the garden. She doesn't wait for anyone to agree, just unclicks the latch and pushes the window wide. A gentle breeze ruffles the rolled-up blinds. The sound of Holly's laughter slips inside, and Chrissie feels her heart lurch. She is there. She is safe.

'I should go and get her,' she says.

'Maybe best leave her for a bit longer,' Wendy says gently. 'She sounds happy enough next door.'

Chrissie agrees, but she doesn't reply. There's a lot she wants to say, but having him here, right now, her anger has melted to insignificance. She glances across at her father. He's older, of course, and under that steely determination of his, there's vulnerability too. The recriminations can wait. 'Can I get you a coffee, Dad? Sorry, I don't know how you take it.' She pauses, catches his eye. 'I don't think I've made you a coffee for, oh, what is it . . . Twenty years?'

'I actually thought you were dead,' Nathan says. 'She's said so little about you all these years. I was thinking prison, or dead, actually. I suppose it might've been the former. Maybe you just got out?' He sits back down on the chair, his face etched in a frown.

Chrissie feels torn that she's never explained the situation with her dad. As far as anyone's been told, the last time she saw him was at her mum's funeral – and that's completely true. He'd sent her a couple of letters after that, trying to apologise. Asking her to meet up. But she'd ignored them, and when she moved house, the letters had stopped. Should she have given him the opportunity to explain?

'How did you find me?' she says.

Wendy slides past them as they stand by the doorway, and into the kitchen. 'Let me get your drink. You should sit down.'

Michael nods his thanks and takes a seat on the far edge of the sofa where Andy sits. 'Like I said, the alert. Your IP address was flagged.' He nods towards Andy's laptop. 'But to be honest, I knew where you were before that. I've always known.'

Chrissie sits on the small sofa that Wendy has vacated. She pushes a scatter cushion out of the way, leans her elbows on her knees. 'Maybe you should start at the beginning. This is all connected to Joseph, isn't it?'

Michael shifts in his seat, looking uncomfortable. 'We didn't know he was looking for you. Not at first.' He locks eyes with his daughter's. 'I take it you've worked out who he is?'

'He left a clue. Except it took me a while to find it.' She lets out a long sigh. 'In the meantime, my next-door neighbour is dead.'

'Wait, what?' Nathan pipes up. 'Who's Holly with? I thought you said—'

'She's with Maureen. You just heard her – she's having a ball out there.' The room falls silent, listening. There are no giggles coming from the garden now. 'Well, she must've gone back inside.' She turns to Nathan. 'Arthur had a heart attack on Saturday night, not long after I was brought home. I spoke to Maureen the next day, but then . . . Well, we haven't really had a chance to talk much since then. You weren't here.'

Michael looks from Chrissie to Nathan, and back. She flashes him a look that says 'Don't ask about this right now', and he turns back to Andy.

'I've been working in a lab in the basement of the restaurant that Chrissie has been designing logos for. We own the building, we rent out the space above.' He turns back to Chrissie. 'It never works out for long. Too many conditions attached to the lease. Not least that we – that is, *I* – am allowed to deal with the creative side. Sort out the branding and whatnot . . . They don't seem to like that, but it keeps the designer in business.'

'You set that up just to give me a job? Was that *you* on the phone, that weird crackly line?'

Wendy lays a mug of coffee on the table and lets out a small burst of laughter. 'I'm sorry. It's just – I always said there was something funny about that whole set-up. Meet-4-Meat? That was definitely not something that anyone with a creative bone in their body would've come up with. No offence.'

Michael smiles. 'Actually, that was their real name. But they pulled out before they even finished refitting the kitchen with a new barbecue grill. I think they were a money-laundering front. They got spooked when they saw some of my official-looking colleagues heading down to the basement. Probably a good thing.'

Chrissie isn't happy about the light-hearted tone. She feels a bubble of rage getting ready to burst. 'I don't really give a shit about any of that right now. I want to know what's going on with Joseph. Did he really get Arthur killed? What's this drug that they gave to Wendy and Holly—'

Michael raises a hand. 'I think you're right. I need to start at the beginning. I need to tell you everything.' He sits back in his seat and crosses one leg over the other. 'It started when I was a post-doctoral student at Cambridge. I was fiddling about with a virus, trying to decipher it. Work out its genetic code. Long story short, I modified it, and I put it into a cell culture – a Petri dish. I watched it grow. Multiply. Then something happened to it. It mutated. I understand a lot more about it now than I did then.' He pauses to take a sip of his coffee. 'It was the eighties. So much of this was new. When I got it to trigger regeneration in cells that I had grown and then killed, I thought I had cracked it. I thought I was going to find a cure for – well, for everything. I was imagining the Nobel Prize for Medicine.' He sighs, and his face falls. 'But Edward had other ideas . . .'

He talks for nearly an hour. No one interrupts. Because what he tells them is something that none of them could ever have imagined. Even Andy looks shocked, and he's the one who's found out the most about it all. Nathan and Wendy are stunned into silence. They'd thought their affair was the biggest thing to rock the boat of this family this week.

Chrissie almost feels relieved. She'd been starting to think she was going mad. She's sad about Joseph, or Edward – both of them, and what a waste of life it all was. But she's still confused about what Joseph wants. She turns to Michael. 'But what I don't really understand is, why this "choose your three" thing? It doesn't really make any sense.'

'Little of what Joseph has done over the years has made sense. There was an early programme, with the rule of three, but I got it scrapped as soon as I could. Some power-hungry top brass came up with it, I think, and Joseph clung on to it. Something fundamentally changed in his brain after what happened to him. He's conflating various theories and jumbling them up into what he thinks is something scientifically sound. He's been monitored, of course, but he's managed to do a lot of this off-grid. I'm sorry, Chrissie. He must've had someone helping him, and we are trying to get to the bottom of it. I'm so very sorry about your neighbour . . .'

'Can you tell me how he died? How he really died?'

Michael looks uncomfortable. 'When we were first working on the kill spray, the idea was to use it as a biological weapon. I'm not part of that group now, but I think maybe Joseph still has a contact there. Someone he's managed to keep on-side. They would've dispatched an operative to Arthur's door that night, and administered it. It's very quick. I'm sure that your neighbour felt no pain.'

'But what does he want from me?' Chrissie crosses her arms. 'I'd assumed he was trying to use me to get to you?'

'He's dying, Chrissie. He's desperate. Our doctors have tried to help him, but it's not working. He . . . Well, he would've been barred from accessing any of your official records, but there must've been enough information for him somewhere. He's managed to track down the three babies called Christina born in Cambridge on the fourth of April 1981—'

'Three of us? With the same birthday?'

Michael shrugs. 'There are probably more. It was a popular name. He ruled the other two out, but they wouldn't play ball. They called the police on him and it flagged up in our system. Why didn't *you* call the police?'

Chrissie swallows. 'I don't know. I haven't really been thinking straight. Besides – I was sure they wouldn't believe me.'

'Well, it doesn't matter now. Anyway, the thing is – I suspect he might be more interested in Holly.'

'Holly? Why?' Nathan jumps up from the sofa.

'Because . . .' He pauses, blows out a long, slow sigh. 'Because Holly seems to have inherited the genetic ability to regenerate her own cells.' He looks Chrissie in the eye. 'From you.'

'Genetic? You mean she *wasn't* given the drug? When she choked? When I pressed the pager . . .'

Michael shakes his head. 'Holly never needed the drug. The paramedic logged it with us. Said she came back by herself. He thought that maybe she'd been OK. That maybe she just hadn't needed it. But, well. We have lots of tests on this programme. We ran them all on Holly. We know that she died, for a split second, and then she came back. By herself. It's extraordinary. I hope you'll let us—'

'So Joseph has been testing her? Trying to kill her . . . twice. I'm sure he was behind that phone call that distracted me when she fell from the treehouse. And Holly may have said there was a man there when she choked at Amanda's, but I didn't make the connection before now, so I haven't asked her about it yet . . .'

Michael pales. 'This is worse than I thought. And yes, you're right. He's been testing her – and now, I think, he'll want to move to the next level.'

'And what exactly is that?' Andy says, coming to stand beside her. 'Is Holly in danger?'

'Holly's blood is a source of genetically transferred Cellregenix. Whether the theory holds or not, I suspect Joseph may want to find out if she can help cure him—'

Chrissie gasps. 'You mean . . .'

'Yes,' Michael says. 'It's not about you anymore. I think Joseph wants to get hold of Holly's blood.'

# Forty-Two

## Joseph (Now)

Joseph leans back against the bench, forcing himself to sit up straighter. His back has been giving him problems lately. It feels weak. More of an effort to straighten his spine. And he hates to slump. A small yellowing leaf flutters down from the tree above him. Five spiked lobes, a bit like a sycamore but he knows it's a plane. He recognises the spiky, balled fruits that are scattered around his feet, some split and squashed, revealing smears of crushed, green innards. The leaf is crispy, but spotted with black. Diseased. The tree will stay there, slowly dying. Unnoticed, unloved.

He crushes the leaf in his palm and tosses it on to the ground.

The children are starting to spill into the playground. The teachers are there, watching them, always vigilant now for predators in their midst. And at the gates, the parents stand chattering among themselves. Boasting about their little angels' achievements.

He watches them coming out of the door, and he smiles, and stands up and walks towards the gates. The parents mostly ignore him, but one or two smile. They're used to him now. He's been coming here every day for months, just to chat briefly to his granddaughter.

*Isn't it so sad that your daughter won't let you come round any-more . . . That husband sounds like a nightmare.*

*It's so lovely of you to visit like this. She'll not forget you . . .*

He'd chosen the right ones to spin his tale to. The ones that he knew were more interested in themselves than anyone else's children. Even the ones who'd looked wary had soon got bored. He looked like a sad old granddad, nothing more. They watched him as he said a few words to the girl every day, then went on his way.

His efforts at playing the doting granddad will be rewarded today.

The children's chatter is loud, but he manages to tune it out. He thinks back to that first time he spoke to her. Several days after he'd first started to come and sit here, watching her, waiting. He hadn't known then how important she would turn out to be. But it doesn't hurt to do some groundwork.

He'd spoken to her at the fence, while she'd been playing alone, running a stick along the railings and singing to herself. The nursery worker – the one who is also Christina Tate's friend, and who is meant to bring her safely to and from nursery every other day – had been busy chattering to the nursery manager. The occasional glance over to make sure that the girl was still there, but nothing more.

They weren't alarmed by the old man on the bench. He was outside the gates. He wasn't a threat.

'Hello,' he'd said.

Holly had eyed him carefully before responding. 'Mummy says I'm not allowed to talk to peoples I don't know.'

'Very wise, your mummy. Only, you do know me, Holly. Well, your mummy does. She's a lovely lady, your mummy.'

Her little face had lit up. 'My mummy is the loveliest. Auntie Wendy is nice too, but I think if I had to pick one of them, I would pick Mummy always.'

'I'm sure she would be very glad to hear that.'

259

'Holly, are you ready to go?' The call comes from the other side of the playground. The nursery worker getting set to leave.

'Bye-bye, Mr Man.' Holly had grinned then scurried off on her pudgy little legs.

And that was how it had started. A little chat, every day. Only a few minutes. Never long enough to cause any suspicion. And he had a cover story, for any of the nosy mums.

But something is wrong today. The playground is already empty, and there's no sound of Holly, or of the playground worker. Wendy. That's her name. Well, he knows that she is still in hospital. Or else, she was. Either way, she is clearly not ready to be back at work.

But Holly – he had expected her to be here today. She was fine after her little choking accident. His theory had held. She had no reason not to be here. Unless they had decided to keep her at home.

Unless they had started to work out what all this was about.

With a small sigh, Joseph stands and walks away from the nursery. He'd hoped it would be simple, but he's going to have to revert to Plan B. If she's at home, then he'll just have to get her from there.

As it turns out, he's due another stroke of luck.

He sees Christina Tate rushing out of the house, rushing up the path to her neighbour. Even after what she has done – causing the death of the woman's husband – she's happy to foist her child into her care.

Well. The old woman will no doubt be distracted. And Joseph knows this area well. He's been watching it for long enough. He knows that there is a path by the park that leads to an alley behind the houses. They all have gates, locked, presumably – but not too hard to break into. He has the letter opener. It will function as a tool to release a padlock, if needs be. Or he might be luckier yet, and find an old gate, owned by an old couple. A gate that hasn't been maintained, perhaps.

He steps out of the shadows of the trees opposite the Tate house and walks along to the small park, quickening his step as he makes his way up the narrow path. He has no idea how long he has. He has no idea when they will come back to collect their child.

He has no idea if the girl will go along with his plan, but he hopes that by laying the groundwork, having the foundations in place, it will be simple.

He hears her in the garden as he makes his way carefully along the alleyway.

'Maureen, Maureen, we need more blankets for the den!'

He was right about the gate. It's weather-beaten, with a couple of missing slats. A light kick, and a third one will pop out of place. He can see her through the gap. She's fussing with a couple of old woollen blankets, trying to attach them to a pile of paving stones that are stacked up behind an old shed. She can't get the edge of the blanket into the gap, and she can't lift the stones to make it easier.

This is dangerous. Does the old woman not realise she could hurt herself down here in this neglected corner of her garden? Does the old woman not realise she could squeeze through that gap in the gate and disappear forever?

He crouches down, so that his face is almost at her height. 'Hello, Holly!' he says brightly.

She whirls around, her face confused at first, and then she sees him. Recognises him. 'Mr Man! You're here!'

'I am, Holly. It's so nice to see you today. How are you?'

She frowns. 'I's not allowed at nursery today because I was in hospital before but I'm fine!' Then her face lights up into a smile. 'You can help me, Mr Man? You want to play here with me?'

'That sounds wonderful, Holly,' he says. 'But I've got an even better idea.'

'Oh?' She crouches down now, mirroring him.

'Well . . . For a special treat, Mummy said you could come to my house today for a special party. I've got cake . . .'

She scrunches up her face. 'What about pizza?'

He nods. 'Of course.'

He doesn't need to say anything more.

Holly grins, and squeezes her way through the gap in the gate. When she reaches up to take his hand, her innocent little face makes his stomach flip. It almost breaks his resolve. But he pushes on. They walk hand in hand along the alleyway, down past the park, then away in the opposite direction to the Tate house. His heart is in his throat until they turn the corner into the next street. So close, yet so far. Holly chatters away to herself, occasionally trying to swing his hand in hers. Happy. Oblivious.

Children are far too trusting. Aren't they?

With his free hand, he fingers the box in his pocket, the letter opener safely inside. He doesn't need to use it now, to sully it with this difficult task. Because she is coming home with him – and he has everything that he needs right there.

In his special room.

# Forty-Three

## MICHAEL (OCTOBER 1999)

Michael is sitting on the sofa in Sandy's parents' house. It's the same sofa they've always had, and even when they died, Sandy didn't replace it. She's added a couple of throws and some cushions to make it look more modern, and the place is a lot less cluttered than it used to be. Freshly painted too, although the woodchip wallpaper is still lurking underneath. He doesn't blame her for not attempting to strip that stuff off.

'Like what I've done with the place, do you?' Sandy smiles. 'I know it's not fancy, but I like it.'

'It's great,' Michael says. His own place is stark and functional. A flat in a new development, equal distance to two of the clinics and his main lab. The company bought it for him after he split up with Sandy and it was clear that it was going to be a permanent thing. It came fully supplied with all the basics, and he's glad not to have to think about it. Even the spare room that Christina had stayed in when she came for the weekend was standard issue. Characterless. He doesn't need it to be anything other than that.

'Christina was horrified that I decided to paint over the wallpaper rather than strip it off, but you know, I kind of like it.' She pauses, as another coughing fit wracks her frail body.

He leans across to the side table and pushes a glass of water closer to her. 'Sandy . . . ?'

She raises a hand, and in another moment, the coughing stops. 'This is the worst of it, you know. Bloody cheek, too, spreading into my lungs and making me cough like this. I've never smoked a cigarette in my life.' She smiles at him again, but it's forced. Her skin is tinged grey. Her face is sunken. All the youthful beauty sucked out of her thanks to this cruel disease. She leans back into the cushions. 'Just need to close my eyes for a minute.'

He lays a blanket over her, then stands up, picking up the mugs and plates and taking them through to the kitchen. His eyes are drawn to the free-standing fridge-freezer, covered with souvenir magnets and photographs. There's one of the three of them from when Christina was only a toddler. A day at the beach. Clacton. He remembers it well. It was before everything changed.

He is torn. He knows he should call Christina, tell her the truth. But Sandy had begged him not to. Christina has been in the south of France for a month, her and a couple of friends from university. She'd called him one day to say she had served ice cream to David Schwimmer and he'd laughed and been as excited as she was, even though he had no idea who this man was and had had to ask Todd, one of the junior researchers, in the lab afterwards. Todd had been as excited as Christina, and he wasn't even there. Apparently Mr Schwimmer had left a large tip, and winked as he'd licked his cornet. Michael was a little disturbed by that, but he hadn't said anything.

Sandy has told Christina nothing about the cancer coming back. She'd successfully gone into remission after that first lump back in 1995, but four years later, it's back and it's not going away this time. Christina is due home for Christmas – which is more than two months away, and Michael, seeing her today, is not at all convinced that Sandy is going to make it.

'She's having the time of her life, Michael. I don't want her to come back and see me like this. It's not as if she can do anything to help. Promise me, please. That you won't tell her.' Sandy had said this two weeks ago, when things had begun to progress faster than expected. There was no treatment, her oncologist had said, only palliative care. A nurse comes to see her twice a day. Michael once. It's a bittersweet feeling that he's back in her life like this, just as she's about to lose it.

He rinses the mugs and leaves them on the drainer, then heads back through to the living room. He'll check on her, then he'll go. This'll be her now for a few hours, until the nurse comes. Once she's asleep, she's asleep.

It's the morphine. She asks him to give her a little bit extra, and he pretends that he has, but he hasn't. He knows what she's doing. Knows what she wants. But he can't give her that. 'Let me drift away, Michael . . .' she begs.

He wants the opposite. He'd asked her again if he could take her to the clinic. Give her the drug – see what happens. But his colleague had been against it as much as Sandy. His colleague, Dr Mason, has only worked on the programme since it became ethically minded. Dr Mason has no idea what he and Edward got up to in those early days.

Michael leans over to kiss his wife on the forehead, and as he does, her eyes fly open, full of terror. She grips on to his collar with her bony little hands.

'Help me, Michael! Help me!'

The morphine gives her sleep, but it also gives her dreams. He's watched her, as her eyes under closed lids have flicked rapidly from left to right. Small groans escaping her throat.

'It's OK,' he says, gently unfurling her hands from his throat and taking hold of them. Squeezing gently.

'Don't leave me, Michael. I don't want to be alone. The darkness is coming for me, Michael.'

He can't watch this anymore. But he can't leave her to suffer.

Sandy still has the old Bakelite phone that they'd chosen together when they'd first got married. She'd brought it here, and her parents' own phone had become the second phone, in the bedroom. Michael watches as Sandy shifts in her seat, her eyes closed, the discomfort etched on her face. She's not fully conscious, but she's clearly in pain.

He lifts the receiver and dials the number on the phone. Mason picks up after two rings. The man rarely leaves the clinic. His dedication borders on obsession.

'Gavin? It's me. Michael. Look – I know you're against it, but she needs help. I need to bring her in.'

'You know we can't give it to her,' Dr Gavin Mason says, his broad Glaswegian accent clipped and firm.

'Maybe not – but we can make her more comfortable than she is here.'

'We're not a hospice, Michael. We can't provide the care that she needs.'

Michael sucks in a breath. 'She's my wife, Gav. Have some fucking humanity.'

Dead air. Michael rarely swears. Finally, the other man speaks. 'I'll send an ambulance.'

# Forty-Four

## CHRISSIE (NOW)

It seems to take an age for Maureen to answer the door, and when she sees the sea of anxious faces, she blinks in shock.

'Chrissie? Is everything OK? Who—'

Chrissie tries to smile. 'Sorry to panic you, Maureen. This is my dad . . . We just wanted to collect Holly so she can finally get to meet her grandfather.'

'Michael,' her dad says, taking a step forward. 'It's lovely to meet you.'

Maureen looks hesitant. Her eyes flit from Chrissie to Michael, then she peers through the gap between them at the faces behind.

'Oh, and my friend Andy from work popped round. You know Wendy?'

Maureen looks suspicious now, keeping the door open only a fraction. 'Holly's out the back. She's had a lovely day. I hope you're not going to upset her with something.'

'No, no, of course not. Just a bit of a surprise. We're all going to go out for lunch to celebrate. Would you like to come?' She takes a step forward. 'If I can just grab Holly and get her changed, then we'll pop back round and pick you up in about' – she turns to Michael, urging him to play along – 'an hour or so?'

Michael nods. 'I'm so excited to meet her.'

Maureen opens the door slightly wider, but her expression remains cautious. 'To be honest I didn't realise you still had a dad, Chrissie. You've never mentioned him.'

'Long story. I'll tell you all about it later.' She forces her smile wider. The anxiety about what Michael has told her is bubbling fast, getting ready to erupt. She's trying hard to stay calm. They heard Holly in the garden a while ago, but they can't hear anything from the front of the house. She takes a step forward and Maureen finally relents, moving out of the way as she pulls the door open.

'She's in the garden.'

Chrissie tries to walk through the house, the layout a mirror image of her own, without speeding up. But it's hard to stay calm when she has a million terrifying thoughts whizzing around in her head. She feels a hand on her arm.

'Stay calm, love. I'm sure she's just playing . . .'

Chrissie had expected it to be her dad behind her, not Nathan. But she's glad to have him beside her for this. Because it's sure to be a false alarm, isn't it? But at least he's stepping up to look out for his daughter.

The back door is wide open. Maureen has one of those beaded curtains that are meant to stop flies from coming in, and it is blowing gently in the breeze – the plastic beads click-clacking together. She imagines the sound would be quite soothing, on a normal day. But right now it just feels ominous. She pushes the strands of beads apart.

'Holly? Mummy and Daddy are here! And we've got a *big* surprise for you!'

She steps out into the garden.

'Holly? Are you hiding from me, you little monkey . . .'

Nathan follows her into the garden. The layout is the same as theirs, but with little in it apart from a couple of chairs by the back door, and down the far end, a shed that has seen better days – the wood stain worn away and damp patches creeping up the sides. The window is broken and partially taped over. She hopes there's nothing dangerous in there.

'Nathan, the shed,' she says, but he is already halfway down the garden.

The shed door is closed. A flurry of fright squeezes her chest. What if Holly is trapped inside?

'Maureen, has she been playing in the shed?' she calls back into the house.

Maureen appears at the doorway. 'No, it's locked. No idea what's in there, to be honest. That was Arthur's place.' Her eyes fill with tears. 'He was planning to get it all sorted soon. He was meant to be ordering a pane of glass . . .' She sniffs, wipes her eyes. 'She was making a den behind it. I gave her some old blankets—'

'Fuck!' Nathan's voice comes from behind the shed.

Chrissie is running down the lawn towards him, but she already knows what's happened. Because she knows what's behind the shed. Same as theirs, just in the mirror image.

The back gate.

'Maureen, was the gate locked too?' Chrissie calls over her shoulder, just as she arrives at the shed. But she doesn't need an answer now.

There's a pile of blankets in the far corner, but no sign of Holly. The gate is wide open, and Nathan has disappeared. She hears him calling her name, down the little alley that connects along the back of the houses. 'Holly? Where are you, princess?'

She turns back and runs towards the house. Michael is in the garden now, having heard the commotion. 'No, get out the front. Out the front!'

Chrissie pushes past, and runs through the kitchen and the lounge, where Andy and Wendy are standing with Maureen, a little awkwardly, not sure what their roles are right now.

'Out the front!' she yells again. 'That passageway comes out by the park. We need to get along there. We don't know how far she's gone, or how long she's been out there . . .'

'I only came in to answer the door.' Maureen's voice is thin, wavering. 'I was watching her the whole time.'

Chrissie ignores her and starts to jog down the driveway.

'We need to call the police,' Wendy says from behind her. 'We need to . . .'

Chrissie stops and turns towards the house, just as Michael appears on the front doorstep. 'No,' he says. 'No police.' He already has his phone to his ear. 'You need to let *me* handle this now.'

# Forty-Five

## Joseph (Now)

Once they are inside his house, Holly looks doubtful. 'When is Mummy coming here?'

Joseph pats the little girl on the head gently, like he's seen people do. 'Soon, Holly. She asked me to look after you for a while because she's got to do lots of work today.' His patting turns to stroking. Her hair is so soft.

Holly frowns and pulls away. 'But Maureen was looking after me. She was getting lots more blankets. I was making a den. Can I make a den here?'

'I'm not sure we have things for making a den. We can play—'

'Don't be silly. There's lots of things here.' She runs out of the living room into the hallway. He hears the squeak as she tries to open one of the closed doors.

He doesn't expect that she'll manage, but better safe than sorry. He follows her out into the hall. She's given up on the door with the stiffest handle. Good. But she's disappeared.

'Holly?'

He hears a muffled, fabric-y sound. Blankets and sheets being yanked off his bed. He hurries through.

'Oh, I see,' he says. 'Better let me help you . . .' She has a pile of bedding in both hands, a pillow perched on top. She can barely see over it, and one of the sheets is trailing on the ground. She might trip on it and fall. Hurt herself. He can't have her hurting herself.

He takes the pile and she picks up another pillow and runs out of the room. Joseph follows her into the living room. He doesn't like this disruption of his house. He's going to have to wash all the bedding now, before he goes to bed tonight. He can't sleep in it after it's been dragged all over the house, even if the carpets are immaculate. He only steamed them last week. He does it once a month. For the germs. He's read a lot on allergies, and had wondered for a long time if dust mites were the cause of his itching rash and aching joints – apparently allergies of this type can be quite severe. And it is an old house. But he knows he's clutching at straws. Still, once you're in the habit of something, it can be quite hard to break.

'First you need to 'tatch it to the back of the sofa, 'K?' She pulls the corner of the blanket from the pile, but it's large and heavy, and it's tangled in the sheet.

Joseph sighs. Then he decides to help her. Why not? If he plays along with this, it should be easier to get her to play along with his little game that he has planned for later. He glances at the clock. Soon, in fact. Because it can only be a matter of time before Maureen realises that Holly is not hiding in her den behind her shed.

He helps her pin the blanket along the back of the sofa, sticking it down the back of the cushions to keep it in place. Then he carries his dining-room chair – he only has one – never been any need for another – and places it far enough away behind the sofa to make a space for her to crawl into. Then he folds it over the chair and under the legs, pinning it in place.

'Perfick!' she says. She grabs a pillow and crawls inside, pulling it in behind her. 'You come in too?' Her voice is muffled by the blanket.

He hesitates. Then he picks up a pillow and kneels down at the entrance to her den. His knees crack, and he winces at the pain. But he crawls in, then twists himself around and leans on the pillow.

'You like making dens, do you?'

She nods her head vigorously. 'I love them! I like to make them in my bedroom for all my teddies. Have you got any teddies?' She cocks her little head to the side, questioning.

'I'm afraid not. My house isn't very exciting really. But you know what?' He leans closer, and lowers his voice. 'I do have a very special den of my own. Would you like to see it?'

Her eyes widen. 'Oh, yes please!' She's already scurrying out, the pillow abandoned. 'Where is it? Is it in your bedroom? I didn't see any dens in there but maybe it's a secret hidden one?'

He closes his eyes, and his knees creak and crack as he crawls back out from under the blanket. 'No, it's not in there. It's in another room. It's a really big den, you know. It has its own room.'

'Wow,' she says, elongating the 'ow' for a very long time.

Joseph smiles at her. It's an odd sensation on his face. His cheeks bunching, his lips curling up at the ends. It's been a long time since he smiled naturally. He hasn't had much call for smiling over the years.

'I think you knew about my den, didn't you?' he says. 'I think you tried to get in there earlier . . .'

'Ohhh,' she says, 'in the room with the door handle that was really, really hard? I couldn't make it move.'

'That's right.'

She scampers across the hallway and stands by the door, grinning. 'Can you open it up, please?'

He takes the key from his pocket and unlocks the door. Then pushes the handle hard, and shoves the door open.

She runs inside, then stops. Turns back to him. 'This isn't a den.' She crosses her arms and her face is knitted in a frown. 'I know what this is, 'cause I've just been in one like this. I don't like it . . .' She turns away from him.

He watches her as she scans the equipment in the room, taking it all in. The hospital bed, with the drip-stand next to it. The ECG machine. The high metal table, lined with neat rows of instruments. Syringes. Needles. The machine that administers analgesia.

'I don't want to go back in hospital,' she says, her voice barely a whisper.

He steps into the room after her and pushes the door closed behind him. 'Don't worry, Holly. It's just a little game . . .'

# Forty-Six

## CHRISSIE (NOW)

'I need to go to the lab. Chrissie, you come with me. The others can follow?'

Chrissie nods, turns to Nathan. 'I'll go with Dad, OK?'

'Fine.'

Chrissie jumps into the passenger seat and clips her seat belt. That same horrible thought from before swims into her vision as Michael revs the engine and pulls away. 'I think he might've done something to my car. I mean, the seat-belt clip was loose, but it was still connecting. When we had the accident, it came right out. And I don't think it would've been too hard for him to engineer the rest. He must've been watching . . .'

Michael is driving too fast. He swerves to avoid a car pulling out of its drive, then slows slightly, swearing under his breath. 'I'd like to say you were just unlucky, but I'd be lying. We found a listening device stuck under the passenger seat. As for the rest, well, I wouldn't put much past him, Chrissie. He's desperate.'

'But I still don't understand . . .'

'I'm pretty sure he thinks your blood, or more likely now, Holly's, will save him. He wanted you on board with this scheme of his so that you would trust him.'

'But if he has these contacts . . . these people in the MOD . . . couldn't he just have arranged for someone to hurt me, like they hurt Arthur? Or, I don't know – kidnap me or something.'

'Yes. But that would've drawn too much attention. You'd hardly have not reported that to the police, would you?' He glances at her as he waits for a traffic light to change to green. 'I'm still not sure why you didn't go to the police in the first place. The other *Christinas* did.'

Chrissie sighs, pushes her hair back and tries to smooth it behind her head. 'I don't know either. Something about it was off, for sure. But it seemed too outlandish. I was worried the police wouldn't believe me. That they might think I was losing my mind . . . That they might take Holly away.'

'Why would they do that?'

'I had a bit of an episode before. Postnatal depression. I didn't know what I was doing. Nathan . . . Nathan looked after me, and Holly. But I think that's what broke us.' She looks out of the side window. 'To be honest, I think we were broken before.'

Michael lays a hand on her knee. 'I know how that feels.' He takes his hand away again and changes gear as they turn on to the Broadway. 'Once this is all over, I hope we can sit down and talk properly. About everything.'

Chrissie nods, but says nothing.

Michael turns off the Broadway and into a smaller side road, then takes another sharp turn and drives into an underground car park. It's not a street she's had any reason to drive down before, but she sees now where he is going. This car park is on the back of the Broadway, under a row of shops. And a restaurant. The ridiculously named Meet-4-Meat. He stops the car.

Behind them, Andy pulls into the space next to them.

'Wait here,' Michael tells Nathan, who is in Andy's passenger seat. 'I'll be quick.' Then he turns to Chrissie. 'You need to come with me.'

She follows him to an unmarked steel door, which he opens via a fingerprint ID pad. It clanks shut behind them. Inside is a long corridor, with sensor-activated strip lights that come on as they hurry down it, their feet slapping on the polished tiled floor. On either side of them are several other steel doors, with the same fingerprint-recognition entry systems.

He stops at a door near the end and presses the pad to let them both in.

Inside is something she would never in a million years have imagined was sitting there under the scuzzy failed restaurant and the row of drab shops above. The laboratory is pristine, all gleaming metal benches down the centre, then smaller ones at the side with filtration hoods over them. In between the side benches are tall stainless-steel fridges – some with glass fronts, some not. And all around the place there is swanky-looking equipment that she can't identify, but that she knows costs a hell of a lot of money. The room is bathed in a lilac glow, from purple bulbs dotted around the walls. The place is silent, except for a muted buzz of electricity.

At the end, floor-to-ceiling glass separates the room from a smaller one – an office, with two wide desks and a couple of Macs. Filing cabinets at either end, and in the middle, a huge mural of what she recognises as Cambridge – an aerial shot showing the River Cam and the backs of some of the colleges.

'Wow.' She can't think of what else to say. She's quite speechless.

'It's a lot fancier than the lab I was in there.' He tips his head towards the photograph of his old university town. A city, not a town. The place where Chrissie grew up. She feels a pang of longing for something that she only has vague memories of. She'd left straight after school, gone to London and rarely returned.

'I just can't believe . . . all this.' She gestures to the room, turning a 360. 'All this, and you were here, all along. And I never knew.'

'You didn't want to know, love. But I kept an eye on you as best I could. If you'd answered my letters—'

'Maybe you should've tried harder.'

He nods. Looks sad. 'You're right. But you were so angry, Chrissie. After your mum . . .'

'You're right. I was angry. But listen, can we do this later? We need to find Holly first.'

'Of course.' Michael sits down at one of the desks and moves the mouse, waking up the Mac. Then he opens a window and logs in via another fingerprint reader, and starts tapping furiously at the keys. 'OK. I've got Joseph's location.' He taps again. 'Everdean Road.' He sighs. 'They must've moved him. He was never meant to be near me . . .'

'Wait, so he's near here?'

'Yes.' He taps again. 'And Holly. I've got them both via GPS. Joseph didn't have a tracker like that originally, of course – they didn't exist back then . . .'

Chrissie runs a hand down behind her ear. 'Mine . . .'

'Yes, yours is the original one.' He turns to her. 'It's not a whole lot of use to us, really. All we can tell is that your vital signs are fine. Obviously they wanted me to bring you in and get a new tracker, but I said no. I suppose that's part of the reason for them letting me set up this clinic here. So I could at least keep an eye on you somehow.'

'By spying on me?'

He swallows. 'In the end, we managed to track you via your phone.' He shrugs. 'Sorry.'

She wants to be angry, but it doesn't matter right now. The more important thing is that they find Holly. 'And Holly,' she says, 'where is she?'

'Now, that's a lot easier.' He taps the keyboard again. 'Holly has the latest model of tracker. Like your friend Wendy.'

'Dad!' she snaps. 'Just tell me where the hell she is.'

He clicks something and the screen closes. 'She's with Joseph. They're about five minutes' drive from here.'

She's already running out of the office. 'Let's go then.'

'Wait!' he says. He takes his phone out of his pocket. 'I need to make a call. I need to do it in here, using the secure Wi-Fi.' He puts the phone on speaker and presses a number on speed dial. She answers immediately.

'Michael. What's happened?'

'Anne. Sorry to call you on this number but it's an emergency. It's Joseph—'

The woman he called Anne sighs. 'We've been watching him, Michael. He's becoming a problem. I can't tell you how many red flags have been raised from something connected to his ID in the last week—'

'I've got Chrissie with me, Anne.' He glances over at her. 'He's taken Holly.'

Anne swears under her breath, vicious words hissing out of the phone like a snake. 'I'll meet you there.'

# Forty-Seven

## Joseph (Now)

'I want to go home now. I don't like it here.'

Joseph tries that smile again. It worked so well last time, but this time it feels forced, and it must look forced too, as the child bursts into tears.

'I want my mummy.'

'Yes, yes. I know.' He tries to pat her on the head again, but she grabs his hand and sinks her teeth into it, biting hard. Then she takes off towards the door.

Except the door is shut, and there's no handle on the inside. It only opens via fingerprint sensor. Something that he'd procured from his woman on the inside when they'd been refitting the new labs with additional security. The idiots in charge think he's stupid. That his brain doesn't work properly anymore. But she'd managed to find a way to help him . . . until she'd got spooked and decided that her job was more important than him.

They're partly right. But his brain just works *differently* now. And over the years, he's learned to train it to his own advantage. The irony is, this brain would've been a perfect one for Edward. But Edward was a different kettle of fish altogether. All he'd wanted was power and money. He didn't even care about being recognised for his achievements.

The polar opposite to Michael.

Although Michael had shown his true colours soon enough after Edward died and Joseph was reborn. Joseph might've been kept away from Michael, but Joseph knew what was going on. Those idiots didn't know whose loyalty lay where. It only took one of them – Melissa – to stand by *Joseph*.

He watches the child as she pummels on the steel door, screaming for her mummy. She's got a sharp set of teeth on her. His hand throbs. He has to hope the bite doesn't get infected. He has enough to deal with without that. After he's carried out the procedure, he shouldn't have to worry about little things like infections anymore.

Then he ignores her, and surveys his handiwork. He's done a good job with this little clinical laboratory set-up. Better than good, thanks to Melissa and her bits and pieces over the years. He's going to miss having her there to call on, but he'll find someone else. Initially, he'd created the lab to support his intention to start the programme again, back to the days of the tramps in Cambridge. But he'd tried making the compound just like Michael did, to no avail. He concedes that he was never as good a scientist as Michael, and that's fine. Because now he has something that Michael wants. And he's going to make sure he doesn't get it.

The child gives up trying to escape. She's tired herself out. 'You're a bad man,' she says, sniffling through her snotty little nose. 'My daddy will come and get you.'

He laughs to himself at that. Her daddy is the last person who's going to save her. Too busy carrying on with the nanny, or whatever she is – the one who was meant to be Chrissie's friend.

That crash had been fun to orchestrate. And it was just what he needed to ensure that Christina Tate took him seriously. Because up to that point, he wasn't fully convinced that she was on board with the programme. Leaving her whiny little messages asking if she could cancel.

And yet she had complied anyway. He'd been a little surprised by her acquiescence – more than that, her ready agreement to sign on with the programme he'd created. This was a woman who was terrified of losing what she loved. And what she loved, more than anything else in the world, was her daughter.

As soon as he realised that Christina Tate had a child, it had become all about that child. If the child had inherited the traits that had been bestowed on her mother via Cellregenix, then she was proof, at least in his mind, that the traits could be transferred to another. It made sense that Holly contained some sort of super-blood. It explained why she seemed to have no fear. No fear of jumping from heights, of taking sweets from strangers, of allowing someone to snatch her away from a place of safety. Somewhere deep inside Holly Tate was a survival gene – and this is what would save him.

The other two – the women calling themselves 'Tina' and 'Ris' – which was ridiculous, wasn't it? What was wrong with 'Christina'? Why did people choose to shorten their names like that? He'd hated it as Edward, when anyone had tried to call him Ed. 'Ed' was the guy who filled up your car with petrol in one of those little garages in the country. 'Ed' was the guy who collected trolleys in supermarket car parks. Now, 'Edward' – that name had class. A name of breeding and nobility.

That was him.

He picks up a pre-filled syringe from the table, slides it up his sleeve.

He hated being called Joseph. Joseph was the carpenter from the Bible who let his wife become impregnated by another man. Joseph was the tramp who'd been so desperate for drugs that he'd agreed to test unlicensed ones in a secret laboratory. Joseph was weak.

He was not weak.

He knew what he needed to do.

As soon as he discovered that Christina Tate had a child. As soon as he realised that Christina Tate was healthy – that minor rash on her inner forearm aside – he knew what he needed to do.

'Come over here, please, Holly,' he says now, crouching down to her height. Speaking quietly and trying not to scare her. 'I told you we would play a really good game, didn't I? The best game you've ever played?'

She nods, but her eyes are wary.

'Well, how about we play my game for a little while – then after that, we can have that lovely chocolate cake I promised you . . .'

'And then you'll phone my mummy? Can she have chocolate cake too?'

He nods enthusiastically, mirroring her action from earlier, in the warm confines of the blanket-den behind his couch. He turns away just enough to conceal it, then uncaps the syringe.

'OK.' She pulls herself to her feet. 'Where's your game?'

'It's right here, sweetheart.'

She takes a step towards him. Again, that innate fearlessness that he admires so much in her.

'It's one of those games where you have to close your eyes, Holly,' he says, and she frowns, briefly, before complying. She screws her eyes tightly shut, and in one deft move, he plunges the syringe into the soft skin of her neck. Her eyes fly open and she cries out once, but puts up no real resistance. Sedatives always work quickly on children. He lets the syringe fall to the floor, and he catches Holly as she wobbles and falls into his waiting arms.

At first, he'd thought he could just take a sample of blood from her – extract the DNA and amplify it to create his own batch of Cellregenix. The purest kind – passed down from an original, healthy recipient. But what if it didn't work? He'd have given up his only chance at a cure for his own cellular degeneration.

He lifts the child on to the bed and attaches the ankle straps, then the wrists. He'd already made extra holes in them to account for her tiny limbs.

No, a sample wouldn't be enough. He would need to take a lot more than that. Just in case. And besides, killing her to save him – that would redress the balance.

One death. One life.

The balance was very important.

He takes a cannula from his table of tools.

Whispers, 'Thank you, my dear little Holly. Sweet dreams.'

# Forty-Eight

## CHRISSIE (NOW)

Michael and Chrissie arrive first. It's a normal-looking house, on a normal-looking street – not much different to Chrissie's. Except no one is supposed to live on this street. The whole street was subject to a compulsory purchase order several years ago, and all the residents moved on – in preparation for the demolition that keeps being delayed. But in this one house, Chrissie realises now, there are signs of life. The small front garden is neat and tidy. The curtains are pulled shut in all of the windows, even though it's still daylight.

All this time, Joseph Marshall has been living around the corner. He must've watched as she crashed her Mini into that planter. Chrissie jumps out of the car.

'Hang on, wait,' Michael says. 'Don't go blundering in there. We don't know what's going on—'

Her jaw drops. 'Are you serious? He's got my daughter in there!'

Michael raises a hand, trying to placate her, just as the others pull in behind them in Andy's car and he, Nathan and Wendy climb out.

Then Nathan is by her side. 'Is this it? Is this where the bastard is hiding—'

'Please,' Michael says. He sounds calm. Too calm. This scares Chrissie even more. He knows more than he's letting on, doesn't he? He knows exactly what Joseph is planning to do. 'What you have to understand is, Joseph is a very methodical man. He's very different to the gung-ho Edward that I counted as a friend. Joseph is the scientist that Edward never really was. Edward fluked his way through his exams. Charmed his way through the oral presentations. Talked his way into the post-doc fellowship programme. He initiated contact with the MOD. He wasn't interested in the ethics, or even the mechanics of the science of all this.' He pauses. They are all watching him. A nervous energy floats in the air around them. 'Edward could have been a wonderful scientist. But something misfired in his brain when we brought him back. He confuses things. His logic is very skewed. What he's doing in there is what he believes to be the right thing.'

The group turns in unison as a car door slams shut nearby. Clipped footsteps make their way towards them. A petite, smartly dressed woman with a perfectly styled bob begins speaking as she nears them. 'Just as T.S. Eliot once said, "Most of the evil in this world is done by people with good intentions."'

She stops walking.

'There was a day I'd have included myself in that,' she says. 'But Michael showed me the error of my ways.' The woman raises one neatly arched eyebrow and gives them all a brief smile, before extending a hand to Chrissie. 'Dr Anne Cater. I'm sure your father has told you absolutely *nothing* about me.'

'I haven't really had a chance yet,' Michael says. 'Everyone – Anne is in charge of this thing. Anne – I'm sure we can do the formal introductions later.'

Anne nods. 'Have you made contact yet?'

'No.' Michael walks up the short path towards the front door. 'Maybe the others should stay out here?'

Nathan marches up behind him. 'I'm going in, Michael. You're not going to stop me.'

Chrissie is holding it together, but she feels like she might throw up at any minute. She goes to join her husband, glancing round at Wendy and Andy, who gives her a little nod. 'We're all going in,' she says. 'I want to speak to this piece of shit. I have a few things to say.'

Before anyone can stop him, Nathan starts banging on the door.

# Forty-Nine

## JOSEPH (NOW)

He has just inserted the cannula into Holly's arm when he hears the banging. It's muffled by the soundproofing in his special room, but he hears it nonetheless.

Someone is at the door.

He swallows, a hard lump of saliva sticking in his throat. He knew they would find him. He just thought he had a bit more time.

He turns back to his patient. She looks so peaceful lying there. Her skin is pale and unblemished. Her little rosebud mouth is perfect. He almost feels sad about it. But he has no other choice.

The banging starts again.

Joseph sighs. He could try and get rid of them, but he knows that whoever they have sent will not leave. He imagines they will deal with him quickly, which will be a blessing, in the end.

But he still has a chance.

There is another door in his special room, one that leads out into the back garden. If he can do it, and take what he needs – then he can get away. He can make a start elsewhere. He has some money saved. And he will have the most important thing in the world – a second chance at life.

He connects the tube to the cannula and releases the valve. Blood shoots up the tube and into the bag. It will take some time to drain her, but maybe if he can just get enough . . .

He cocks his head, listening. Expecting the banging to start again. But there's nothing. Have they given up? Maybe it wasn't them after all. A giggle escapes him. Maybe it was an Amazon delivery man.

He turns back to Holly. Still. Peaceful. Then he watches the bag as it slowly fills. Perhaps he does have enough time after all.

Then there's an almighty crash, and the whole room shakes.

# Fifty

## MICHAEL (NOW)

Michael surveys the scene. The reinforcements arrived shortly after Anne. Four men in white coveralls, carrying various pieces of equipment, including their first tool of choice. A battering ram – or 'the enforcer', as they call it. Mostly used by police, but expertly deployed by these men in their biohazard suits.

They await their instructions from Anne, and as soon as she gives the nod, they take action. The door splinters and breaks with one blow, but they give it another for good measure, then yank it off its hinges.

Four other men have arrived now, dressed in army combats, setting up a cordon for the inevitable neighbour enquiries. They will have a cover story ready. Chemical leak. Hazardous waste. Not too difficult when the house, and the whole street, is supposed to be unoccupied anyway. Michael trusts that Anne has seen all this before and will ensure that all bases are covered.

'Here,' Anne says, tossing a box at Michael. 'Get suited up. We don't know what he's got in there.'

He grabs a suit from the box, and he takes a moment to step inside and seal himself in, as he's had to do many times before. Anne does the same, her expression steely.

'Should they all . . . ?' He points from the box to the group. She nods, and he passes it to the others. It's full of paper suits and gloves, plus surgical masks.

'Dad, what is all this?' Chrissie is holding up one of the suits, her eyes wide with fear. 'What's he doing to her in there?'

'Don't worry, love. This is just to help when we need to sort out a story. Anne's team will give you a full debrief when we're done.' He squeezes her hand. 'Trust me.'

One of the suited operatives hands Anne a small, narrow box, and she slips it up her sleeve, the elastic cuff keeping it in place. She catches Michael's eye. Nods. They enter the house, and Michael glances back at the others, fumbling with the suits. He can't waste time waiting for them.

'Joseph, are you in here? It's over. You might as well come out . . .' Anne calls up the stairs.

Michael walks into the living room, sees the blankets in a heap behind the sofa. He hesitates. 'Edward,' he calls. 'It's me. I just want to talk to you.'

The suited operatives check the rest of the house. 'All clear,' says one of them. 'Except for this room here.'

Michael stares at the door. He tries the handle, but of course it is locked.

'Dad?' Chrissie is suited, and at his side. 'Is she here?'

Her voice is small and childlike, and Michael's heart aches. He wants to grab her and hug her tight. 'If she is, we'll find her.'

The house is eerily quiet.

'Ready?' Anne says.

He nods and she gives the command.

One of the operatives rams the enforcer into the locked door. 'Solid,' he says. 'Reckon there's a steel reinforcement behind it.'

'What now?' Michael says.

The operative turns to face him. 'We've got other methods.' He turns to Anne. 'Make sure we're clear.'

'Tell the rest not to come inside,' she says to Michael, then she goes off to check the other rooms again.

Michael turns to Chrissie. He holds up a hand. 'I need you all to stay outside for a bit longer.'

'You too, sir,' another of the operatives says.

Anne joins them and ushers Michael outside the front door, then follows him out.

In another moment, they're joined by the other operatives. 'Clear!' calls the last one to leave, loudly and firmly.

'You might want to cover your ears,' Anne says, beside him.

But before he gets the chance, there's an almighty bang.

# Fifty-One

## Joseph (Now)

He hears the front door being smashed in. The whole room shudders. He knows what they are going to do next. How long does he have? Two minutes? Less?

The first blood bag is almost full.

He closes the valve to stop the flow, then he closes the valve on the bag end and lifts it away. He seals it quickly, then grabs another bag from the metal table, clipping it in place. He opens the valve on Holly's arm again and watches as more blood shoots up the tube.

Can he wait for this one? Will one bag be enough?

He heads across to the other door and presses his finger on the door-release pad.

Nothing happens.

He takes a breath. Rubs his hand on his shirt. Even a tiny bit of dirt or sweat can stop it from working. And it has been a while since he used this door. Maybe the sensor is faulty.

He touches it again. Nothing. Tries his other hand, just in case, for some reason that he's forgotten, he used his left hand for this one.

Still nothing.

He glances around at Holly. At the drip-stand. The blood is filling more quickly this time. Maybe he should wait a minute longer, get the second bag. She must be close to dying now, too. How much blood does a three-year-old body actually hold? He should know this, but it is somewhere deep in the recesses of his mind. He's not sure he ever paid that much attention to the basics of human biology.

It comes to him then. Two litres. Two bags. He smiles at his memory recall, just as the lab door explodes and comes hurtling into the room.

# Fifty-Two

## CHRISSIE (NOW)

The four operatives run through the smoking rubble of the living room and burst into the now doorless room, with Michael following close behind. Nathan grabs Chrissie's hand and drags her inside.

Chrissie gasps as she sees what is in front of her.

It's a fully equipped theatre. Everything is there, right down to the bright overhead lamp that is angled over the bed, where a tiny patient is strapped down, hooked up to a drip.

Holly!

She runs to her daughter. 'Oh my God, Holly?' She grabs her tight, and Michael pulls her away. She falls back against him in shock, and then she sees Joseph. He is cowering over by another door, clutching a bag filled with blood. Holly's blood.

Rage burns through her like fire. She yanks herself away from her dad and practically flies across the room, avoiding the remnants of the door and the upturned equipment around it. She grabs Joseph by the throat. 'You!' she screams into his face. 'What the hell have you done?'

'Chrissie, no!' Michael shouts.

She's barely aware of the sound of Anne's heels on the tiled floor as she marches across the room. Then she feels the woman's small hands on top of her own as she tries to prise them off Joseph's neck.

Chrissie falls back on to the floor, shuffles out of the way. She is shaking all over. 'What do—'

'First things first,' Anne says. She grabs the bag of blood from Joseph's hands. 'This belongs to the child, I presume?'

Joseph gives her a small nod.

'Restrain him,' Anne says. 'Keep him alert. We might need him.' She marches back to the bed, takes in the scene. Chrissie watches her as she fiddles around with the bag that is still hanging up on the stand – it's almost full now. But Anne does something and the blood stops flowing. She turns back to Holly and leans down, holding two fingers to her throat to check for a pulse, listening for breathing.

'What have you given her?' she snaps. 'Not T7843Y, I hope?'

'No.' Joseph's voice is thin and wavery. 'Just a little pentobarbital.'

'Michael – check the fridges. I need some methylphenidate.'

'What's happening?' Chrissie asks. She's pulled herself to her feet and is now standing by Holly's side. She takes her small hand, squeezes it. 'She's so pale. She's . . . She's almost blue . . .'

By the door, two of the suited operatives are strapping Joseph to a chair.

'OK, here we go.' Anne adjusts something on the tube that is attached to the blood bag, then the blood that's halfway up the tube starts to slide down. Back towards Holly. Slowly. Much slower than it was filling up. 'I'll infuse this bag back into her before I wake her.' She turns to Chrissie. 'If I try to wake her too soon, it might not work.'

Michael hands her a vial. 'Are . . . What kind of doctor are you? I thought . . .'

'Just because I run this programme doesn't mean I don't know how to do the basics, Michael. All these years, and you've never actually asked me what my background was.'

'It seemed clear you didn't want to share it.'

She sighs. 'It didn't seem important. Not day to day. I chose not to work in a hospital because I didn't fancy all that stress for little reward. As for being a GP? Listening to people's moans and gripes all day? No thanks.'

'But you could've taken more of a front seat on the medical side, Anne. I'm sure the clinical team—'

She raises a hand. 'We're here to sort this mess out now.'

Chrissie watches her dad's face. Michael doesn't want to give up. 'But that day, when Edward . . . You injected it into his heart. I told you it was the wrong location . . .' He lets his sentence trail off. The implication is clear. She knew exactly what she was doing.

'It all would've been fine, Michael. But you just had to play the hero, didn't you? You had to bring him back.'

'I don't understand. You wanted him dead? Why?'

Anne points at Joseph as he sits on the chair, arms tied behind him. A defiant look on his face now.

'Look at him!' Anne yells, the composure that's been evident up to now completely out of the window. 'He's loving this.' She addresses him. 'You're loving this, aren't you?'

She turns to Michael. 'He was behind all the unethical practices, you know. He was the one who suggested that ridiculous "rule of three".'

'The rule of three is a perfect scientific construct,' Joseph says.

'You're not well,' she says, her calmness returning. 'You never were. What you did to yourself in the lab proved that. I just wish we'd got rid of you back then instead of letting you play your little games just so we could monitor you as our own damn experiment.

You're a monster, Joseph. No.' She shakes her head. 'You're a monster, *Edward*.'

The man in the chair – Joseph, or Edward, or whoever he really is – grins.

Then Anne slides something out from inside the cuff of her sleeve. She walks over to him slowly, opening the box.

'No,' Michael says. 'Wait.' He tries to grab her wrist but he is too late.

She takes out a small bottle and sprays two pumps into Joseph's face.

The suited pair of operatives behind the chair remain impassive as Joseph's face contorts briefly with pain. Then it falls slack, and he slumps in the chair. Something falls from his hand and rolls under his chair. A rectangular velvet box. On the side, the initials 'EL'.

The room falls silent for a moment.

Then Anne is back in action. 'Right. It'll soon be time for the second bag. Then we can wake this little sweetheart up. What do you say to that?'

Chrissie watches. Her daughter's colour seems to be changing already, no longer so blue. No longer so pale – as her blood flows back into her little body.

The operatives gather round Joseph, preparing to take him away.

Everyone else gathers around Holly.

Anne picks up the syringe filled with methylphenidate, injects it carefully.

Then they wait.

# Epilogue

## CHRISSIE (SIX WEEKS LATER)

Chrissie sits in the waiting room, flicking through a magazine. It's full of winter coats, and when she checks the date, it's nearly six months old. She smiles, remembering Wendy flicking through an old magazine just like this.

It was only a couple of months ago that Chrissie's biggest drama was arranging a much-needed night out. Funny how that turned out.

This is one of the fancier clinics, her dad had told her. One of the 'above board' ones that they use for parallel research. For every secret programme they run, there's a well-funded medical one in place too.

That had been one of his ideas, when he'd taken over from Edward.

The last six weeks have flown by, with so much going on. Getting to know her dad again. Getting to know Andy again. Working out a way for Nathan – and Wendy – to stay in Holly's life.

They're a blended family now, she supposes. Although there is only one child – for now, anyway. And they are all quite happy to share her.

Maureen is happy to babysit, too. Michael had arranged some 'compensation' money for her, somehow wangling it that one of Arthur's daily drugs had caused his heart attack, and while she is still desperately sad to be without him, she is glad to be part of Holly's life.

Because it's all about Holly now.

Chrissie smiles as the doors swing open and Andy appears with two coffees. 'Nathan's on his way. I just bumped into him by the vending machine.'

It's been an easy transition with Nathan and Andy. First off, Nathan didn't really have any room to be angry about it, considering that he and Wendy had been seeing each other for almost two years. Chrissie wanted to be furious when she found that part out, but she couldn't. She knew it stemmed from both of their frustrations at not being able to make Chrissie better. The pregnancy had triggered a lot of things inside her that she never knew were there. About her own childhood, her accident, that she had tried to block out – and then her mother's illness and subsequent death.

There's a lot of guilt. She remembers that summer in the south of France. She could remember hearing her mum's voice on the phone, and she knew that something was wrong. But her mum chose not to tell her – to protect her – to give her that summer. And Chrissie had chosen to take it.

But the guilt had manifested itself in blaming her dad for everything – that he didn't tell her to come home; that he didn't do anything to save his wife. She'd pushed all the blame on to his shoulders, and to protect her, he had taken it.

She feels so much love for him now. She's determined to make up for lost time.

'You OK?' Andy says. He lays the coffees on the small table between them. She's about to answer when the doors swing open again and Nathan appears. He's carrying a massive pink teddy bear. He sits it on the chair next to the smaller one that Andy has brought, and gives him a good-natured nudge with his shoulder.

It's a relief that they've become friends. Both of them more interested in Chrissie and Holly than fighting among themselves. Which is why she's decided that she's not going to do a paternity test. She and Andy had spoken about it, and decided that it really didn't matter what the DNA said – Nathan would always be Holly's dad, and there was enough for them all to deal with without adding that doubt to the mix. It's better this way. Besides, Holly could do worse than have two father figures in her life. And two mums – although Wendy will always be Auntie Wendy.'

Holly hasn't been drawing much recently, but Chrissie hopes that there will soon be four of them in those pictures, plus Holly, of course. And her new granddad too.

'Wendy couldn't get away from work early,' Nathan says, slurping his coffee. 'Says she'll come round after.'

The doors at the other end of the waiting room open now, and Holly comes barrelling through. 'Looook! I got two lollipops!' She is holding one in each hand, her ponytail bouncing as she runs towards them all, grinning.

Chrissie stands up to greet her dad, who follows behind Holly, with a white-coated man beside him. 'All done?'

He nods. 'This is my colleague, Dr Mason. He's the best there is.'

The man steps forward and holds out his hand. 'Gavin, please. And she's fine. You have one very healthy little girl right there.'

Chrissie smiles. 'I'm very glad to hear that.'

Dr Mason smiles back. 'I'm very glad you've allowed us to monitor her more closely. Six-weekly would be great for blood sampling, but if you think that's too much?'

She shakes her head. 'As you can see, she loves the attention.'

He nods. 'Perhaps you'd reconsider about yourself, too? I do think we could learn a lot from genetically profiling both of you. Tracking any changes on a regular basis.'

'Maybe. Not right now, but—'

He holds up a hand. 'My apologies. Absolutely no pressure.' He turns to Michael and slaps him on the back. 'You guys have a nice rest of the day now, OK? Some of us need to do some work around here.'

Michael slaps his colleague back. 'Right then,' he says, turning to the rest of them. 'Who's up for some ice cream?'

'Meeee!' Holly says, jumping up and down.

'Hey.' Nathan grabs her around the waist. 'What about *this* first?' He twirls her around so she is facing the soft toys on the seat.

'And *this*,' Andy says, pushing his smaller bear to nudge the bigger one out of the way.

Holly's face scrunches up, and she giggles. She looks up at Chrissie. '*Two* bears isn't enough, Mummy.'

'It's not?' Chrissie grabs her daughter by the shoulders and pulls her in close for a cuddle. She smells of strawberry sweets, with just a hint of antiseptic underneath.

Holly pulls back, her face serious. 'No, Mummy.' She leans in, whispers so that only Chrissie can hear. 'Mr Man says you always need to have *three*.'

# ACKNOWLEDGMENTS

I first had the idea for this book back in 2015, just after I got a publishing deal for my first novel. At the time, I had no idea what my second book was going to be, and I started and abandoned several, including *Substitute*. The idea was partly influenced by a short story I read, where a mysterious caller turned up offering seemingly impossible things. I knew I wanted *my* impossible thing to involve my main character making a difficult choice – and I also knew that the title was going to be a homage to one of my favourite songs by The Who. Anyway, my second book turned out to be something else altogether, but I couldn't get this idea out of my head – so in 2018, I finally started writing it again, and by early 2019, a partial manuscript had secured me a new and exciting contract with Thomas and Mercer. Yes – this book actually came out of my head first, but we decided that it would swap places with *The Last Resort* – very on-brand!

Which leads me to my first thank you . . . to my former editor, Jack Butler, for being excited enough about this book to take me on before I had written it. To everyone at T&M – who've all done such a brilliant job with this book and the one before; and to my new editor, Victoria Haslam – I'm so pleased to be working with you!

Big thanks to Sophie Goodfellow, for wonderful PR opportunities and lots of laughs; to the one and only Agent Phil (aka the Wildman of Borneo), and all at Marjacq, for always being brilliant.

To all the bloggers, reviewers, readers, fellow crime writers and every single person who has supported me along the way. I couldn't do this without you!

Huge thanks to Anne Cater for her generous CLIC Sargent winning bid to have a character name in the book, and to Karen Cole, who won hers at my last book launch – hope you're both OK with what I did with you! Secret thanks to the other people whose names I stole – let me know when you find yourselves!

Massive thanks, as always, to my friends and family – especially the ones who don't read much, but manage to find the time to read my books – this means everything to me, and I promise to try to keep the word counts as low as possible for you (ha!).

And final thanks, as is tradition: to JLOH. You know why.

If you want to find out more about me, you can go to my website: www.susiholliday.com, or have a look here: linktr.ee/susi-holliday for my social media links. I'd love to hear from you!

And of course, if you enjoyed my book, I would really appreciate it if you could leave a review . . .

Love, Susi

# FREE *DARK HEARTS* BOX SET

Join my readers' club and you'll get a free box set of stories: 'As Black as Snow', 'The Outhouse' and 'Pretty Woman'. You'll also receive occasional news updates and be entered into exclusive give-aways. It's all completely free, and you can opt out at any time.

Join here: sjihollidayblog.wordpress.com/sign-up-here

# ABOUT THE AUTHOR

Susi Holliday grew up near Edinburgh and worked in the pharmaceutical industry for many years before she started writing. A life-long fan of crime and horror, her short stories have been published in various places, and she was shortlisted for the inaugural CWA Margery Allingham Prize. She is the bestselling novels and a novella, several of them written as SJI Holliday. Along with three other female authors, she provides coaching for new crime writers via www.crimefiction-coach.com.

You can find out more at her website, www.susiholliday.com, on Facebook at www.facebook.com/SJIHolliday, on Twitter @SJIHolliday, and on Instagram @susijholliday.

Did you enjoy this book and would like to get informed when Susi Holliday publishes her next work? Just follow the author on Amazon!

1) Search for the book you were just reading on Amazon or in the Amazon App.

2) Go to the Author Page by clicking on the author's name.

3) Click the 'Follow' button.

If you enjoyed this book on a Kindle eReader or in the Kindle App, you will be automatically invited to follow the author when arriving at the last page.

 **THOMAS & MERCER**